MEET THE DAUG

LUCIA, the eldest, Daddy's favorite ~~....~~ ng a
profession worthy of her heritage—she's an assassin.

JEZEBEL, never a female more suitably named.
Thank her half-demon blood for that—and pity the
poor guy who crosses her.

LOLA, the baby of the family, so beautiful to look at.
Men would do anything to have her, making it that
much easier—and fun—to steal their souls.

Never has man met such a desirable challenge...

Three all-new stories by

**National bestselling author
JULIE KENNER**
"One of my favorite writers. Funny and sassy,
her books are a cherished delight."
—Sherrilyn Kenyon

KATHLEEN O'REILLY
"O'Reilly's engaging voice and talent for combining
humor and pathos suggest a promising future."
—*Romantic Times*

DEE DAVIS
"Don't miss any book by Dee Davis."
—Christina Skye

HELL on HEELS

Julie Kenner
Kathleen O'Reilly
Dee Davis

BERKLEY SENSATION, NEW YORK

THE BERKLEY PUBLISHING GROUP
Published by the Penguin Group
Penguin Group (USA) Inc.
375 Hudson Street, New York, New York 10014, USA
Penguin Group (Canada), 90 Eglinton Avenue East, Suite 700, Toronto, Ontario M4P 2Y3, Canada
(a division of Pearson Penguin Canada Inc.)
Penguin Books Ltd., 80 Strand, London WC2R 0RL, England
Penguin Group Ireland, 25 St. Stephen's Green, Dublin 2, Ireland (a division of Penguin Books Ltd.)
Penguin Group (Australia), 250 Camberwell Road, Camberwell, Victoria 3124, Australia (a division of
Pearson Australia Group Pty. Ltd.)
Penguin Books India Pvt. Ltd., 11 Community Centre, Panchsheel Park, New Delhi—110 017, India
Penguin Group (NZ), 67 Apollo Drive, Rosedale, North Shore 0745, Auckland, New Zealand (a division of
Pearson New Zealand Ltd.)
Penguin Books (South Africa) (Pty.) Ltd., 24 Sturdee Avenue, Rosebank, Johannesburg 2196, South Africa

Penguin Books Ltd., Registered Offices: 80 Strand, London WC2R 0RL, England

This is a work of fiction. Names, characters, places, and incidents either are the product of the authors' imagination or are used fictitiously, and any resemblance to actual persons, living or dead, business establishments, events, or locales is entirely coincidental. The publisher does not have any control over and does not assume any responsibility for author or third-party websites or their content.

PRINTING HISTORY
Berkley Sensation trade paperback edition / June 2007

Library of Congress Cataloging-in-Publication Data

Kenner, Julie.
    Hell on heels / Julie Kenner, Kathleen O' Reilly, Dee Davis.— Berkley Sensation trade pbk. ed.
        p. cm.
    ISBN 978-0-425-21527-2 (alk. paper)
1. Love stories, American.   2. Devil—Fiction.   3. Fathers and daughters—Fiction.
4. Inheritance and succession—Fiction.   I. O'Reilly, Kathleen.   II. Davis, Dee, 1959–   III. Title.
    PS648. L6K46 2007
    813'. 6—dc22

                                                                          2007000499
PRINTED IN THE UNITED STATES OF AMERICA

10   9   8   7   6   5   4   3   2   1

CONTENTS

Prologue

The devil stood in his bedroom, examining the two shirts laid out on the bed. "What do you think, Eustace? The Hawaiian print or my 'Hell's Angel' tank top?"

His servant, the ever-faithful Eustace, looked at the two shirts, and then looked around at the shambles that his boss had made of what was normally a neat and tidy bedroom and sighed. Four suitcases were laid out, piled high with clothes, beachwear and formal wear alike. Ties were tossed over the antique hand-carved headboard and the Chippendale chairs were laden with rubber floats and scuba gear. "The Hawaiian, sir. It will go nicely with your complexion."

Lucifer rubbed his hands together with glee. "I thought so, too."

"I'm sorry to intrude on this moment of joy, but you do need to prepare the tests for your daughters."

"Tests? Oh, yes, yes, the tests!" In all the strategic planning for his first vacation getaway, he had completely forgotten about his real job. Hell. Literally. Running a multigazillion-dollar enterprise, along with the entire torment and temptation of the planet was a huge mind-suck and took all of his energies, but now the devil had a new goal: to figure out which of his daughters was worthy of succession—and then he was out of here.

Of course there was always the possibility that they'd disappoint him. His sons, Jack, Nick, and Marcus, had certainly let him down. But hell hath no fury—or something like that—and his daughters were not to be trifled with. To be brutally honest, he was looking forward to kicking back with a case of Dos Equis and a couple of bikini-clad blondes—or brunettes—or maybe both. Point was, it was time to get the hell out of—well, hell.

"What do you have for me, Eustace?" Lucifer asked.

"I found a way to ensure that your business interests remain secure."

Lucifer turned, looking down his nose at his servant. "Considering the troubles I've been having in Monte Carlo recently, I hope you're not making a joke."

"Jacques Moreau," Eustace said, with the appropriate flourish. "He seems particularly suited to be the recipient of Lucia's unique talents."

"Very nice," the devil said, in a rare tribute to Eustace's loyalty and skill. "And what about Jezebel?" he asked.

"Well, hopefully you won't need this, sir. But just in case, I've put together a complete dossier on the Protector of Armageddon."

"And Lola?"

Eustace handed him a newspaper clipping. FREAK ACCIDENT, WALL COLLAPSES AT BANK: 1 SURVIVOR, 14 DEAD.

"Sounds marvelous," he said. "You wrote up my notes as well?"

Eustace barely refrained from rolling his eyes.

"I saw that, Eustace," Lucifer said, lifting a hand. Eustace ducked as a plume of smoke sailed over his head; then he straightened and with a courtly bow handed his master a manila folder.

"Double-spaced, just as you like it, sir."

Lucifer slapped him on the back. "Excellent," he said, pulling some Mardi Gras beads from a suitcase and slinging them around Eustace's neck. "First, we find Lucia."

"And after that?" Eustace asked with a sigh.

"Unless I miss my guess, it'll be time for me to drink a few margaritas—preferably served by a naked redhead. Or a naked blonde. Or," he added, collapsing happily onto the bed, "perhaps both. That, my dear Eustace, is *my* idea of heaven."

LUCIA'S STORY

Julie Kenner

Chapter One

She was off her game.

Lucia Faucheaux sighed, and slipped the syringe back into her cleavage. Its weight was negligible, but the press of the cylinder against her skin fortified her.

And she sure as hell needed fortification at the moment.

Around her, women in ornate ball gowns swirled in the arms of men in tuxes. The music of Strauss filled the room and the mouth-watering scent of exotic appetizers seemed to dance on the gentle breeze kicked up by the open patio doors. Across the marble dance floor, her gray-haired quarry sipped scotch and traded political stories with the ambassador to Spain.

The opportunity had been *right there*. They'd been alone on the side balcony. The better, he'd said, to see the view of the Rhine. She'd thought that she had engaged him, that he was taking her outside for an amorous interlude despite his new wife back home in Vienna. And why wouldn't she think that? That was her special talent, after all. Getting close to men.

As a child, her father had taught her how to make the most of her dark, aristocratic good looks. She'd inherited her father's midnight black hair, but her mother's violet eyes were what really drew the men in. Under her father's tutelage, she'd learned how to move through the world with the grace and skill of royalty. She'd always been a bit of an actress, and that had helped. She'd adapted to her environment, easily picking up manners of speech, turns of phrase, and nuances of etiquette.

Even now, she was smiling gracefully, gliding through the ballroom with a smile and a nod, even though her mind was anywhere but the festivities.

She had her father to thank for that skill. He had ensured that she gracefully mingled easily with kings, princes, pharaohs, and the like. She could make small talk in twenty-three languages, interpret political conversations, and insert herself into the most touchy of diplomatic situations.

All with a single goal: getting close enough for the kill.

Because from the day he'd come to claim her, her father had raised her to be his own personal assassin. An assassin who could get close to any victim. Be it a lowly country preacher or a politician having a crisis of conscience and considering doing a little good for the country.

Lucia was, quite simply, the best. And she had been for an eternity, it seemed.

Not tonight.

Frustrated, she reached out and snagged a flute of champagne from the tray of a passing waiter. She swallowed it in one gulp, then turned away from the baron, unable to look at him and the failure that he represented.

It had all been so easy. So run-of-the-mill. So . . . *dull.*

Just another one of her father's targets. A politically connected Austrian baron with ties to significant social welfare programs. A straightforward elimination request, complete with the perfect event for the assassination: a private party thrown by a wealthy American entrepreneur who had purchased and renovated a dilapidated German castle. All of society had been invited to ooh and aah over the excellent restoration. And Lucia's name was, of course, at the top of the guest list.

Simple. Straightforward.

Just get in, nail the guy, and get out.

She'd done the same thing countless times over the centuries. So why in Hades was the job suddenly so difficult? Why had she dragged her feet preparing for this kill? Why had she not experienced that tingle of anticipation as her driver had chauffeured her to the party?

Why had she lost her focus?

It was a question she hated to pose because she feared the answer. Self-analysis had never been one of her strong suits for exactly this reason: look too closely at yourself and you'll surely find a flaw.

Flawed. She fought a shudder. The very word disgusted her. She'd been raised to be perfect, and to now find herself at such loose ends . . . well, to say the situation was unnerving would be one hell of an understatement.

She thought back over the evening with the baron. Yes, she'd been less than enthusiastic about the assignment, but she'd never doubted that she would ultimately pull it off. No doubt, that is, until they'd been on the balcony.

He'd leaned in toward her, and she'd been so certain that he'd fallen for her charms. She'd eased the cap off the syringe, planning to inject it into his thigh, then wait for the massive coronary to hit.

She'd never made it that far. Because instead of leaning in to kiss her, he was leaning in to show her his wallet and the photographs he'd tucked inside. Photos of his wife. Of his kids. Even of his dog.

Utterly pedestrian! But oh, how he loved his family.

Something had twisted in her heart, and she'd hidden the syringe away. She simply couldn't do it.

The failure was completely humiliating and utterly inexplicable.

Was she losing her edge? Was she having a midlife crisis?

The cause of her failure was completely elusive, but one thing was certain: she needed an attitude adjustment. Desperately.

No sooner had the thought entered her head than the movement around her seemed to slow and then, suddenly, freeze. It was as if she were the only living thing in a diorama of the restored ballroom. To some, the effect might be unnerving. Lucia, however, felt only mild irritation.

"I'm not in the mood for hide-and-seek, Daddy," she said, turning in a circle as she surveyed the room, wondering where her bombastic sire would deign to appear.

A flurry of movement by the bandstand caught her eye, and she watched as a whirlwind of black and red seemed to glide across the floor, like a cyclone that couldn't quite touch down. Her skin warmed, and every hair on her body seemed to prickle as threads of lightning shot across the room, converging on the ephemeral column.

A crash, a smash, and then there he was. Her father. Standing in front of her in all his dark glory, looking sharp and seductive in his finely tailored tuxedo and buffed wingtips.

The room snapped back into motion, with none of the occupants being the wiser. And as far as Lucia could tell, no one had noticed her father's unusual arrival. Or, for that matter, the smell of sulfur that still lingered in the air.

"Are the pyrotechnics really necessary?" she asked, moving into his open arms.

"Not in the least," he said as he swept her onto the dance floor. "But they are ever so fun."

She lifted a brow. "Are they? Even when no one knows? You froze them. What's the point of showing off if you're only showing off for me?"

"Perhaps I thought you needed the reminder."

The casual remark hid a hard edge, and Lucia stumbled over it, losing her footing as she debated the best way to answer her father. He'd been stern from day one, expecting only perfection from her. She was the oldest, after all. Even when Jack had come along and— being the oldest boy—completely captivated her father, he'd never stopped demanding her best.

And she'd been more than happy to give it. Her father had needed her, and after the loss of her beloved mother, she'd jumped to the task. While her brothers and sisters followed a myriad of paths, she'd been the only one to really stay in the family business, report directly to her father, *and* get her hands dirty. Even Jack had played the administration game, his occasional parlor trick hardly worthy of his heritage.

She, however, had played an essential role. And up until recently, she'd been damn good at her job.

Lately, though . . .

"Lucia?"

She looked up and saw concern in her father's eyes. She couldn't help but smile. The man was an absolute devil, and yet, like every father, he was completely smitten by his daughters. Even after thousands of years, that inalienable fact still amused her.

"I'm sorry. I blew it. A momentary lapse. Nothing to worry about."

"And I wouldn't be worried," he said, "if this were the first time."

She sucked in an involuntary breath. He couldn't possibly know that! Yes, she'd hesitated on her last four jobs. But she'd forced herself, and managed to handle the assignments, just like she'd expected to handle this one. True, on the last one, she'd been spared by the fact that her target's private plane went down over a Florida swamp, but if he'd landed safely, she would have been right there to—

"The plane," she said, suddenly realizing. "You did that?"

"I wasn't confident the job would get done," he said. "And it *had* to be done."

"Oh." She licked her lips, not at all sure what to say. Finally, she drew in a breath and tried a completely new tactic: the truth. "I don't know what's wrong with me."

Damn, but she hated admitting that. This was what she did, what she'd always done. And the thought that she could be losing her edge—losing her purpose—positively terrified her.

"My dear," he said, "it's so simple. You simply need a change."

"A change?" But even as she said it, she knew he was right. She'd had the same job for thousands of years. Of course she was ready for something different. After all, didn't all the modern psychologists suggest that most people needed to do something new every ten years or so? If that were the case, then she was seriously behind the curve.

"A change," he confirmed. "And a whole new set of priorities."

She cocked her head, intrigued by the tone of his voice. "You have something in mind. You didn't come here to slap my hand for screwing up the baron's assassination. You came for something completely different."

He stroked her cheek. "Such a perceptive woman."

"Come on, Daddy," she crooned, easing closer, "tell me."

The music stopped, and they paused long enough to applaud the orchestra. He held out his hand, and she put her fingertips on his palm. "Have I ever failed to treat you like royalty?"

She considered answering in the affirmative, but decided that now wasn't the time to discuss his parenting skills in detail. "No," she said as he led her off the dance floor. "I've always been a princess to you."

"And now you have the opportunity to be queen."

"I'm listening."

"You say that you are growing weary of your current position. That is a sentiment I am very familiar with, as I have grown weary of mine."

"You've . . . *what*?" Surely she'd heard wrong. Her father, the Prince of Darkness, had grown tired of lording over his subjects? That couldn't be right.

He waved the question away. "It was inevitable. The job pressure. The daily demands of the workplace. I used to have so much free time to enjoy myself. Now I have duties to attend to."

"You make the job sound so appealing," she said, dryly.

"Jack certainly thought it was."

Her head cocked at that. "You offered the position to Jack first. Of course. How foolish of me not to assume so right away."

"I offered," he said, with a slight bow of his head.

"And?"

"And he accepted the challenge. Then he failed."

"And now you've come to me?"

"Essentially."

She fought the urge to roll her eyes by turning to pluck a champagne flute from the tray of a passing waiter. "In other words, you approached Nick, as well. And Marcus, too. I assume they both failed as well, or else you wouldn't be here talking to me." She took a sip of wine to cool her rising temper. "Did you approach the sons I don't know about, too? Surely in all these millennia you have sired more than six children."

"My darling Lucia, you wound me."

"I seriously doubt that."

"As a prince myself, of course I sought a prince to fill my shoes. But after the abysmal performance of your three half brothers, I realized that my thinking was far too narrow. I needed to look for a queen. Regal, beautiful, and able to bear the weight of the position."

"Mmmm." She wasn't about to say more. Her brothers may have been her father's first choice, but they'd failed. And now that she was being handed the opportunity, she wasn't about to risk losing it by criticizing her father's approach. After all, she had two younger sisters. She'd be damned if he'd skip over her and go straight to Jessie. Or, even more humiliating, her baby sister, Lola.

"Are you interested?"

"You know that I am. When do I start?"

"There are a few details that must be attended to first," he said.

She looked at him through narrowed eyes. "I see."

He waved a hand in the air. "Ah, Lucia. Don't fret. It's nothing. A trifle. A task you could handle in your sleep. But I would be remiss if I handed over the keys to my kingdom without requiring a demonstration of your worthiness, don't you think?"

"I think that I've been displaying how worthy I am ever since I slipped the poison to the pharaoh."

"Ah, yes," he said wistfully. "Your first assignment. How young and eager you were."

"And how old and jaded I am now."

"Nonsense. You are as beautiful now as you were then."

"I have good genes," she said, unable to stop her smile.

"Indeed. And I would think you would want to keep them."

She forced herself not to react to that tidbit of information. Her beauty came from both father and mother, but her immortality . . . well, that was from her father alone. And he was in a position to take that gift away.

"What is the task?"

"A simple assassination," he said. "No different from what you have been doing for years."

"That's all?" Surely, it couldn't be so simple.

"That is all."

She licked her lips, both tempted and confident.

Still . . .

She couldn't deny the fact that she'd failed in that very task just moments ago. If she accepted her father's challenge and failed again . . .

She closed her eyes, banishing the thought. This evening on the balcony had been an aberration. One that she could certainly have overcome had the incentive been enough.

She *wouldn't* fail. Not again. Not with stakes this high.

"Who?"

Her father smiled, and Lucia knew that it was all over. She'd shown curiosity; she'd shown weakness. And now the ball was in her father's court.

To his credit, he didn't gloat. Simply held out a hand and allowed her to take the picture that materialized there in a puff of smoke. A distinguished-looking man with a full head of gray hair and a hint of mischief in his eyes. Under other circumstances, Lucia might suspect that she would enjoy dining with the older fellow. As it was, she steeled her heart. This man was her ticket to freedom. She'd do what she had to do.

"Why him?"

"Such a curious mind," her father said with a dismissive wave. "Let's just say that his business interests conflict with mine. He's a nuisance. And I want him eliminated."

"Business interests?" She couldn't keep the hint of amusement from her voice. Her father was forever dabbling in mortal business, and his failures often prompted larger consequences. October 1929 came to mind as one of the more vivid examples of her father's financial wrath.

If this final job could prevent another of her father's meltdowns, well, then surely the world would thank her for taking on the task, no matter how tired she might be of the devilish business.

That, of course, was a shallow excuse, hardly worth the energy to think it up. The truth was she was simply tired of her job. Bone tired. And this gray-haired man was her way out. Yes, he had to die in order for her to get what she wanted, but he would die eventually anyway, whereas she would go on and on and on.

Might as well ensure that her eternity was spent in comfort. Ideally with a position of power to lord over her sisters. And, of course, her brothers.

"All right," she said with a quick nod. "I accept."

"Of course you do," her father replied. "Of you, my dear Lucia, I expect nothing less."

Chapter Two

Monte Carlo. The epitome of wealth and elegance, and Moreau's Sur la Mer hotel and casino stood like an ambassador. Her sleek lines rising toward the sky. Her liveried staff practically prostrating themselves to the clientele. And the guests shone with as much vibrancy as the diamonds they locked away each night in the hotel's vault.

Anyone who was anyone would give his right arm for a week in Monte at the Moreau. And if that week included a stay in one of the premier suites—if that stay included casino privileges at the most exclusive tables—well, then anyone who was anyone would surely give more than one measly limb.

Dante Moreau, however, would have preferred to be anywhere but where he was. And he would have preferred to be doing anything but what he was doing.

He'd come to Monte Carlo for one reason only—his father.

And because of that, he couldn't just simply leave.

And because of *that*, he was currently suffering under the headache to end all headaches.

"You look like a man with a lot on his mind."

With great effort, Dante lifted his head and looked through the red migraine haze into Marcel's chiseled face. The words were in flawless English, but the accent—like that of most Monte Carlo inhabitants—was pure French.

"*Oui,*" Dante replied to the bartender. "That's because I am."

He'd known Marcel for years, and he braced himself for a lecture. A rundown of his blessings. Of how not every man was so fortunate as to be the sole heir to the Moreau fortune.

Of how most men, upon entering the bar in one of Monte Carlo's most elegant hotels, would at least be expected to pay the tab at the end of a drinking binge.

Instead, Marcel said none of that. He simply poured two fingers of scotch into a glass and slid it across the polished bar toward Dante.

"I must look even worse than I feel," Dante said. "You've never once taken pity on me."

"Things change," Marcel said. "And the prodigal son returns even under protest, *n'est-ce pas?*"

Dante sighed. He hadn't realized that the casino staff knew the details of his business. He *should* have realized, of course. Rumors and gossip passed through the staff even faster than through the intelligence community. So the fact that Marcel knew that Dante had reluctantly returned to the glitter of Monte Carlo from his new home in Manhattan should come as no surprise.

"Your father needs you."

Dante slammed back the drink, his eyes never leaving Marcel's. "So he says."

At that, Marcel almost smiled. "Jacques Moreau is a man of few words. If he says so, it must be true."

True enough, Dante supposed, but considering he'd been summoned at three in the morning two days ago, then rushed over on his father's private jet with no explanation other than "your father says so," he was hardly in the mood to be altruistic about his father's motives. He shoved the glass forward, his brows raised in silent demand. Marcel took the hint and poured.

"You don't know what the emergency is?" Marcel asked.

"I'm not even certain there is an emergency."

Jacques Moreau had money, power, and wealth. He also had a rather inflated sense of self-worth, and an absolute certainty that only he knew best for his only son. That certainty had only increased after Jacques had divorced Dante's British mother when Dante had been barely out of diapers. He'd insisted on funding Dante's schooling, then urged his only son to follow through with military and intelligence training. Not bad work, all things considered. With the exception that it wasn't the work Dante wanted.

Still, he'd plodded through the system, ending up doing a stint with British Intelligence before his father crooked his little finger and played the family debt card. In retrospect, Dante supposed that he could have declined, citing his love for his work and the growing respect he'd earned within the intelligence community.

Except, of course, that wouldn't be true.

Oh, the respect was true, all right. He'd never once stepped on a toe that didn't need stepping on. He'd been the epitome of polite Eton upbringing, just as his parents would have wanted. But to stay because he loved his work . . . *that* would have been a blatant lie.

The truth was, Dante had never craved a life in intelligence circles. He'd gone that route because he hadn't known what life he craved, and as jobs landed in his lap because of his skills and family background, he'd accepted them graciously. After all, work was work. And absent passion, a paycheck would easily suffice.

When his father offered him the opportunity to run the security detail for the extensive chain of Moreau hotels . . . well, that was a paycheck, too. And considering the Moreau Corporation paycheck was higher than the British government's, Dante had easily made the decision to move. Why not? Trading one job for another equally passionless job was simple.

The job had been simple, too. Yes, his father had built an empire. But unlike the British Empire, the need for intelligence resources extended not much further than security cameras in the gift shops and private gaming rooms. In other words, a dull job, though a well-paying one.

Still, he couldn't knock it. Because Thomas Murchison would never have approached him while Dante was with the government. And once Thomas *did* lay out the offer, Dante realized what he'd been waiting for. A chance to use his training to make a difference. To help people in impossible situations. And, most of all, to help children.

He'd spent two months wrapping up his business with Moreau Corp., and then he'd flown to Manhattan and the nascent headquarters of M&M Security. The name was dry, but they weren't looking to be flashy. Their clientele was exclusive, and consisted of people who—if they needed Thomas and Dante's particular services—would know where to look.

Their specialty was the recovery of kidnapped children, particularly those taken out of the country. And in the last nine months, Dante had been instrumental in returning two little girls to their mothers. The satisfaction was immense, and the job itself was heaven. Moreover, it took every bit of his skill. From the merce-nary arts he'd learned in the intelligence world to the contacts he'd made in that same shadowy forum to the administrative skills he'd honed working for his father.

It had all come together.

Somehow, in all those years that he'd floundered, he'd known that eventually it would. Eventually, he'd find his purpose. And, once he did, nothing could sway him.

So why the hell was he now back in Monte Carlo, when at least two files were on his desk, waiting for his review and input?

He slammed back his drink, wanting to dull his mind with more scotch as the reality hit him dead-on—*his father.*

"I have a situation," his father had said. "I need you back here."

Dante had protested, of course, but in the end he had come. Even had his father not oh-so-subtly reminded him that Jacques Moreau had essentially paved the way for Dante's current job, Dante still would have come. That was the reality, after all. His father *had* supported his education. His father *had* utilized his con-tacts to get Dante a foot in the intelligence door. And his father *had* paid him a steep enough salary to allow Dante to save enough to live in comfort in Manhattan while the first M&M assignments rolled in.

In other words, even absent the demand, Dante knew that he owed his father. And since Dante didn't shirk his debts, here he was.

Besides, the man was his father. And wasn't that reason enough?

Too bad his father was nowhere to be seen.

He lifted a finger to signal Marcel. "Any word as to when my father will be back?" If anyone would have the latest gossip, it would be Marcel.

"Not even a trickle of a rumor."

"Damn." Dante's instinct was to let loose with a much louder curse, but he managed to rein it in. It was one thing to drop everything and come back to help his father. It was another thing altogether to have his father not be here despite his having demanded Dante's presence.

He half considered going home. He could leave a note for his father, then catch the next plane home. If Jacques needed him that badly, then Jacques could damn well fire up the Learjet and aim it toward Manhattan.

Not a bad idea, actually, and it was becoming more and more appealing as he mulled it over. So appealing, in fact, that he pulled out his cell phone and called his secretary. Nadine was a whirlwind of efficiency, and she quickly got him booked on a flight leaving in the morning.

Perfect.

He turned, intending to go to his room and catch up on reading and paperwork. He never made it that far. Instead, he simply froze, every nerve in his body tingling from the mere sensation of viewing the woman standing in the doorway. Dark and slender, with a bearing of both grace and strength. She assessed the room with a glance, her expression giving nothing away.

For just a hint of an instant, though, her eyes landed on him, and he swore he saw a spark there. A tiny hint of awareness. Of interest.

Lord knew he was interested, and it was that primal tug that kept him in his seat. Because the truth was, he'd been working too damn hard for too damn long.

And he could think of no better salve for his frustrated psyche than buying a drink for a beautiful woman.

Chapter Three

Her target wasn't on the premises.

A frustrating reality, but reality nonetheless, and one that Lucia would simply have to face.

Since facing it would be easier with a glass of cabernet, she eased toward the bar and slid onto one of the empty bar stools. The bartender seemed to materialize in front of her, and she ordered her wine, then sat back with her eyes closed, hoping that Jacques Moreau's absence wasn't a portent that her assignment was doomed. Monaco had never been a good place for her, and just being back sent a wash of bad memories flooding over her.

Stop it.

This was not a mission she could—or would—fail. Monaco meant nothing to her. Centuries had passed. The place had changed.

Moreau's absence meant nothing either. Not even a delay. After all, it wasn't as if she was going to stroll into the casino, guns blazing, and take him out.

No, her work was always much more refined. She had to plan. To prepare.

But part of that planning and preparation involved observing the target, and sometimes even affirmative action to get close to the target. His absence *did* delay that aspect of her preparations.

Didn't matter. He'd come eventually. She'd get close. She'd do the deed. And it would be over. Her father had given her a week to succeed at her task, after all. And Moreau never stayed away from his signature property for more than four days at a time.

So even if she *did* have to come out, guns blazing, well, she could do that. To ensure that this was her last assassination, she'd do it in a second.

That was her only way out, after all. Assassinate Moreau and be free of this life. Take charge of her father's empire . . . and never have to answer to his demands again.

She couldn't prevent the smile that eased across her face. Because as ironic as it might be, *that* situation sounded like a little bit of heaven.

"Nice to see that," a rich voice commented. "I was afraid you had serious things on your mind."

She jerked her head up, surprised. And more than a little unnerved that someone could have eased so close to her without her well-honed wariness kicking in. She opened her mouth to tell the interfering bastard off, but instead found herself holding her tongue, her breath caught fast in her throat.

The man was perfect.

There was, quite simply, no other way to say it.

And, honestly, for Lucia, that was saying a lot. After all, she'd been in a position to be up close and very personal with some of the most attractive men in the world. She'd dined with playboys, danced with film stars, and had wild, passionate affairs with men so beautiful they'd posed for the likes of Da Vinci and Botticelli. Men handpicked to model for sculptors commissioned to chisel likenesses of the gods themselves. Men who were, without question, absolutely beautiful.

She'd brought those men into her bed. Some for pleasure . . . and some for business.

With each of them, she'd enjoyed herself. And with each of them, she'd always felt in control.

Right now, though, control escaped her. And, honestly, she wasn't even sure why.

This man standing in front of her wasn't beautiful. If anything, he was a little too rugged. His lord of the manor European features softened by a day's worth of beard that she longed to reach out and stroke. His brows were thick and dark, and seemed to perfectly frame his ice blue eyes. And his mouth . . . wide and firm.

Perfect.

She shivered a little, because empirically, the man really wasn't perfect. And yet there he was, standing in front of her. And there she was, sitting on her hand so she wouldn't reach out and brush her thumb over the curve of his lower lip.

"Or, perhaps I spoke too soon?" he said.

She shook her head, trying to make sense of his words. "What?"

"You smiled, and I thought that you'd resolved whatever put that serious expression on your face. But now it's returned, and so I have to wonder . . . what could be causing such consternation in a woman as beautiful as you?"

"Beautiful," she repeated, determined to pull herself together. "Hmmm."

"Hmmm, good?" he asked, his voice laced with amusement. "Or hmmm, bad?"

"I'm just a little shocked, I think," she said, working to keep her expression completely deadpan.

She watched his eyes widen. "Are you?" he asked. "Why?"

"I guess I'd hoped you'd be more original."

"Ah, yes. Well, perhaps I'd hoped you'd take pity on me."

"Pity?" she repeated, enjoying the banter. "Trust me. Pity really isn't my style."

"No? Then how about charity? Can I buy you a drink?"

She sighed, putting her whole body into the deep expression of woe.

"Still not original enough for you?" he asked, his voice overflowing with concern.

"Not in the least."

"Damn. And I usually do so well with the ladies."

"Really? With that material?" She was having a hard time not smiling, but she was also having too much fun to break the mood now. And the fact was, it had been a long time since she'd really had fun with a man. Especially one so delicious to look at.

"Nah, I haven't pulled out the tried-and-true stuff on you yet."

"Maybe you should," she said with mock seriousness. "I think you're getting down to the wire."

"Am I?" he said. "I usually have such a good sense of when I'm crashing and burning."

"Trust me," she said. "I've got the inside scoop on how you're doing."

"Good point. All right, then. Time for the big guns." He pulled out the stool next to her, then sat down. He turned to face her, his eyes deadly serious. "So," he finally said, "I have to know." He paused, and she held her breath, wondering what wonder he'd come up with now. "What's a nice girl like you doing in a place like this?"

She burst out laughing. She couldn't help it. The campy line was just too funny. Too unexpected.

And, frankly, way too false. "I think you've got it backwards."

"Have I?"

"The question is, what's a girl like me doing in a nice place like this."

"Ah." He leaned back, his hands together, his fingers steepled. "Interesting."

"What's that?"

"I've managed to hook up with a naughty girl."

"Trust me," she said, looking straight into his eyes. "You don't know the half of it."

His gaze didn't waver, and she felt herself being sucked in. "Why don't you show me?" he asked, his voice holding all sorts of decadent possibilities.

"Is that a proposition?"

"Absolutely."

She leaned back in her seat, a fingertip pressed to the side of her mouth as she made a show of looking him up and down. The view was quite delightful, and she fought the smile that tugged at her lips.

Finally, she met his eyes, and the heat she saw there was almost enough to make her drop the pretense altogether and simply lose herself in his arms. "Convince me."

"This is a casino," he said. "Perhaps you'd fancy a wager?"

"A wager," she repeated. "Like what?"

"Nothing unreasonable," he said. "Roulette. A game of pure chance. I win, you have dinner with me."

"Dinner?"

"That's a metaphor," he said. "But don't ask me for what. That, I have to show you."

"I see." She licked her lips, reveling in the way her body tingled from the decadent promise in his voice. "Only dinner?"

There was a question in her voice, but he couldn't quite interpret the query. She had to know, though, that he wasn't interested in anything more than the one night. That was, after all, only fair. "I'd offer you breakfast as well," he said, "but I have a plane to catch in the morning."

Relief flashed in her eyes, and he congratulated himself for saying the right thing. This woman wanted the same thing he did, and that was perfectly fine with Dante.

"All right," she said. "Dinner if you win. But if you lose?"

"I lose and you can tell me to go jump off a cliff."

She lifted a brow. "You realize that we're in Monte Carlo. There are a lot of cliffs in the vicinity to choose from."

"Believe me," he said, after letting his hot gaze sweep all the way from her toes to her eyes, "I know exactly what's at stake."

His luscious mouth twitched at the corner, and as it did, she shifted in her seat, the warm tingle between her legs evidence of the way she wanted this wager to go. She didn't normally mix business with pleasure, but in this case she'd decided to make an exception the moment she'd first seen him.

After all, her quarry had yet to arrive, and she did have some time to kill. . . .

Dante waited, his breath caught in his chest, as he watched the woman's face. He was certain he was reading her right, certain that their banter was a casual flirting with a not-so-casual intent raging just beneath the surface.

Still, though, that tiny glimmer of doubt remained. The fear that everything he saw in her was fueled by his own desire. A lust-induced fantasy, complete with a willing woman and a few hours to kill before his plane took off in the morning.

The situation truly teetered on the precipice of unbelievability, and he wasn't sure what kept it from tumbling over. The interest in her eyes, perhaps. Or the way her body leaned toward his with a purposeful casualness, as if she was as attuned to him as he was to her.

He didn't know. All he knew was that he hoped his certainty that their attraction was mutual wasn't imaginary. Because if this woman didn't accompany him to the gaming floor—and, ultimately, to his bed—he was going to be one very unhappy man come morning.

He managed a slow smile, and hoped that no edge of apprehension crept into his voice. "Is it that hard to make a decision?"

"I'm just contemplating whether you play fair."

"Never," he said, and saw immediately that he'd said the right thing.

She slipped off the stool, her silk skirt clinging to her thighs, then hooked her arm through his. "Then by all means," she said. "Let's wager."

He signaled to Marcel to put her bill on his tab, and was relieved when she didn't protest. So many women refused to let a man buy them a drink. The fact that this woman did, not only pleased him, it seemed to hone some primitive urge within him.

Nothing about her indicated a need to be protected, and yet he couldn't help but feel that there was a vulnerability in her. And coupled with the smoldering sensuality that had set his senses on fire . . . well, the woman needed only to smile if she wanted to wrap him around her little finger. Or around anywhere else, for that matter.

Stepping from the oak-walled quiet of the bar into the gold leaf and bright lights of the casino was like stepping into a different world. The noise level rose, though not to an obnoxious level. This was, after all, a Moreau casino. And if Jacques Moreau understood anything, it was class and sophistication. The lights were bright—a typical casino trick—and the decibel level increased, but nothing about the room was overwhelming or off-putting. Just the opposite, actually.

The ornate furnishings clustered in corners provided relaxing seating areas where well-trained waiters and waitresses would provide for every whim, from vodka to cigars to a late-night snack of oysters on the half shell. Every need satisfied. Every want fulfilled.

Dante had grown up living half in and half out of this world. His youth spent just outside of London with his mother. Rare weekends and summer months spent here, the beloved "young master" to the staff. At the time, he'd been embarrassed by the attention. Uncomfortable with the power and wealth that went along with being Jacques Moreau's son.

Over time, the monetary part had gotten easier. Even now, though, he wasn't comfortable being his father's son.

The melancholy thought seemed to come from nowhere, and he pushed it away, reaching across himself to close his free hand over hers still hooked to his elbow. They'd been walking in companionable silence, him lost in his thoughts and his companion apparently lost in awe of her surroundings. When he touched her, she started, her gaze pulled away from an examination of the ceiling and the camouflaged catwalk above to land on him with studious intent.

"Hey," she whispered.

"Hey, yourself."

"Do you know the way to the roulette tables?"

"I think I can manage to get us there," he said, fighting a grin. He had no intention of telling her who he was. Not yet, anyway. Too many women had fallen into his bed once they'd learned his family name. This woman he wanted to see only him. Not his paternity.

He stepped back, unhooking their arms, then offered her his palm. She pressed her fingertips against his hand without even hesitating. The familiarity delighted him more than he cared to admit, and he covered his discomfiture with absurd small talk. "Have you been here before?"

A quick shake of her head. "No. You?"

"A few times."

She looked up at him, her eyes twinkling. "Well, then. I guess you've just earned your spot as my guide."

"Gainful employment. Not bad. But what are the terms of the offer?"

"Terms?"

He stopped, then tugged her hand, pulling her close, the delighted surprise he saw in her eyes thrilling him. "For example, are there any perks with the job?"

She lifted an eyebrow. "Well, now, I think that's entirely negotiable."

"Is it?"

"Absolutely." Her voice was like honey, and she capped the word with a seductive grin. "Of course, there's still one thing."

"One thing?"

"You still have to win that wager." She took one step away from him, then flipped her hair and looked back at him over her shoulder, as he looked on in awe, his mouth hanging open like a teenager's in lust. "So are you coming?"

"Oh, yeah," he said. "I'm coming."

And that, he thought, was the understatement of the century.

They finished crossing the main floor, then turned into the west salon, where the roulette tables were set up under ornate gold and jeweled chandeliers. As they approached, Jacob, one of the long-time croupiers, started to raise a hand in greeting. Dante made a subtle cutting gesture with his free hand. And Jacob—who'd been taking cues from the Moreau men for years—turned away without missing a beat.

It was all Dante could do not to smile. Damn, but his father knew how to train his staff.

They approached at the same time as two other couples, and Jacob started the wheel spinning.

"What number?" Dante asked her, as the other couples spread their chips over the numbered grid.

"No way," she said. "Your wager, your responsibility." She leaned in close, then kissed the tip of his nose. "But I will wish you luck."

"And I thank you for that."

They shared a smile, and he put a crisp hundred-euro note on number 17. Then he did something he'd done only once before. He tapped his index finger once on the table, then stepped backward and pressed a finger to his temple. The first time, he'd been an arrogant teenager, trying to win a stupid bet. This time, he was a lust-filled adult, trying to win the girl.

No one suspected as Jacob worked the floor pedal, ensuring that number 17 came up the winner. And as the other players applauded his good luck, the woman on his arm looked at him with wide, intrigued eyes. "Congratulations."

"I have you to thank," he said as he scooped up his winnings, making sure to signal to Jacob to have the rooms of all the players at the table comped.

"Me?"

"You're the one who wished me luck."

"Mmmm." She looked him up and down. "And it worked. I take it you're feeling lucky?"

"Absolutely."

"So it looks as if we'll be having dinner together tonight."

"That was the wager."

"Indeed." She tilted her head to the side, then looked at him through lowered lashes. "And where do you plan on taking me?"

"Actually," he said, swept away on a wave of boldness, "I was thinking room service."

Chapter Four

Lucia was having fun.

There was, quite simply, no other way to describe it.

And while the emotion didn't exactly disturb her, the ramifications did. After all, she needed to be at her best if she was going to pull off this assignment. Distractions—especially of a sexual nature—would simply not do.

And yet . . .

And yet she couldn't bring herself to walk away from this man. There was something about his laugh. Something about the way he was willing to put himself on the line for her. The wager. The banter. All of it delighted her. And, yes, all of it excited her.

And when he'd suggested room service rather than a five-star restaurant . . . well, honestly, the mere thought of being alone with this man in a room was almost more than she could stand. And after several millennia, Lucia had withstood a lot.

"Well?" He was looking at her, the query in his eyes as intent as the need she saw there. She recognized it, absorbed it, and reflected it right back at him.

More than that, though, she realized suddenly that he didn't know her name any more than she knew his. The realization sent shock waves of relief and lust coursing through her. Anonymity meant freedom, and with this man she wanted the freedom to do anything.

And why not? Wasn't she under the absolute worst kind of job stress? She needed a little stress relief. Not only that, she *deserved* it.

"Absolutely," she said, unable to hide her smile. "Room service sounds positively delicious."

His return smile matched hers, and that was all the response she needed to know that she'd made the right decision. After all, this was not a situation where she would be forced to try to complete her task with a clinging male dogging her every move. This man wanted exactly what she wanted—a quick fling. And the freedom to then move on.

"Your room or mine?" she asked, which broke her rule of never inviting a man to her room. But she was already breaking her rule of never seducing a man while on an assignment—unless he was part of the assignment—so she decided one more rule shattered wouldn't hurt. Besides, the room wasn't listed under her real name—or, at least, not under the surname she'd been using for the last dozen or so years.

Still, the fact that she'd so cavalierly offered made her uneasy, and she was about to rescind when he resolved the issue for her.

"Our room," he said, holding up his winnings with one hand while slipping his free arm around her waist and pulling her close.

"Ours?" The word sounded weak, and she had only his touch to blame. The man had already turned her ignition up high. The added heat generated as he pulled her close set her near to combusting.

He urged them forward. "Come with me, Mrs. Smith."

She kept in step with him, fighting a smile, because she had never once bowed to convention and checked in to a hotel with a man under an assumed name. With this man, though, the idea seemed not only brilliant, but erotic. And full of infinite promise.

They strolled through the casino toward the hotel registration desk, his thumb grazing her back, bare from the halter that tied at her neck and waist. Every few strokes, the tip of his thumb would ease below the waistband of her skirt, and each time it did, Lucia wanted to moan and beg.

She didn't show it, though. She prided herself on that. The intense lust was under the surface, as was his. He kept up the playful banter as they walked, his tempting finger the only clue that his mind was on a more decadent form of play.

The dichotomy was overwhelmingly erotic, and by the time they reached the front desk, she knew her panties were soaked. One touch, and she would surely come right there.

Considering her desperate straits, the five-star service was much appreciated. She'd been in many hotels, but never in her life had she seen a hotel staff scurry so fast. This staff did, and all Dante had to do was ask. In less than five minutes, Mr. and Mrs. John Smith were booked into an executive suite on the twenty-fifth floor.

She clasped his hand, practically dragging him to the elevators with a ferocity born of a need that she hadn't experienced in a very long time. Had she ever felt this way about a man? This desperate? This out of control?

Lucia was no stranger to lust. To wild passion and physical abandon. She was, after all, her father's daughter. But the hard-hitting drive of pure sex—while decadently wonderful—had an edge to it unlike what she felt with this man. With him, she wanted . . . what?

She didn't know, and she told herself that there was nothing else to it. She wanted sex. That was all.

Sex. Abandon. To lose herself in this man and in this few hours of freedom before she threw herself hard and heavy into her final assignment.

She told herself all of that, and yet she didn't quite believe it. Still, the truth hardly mattered at the moment, when all she wanted to feel was the press of his skin against hers, and as they moved toward the elevator bank, she barely even noticed the surroundings, the warm gold and dazzling gemstones little more than reflections of her own vibrant emotions.

The mirrored elevator doors reflected their approach—and her need. She could see it in her own eyes, and saw it equally matched in his. And it was that glimpse into the depths of his own desperation that convinced her that she was right to simply go with this. Tomorrow, she could be Lucia again. Tonight, she would lose herself in the heat of anonymity.

The doors opened, and they stepped on together. The car was empty, and they turned, their eyes catching for only a fraction of a second. That was all it took for ignition. He pulled her roughly to him, and she moaned, her body crying out with need. She pressed herself against him, her leg up, suspended by the press of his hand on her thigh. His fingers spayed along the bare skin under her skirt, just inches from her crotch. She pressed her mouth to him and wriggled shamelessly, desperate to feel his fingers stroking her and filling her.

His mouth was hot and firm against hers, his tongue demanding entrance. She opened herself to him, delighting in the warm taste of him and the way his tongue teased and explored.

His thumb made slow circular motions on her thigh, and the teasing touch came near to driving her mad. With one hand, she cupped his neck, pulling him in closer, deepening the kiss. With the other hand she reached down, closing her hand over him and urging his fingers higher, searching for a different kind of depth.

His groan was all the encouragement she needed. "Stop the elevator," she whispered, her tongue flicking at his ear.

"There are cameras in the cars. Security."

She pulled away just long enough to meet his eyes. "I don't care."

He slipped his hand up, his finger sliding easily under the edge of her silky panties. She felt her body tighten as his fingertip explored her folds. Then he pulled back, ever so gently, and kissed the tip of her nose.

"I care," he said.

She wanted to protest. To rant and rage and beg that—cameras be damned—she simply couldn't wait any longer.

But there was no need. The elevator slid to a stop, and the door to their room was right there. She stumbled out, tugging him with her. They edged forward, their bodies so intertwined she wasn't sure where she ended and he began. She wasn't at all sure how, but somehow they got the door open. They tumbled inside, the scent of champagne and strawberries surrounding them, casting their hard-edged lust with a romantic edge.

He kicked his foot back, and the door slammed shut with a resounding thud. That noise was like a cue, and suddenly they were ripping at clothes, pulling and tugging, lips joined, and skin touching.

A few straps and buttons later, and Lucia found herself naked on the bed, this perfect man above her, his body as hard and cut as the statue of a Greek god. She opened her mouth to beg—to demand—but no words came. Instead, she saw the look in his eye and knew that all good things come to girls who wait.

So instead of demanding, she let her head fall back on the pillow, then shivered as his fingers traced over her body, forming slow sensuous circles around her navel, then tracing down, down, down to tease her between her legs.

She gasped as his finger slipped inside her, but the sound barely escaped, blocked by the pressure of his mouth on her lips. His tongue thrust deep inside her even as his finger mimicked the same rhythm and stroked her intimately. She lifted her hips, instinct demanding more of him. She clung to his back, her fingernails digging into his flesh.

He broke the kiss, but didn't stop stroking her. Her body hummed, a tightwire ready to snap, as his mouth closed over her breast. His tongue danced around her nipple and she knew without a shadow of a doubt that this man would be the death of her—an amazing feat, considering her immortality.

He nipped at her, teeth and lips teasing her, and sending a hot coil racing through her to find his fingers, still exploring her secrets. He stroked her in small circles, tensing and tempting and—

Oh, sweet Hades!

She couldn't take it. Had to have him. Had to have release.

And so she reached for him, her fingers twining in that silky black hair. She tugged him toward her, then nipped at his chin, his neck. And then, when she couldn't take it anymore, she shifted her weight, and shifted him as well, rolling him over until she straddled him.

He grinned, slow and satisfied. And completely unperturbed that she'd taken advantage of the situation.

She pressed a kiss to the dimple revealed by his grin, then followed that with another to his chin, his neck, his chest.

She stroked lazy circles on his chest, her fingers twisting in the smattering of chest hair. Enough to be masculine, and yet not too much. He hit, as always, the perfect blend.

In fact, so far nothing about this man had urged her off her first impression—*perfect*.

And, so help her, she was ready for a taste of perfection.

She cast one simmering glance toward his face and saw the need building there. Good. Slowly, she trailed her kisses lower and lower, delighting in the way his body shimmered and stuttered as he fought the building passion. Her fingers teased and stroked, but her mouth tasted and tormented, taking him close to the edge, then back again, and silently daring him to demand more.

His body demanded—bucking and tightening and thrumming with a heat that she could feel and touch and smell. But his lips never begged. Never gave a hint of the sweet agony he was suffering. And, ultimately, that she was suffering, too.

"Damn you," she said, as she eased herself up and over him. And then, when she knew by the tiny smile that played on his lips that he understood the reason for the curse, she impaled herself on him.

Oh, sweet fires of Hades!

Had she ever experienced such delight? They moved together, and Lucia was certain that, somehow, she was going to lose herself. That she was going to come free of this body that she'd known for so many years and simply end up a bit of vapor in the sky, burned up by the heat that they were generating together.

A dangerous heat, and one she couldn't let stop. It built and built as they moved together, bodies damp from the sweat of exertion, limbs gliding and twining. Now, she thought. Now, now, *now*!

She exploded in his arms, the tremors continuing as he milked her orgasm, pulling her further than she'd gone and then bringing her back, gently, to rest in his arms as they watched the moonlight streak in through the window that overlooked the sea.

"I—" She started to speak, but he hushed her with a gentle finger to her lip, and she closed her mouth, gratefully. Minutes had passed, but she was still sated, languid. And the thought of not moving—of not speaking—of simply remaining in his arms held such sweet delight.

That, however, wasn't his plan. A fact that became apparent as he slid off the bed, taking the covers they'd loosened in their erotic fever with him. She started to protest—she didn't want him to leave!—when the point became moot. He gathered her close, then carried her bridelike across the room and into the bathroom. A bath had already been drawn, and now he gently settled her into the overflowing bubble bath, the hot water still flowing so that the water was kept at a perfect temperature.

Rose petals decorated the floor, leading up to the oversized, sunken tub. And the entire thing was surrounded by candles, each already lit.

How had she not noticed this before?

That, of course, was easy. She'd let down her guard. She'd entered the suite with him, and she'd never once examined it, a behavior totally contrary to her well-honed survival skills. Even an innocent liaison can turn dangerous, especially in her profession. And yet she'd never even hesitated in this man's arms.

The thought sent a shiver running through her, but she wasn't sure it was fear. It was . . . she didn't know. And at the moment, she couldn't quite think, because suddenly he was in the tub as well. He settled himself behind her, then leaned her against him, her back against his chest.

"I'm glad you lost the wager," he said.

"Did I lose? It really doesn't feel that way."

He licked the back of her ear. "Good."

"Are we—"

"Shhh. We're bathing. Let me bathe you."

And because she'd never in her life had anyone ask to bathe her, Lucia nodded, then closed her eyes and lost herself to the sweet sensation of the soapy sponge against her bare back.

The attention was undeniably erotic, yet at the same time it was somehow sweet. And it was that sweetness that piqued her senses.

She'd always liked sex fast and hard—and this man had more than delivered. No emotional entanglements for a girl like her. But lately, soft thoughts had been entering her head. Her hesitation to undertake her past jobs. The tug at her heart when the baron had shown her his family pictures. And now this sense of sweetness as a man she barely knew rubbed her back with gentle touches. And during their lovemaking there'd been a gentleness under the heated passion. An emotion that made the act more than simply coupling. It made it special. And damned if she didn't like that, too.

She was a study in contradictions and the direction of her thoughts scared her. Right now was not the time for distractions. She had her purpose, and she needed to follow through quickly and efficiently.

She said a silent thank-you that he'd be gone tomorrow. That knowledge alone quelled her fears. Yes, her reaction to him was uncomfortable and strange. But what did it matter? He'd be gone soon enough. And she could get on with her plan.

And with her future.

Chapter Five

Dante woke up slowly, the woman soft and warm in his arms. He had no desire to be anywhere else. No thoughts of moving, no plan to get on.

And yet that's exactly what he had to do.

He closed his eyes, fighting the inevitable, and instead shifted closer, the heat of her body firing senses that by all rights should have been dulled from sheer exhaustion.

They weren't. They weren't dulled at all.

If anything, his body was ready to stand up, salute, and jump right back into the fray. And it took every ounce of willpower in his body not to kiss her shoulder, roll her over, and do exactly that. He couldn't, though. The bright green numbers on the digital clock made that perfectly clear. He had three hours to get dressed, get packed, and get to the airport.

He actually considered staying. Not for his father, of course, but for this woman. But he knew that wasn't possible. No matter how much he might wish otherwise, the woman beside him was little more than an illusion. A sexy, hot, responsive illusion, but fantasy nonetheless.

His chest tightened with longing, because the truth was that he wanted her name. He wanted her name and her phone number and her address. He wanted to knock on her hotel room door, take her arm, and escort her down to a romantic dinner.

Last night with the anonymous vixen had been beyond incredible, but now he wanted more. He wanted real.

And damned if he couldn't have it.

Best to just go as planned. Besides, if he stayed, he'd just get sucked into some damned power play with his father. Even more, though, he knew that the woman in his bed didn't want the date. Didn't want the romance.

Above all, she didn't want to tell him her name.

They'd uttered no promises, and yet the rules were clear all the same. One night. No names.

And then he'd leave Monte Carlo.

As much as he now regretted that silent promise, he knew that he wouldn't break it. He couldn't.

With a sigh, he moved slowly, curling himself out from under her arm and sitting up. He bent forward, stretching, as he tried to work up the enthusiasm to move to the shower.

A warm palm pressed against his bare back, and all semblance of motivation vanished. Staying here was fine; the bed was just fine.

"Hey." A soft whisper from behind, accompanied by a subtle shift of the mattress. A quick brush of lips on the back of his ear, and soft hands snaking around his body to stroke his chest. "Good morning."

"Good morning to you," he said, his body testifying to just how good a morning it was suddenly becoming.

"It is rather exceptional, isn't it?" Her words were soft, laced with a tease, and punctuated by the fingers dancing over his bare skin.

"And getting better by the second."

"You're getting up. Taking a shower?"

"That was my plan."

"You have a plane to catch," she said. It was a simple statement, and yet Dante ripped it apart, trying to analyze nuances, tone. Did she want him to hurry and leave? To stay? He didn't know. He knew only that he wanted to hold on to the fantasy that this woman wanted him as much as he wanted her.

"I do," he finally said, which was completely inadequate, but the best he could do.

"When do you have to leave?"

A hint of invitation colored her voice, and Dante jumped all over that. "Why do you ask?"

Her hands slipped down, gliding beneath the satin sheets to stroke him. He was already hard as steel, and her little moan of pleasure when she discovered that fact simply made him harder. "Well, I'd hate to make you late, but . . ."

"I'll make up the time somehow," he assured her as he turned, leaning back so that he could see her face. "Actually, I have a better idea."

One perfectly formed brow lifted. "Oh, really?"

He stood, then held out a hand. "Nothing like multitasking," he said with a quick glance toward the bathroom and the eight showerheads that waited for them in the stall.

She grinned wickedly, then slid out of bed. "I'm a big fan of multitasking."

The shower was amazing, even by the Moreau standards, and it was one of the reasons that Dante had wanted this suite. Large enough for even more than two people, with an overhead "rain" showerhead and rows of side heads on either side, the place was both practical, decadent, and potentially erotic.

He turned the water on full blast, then adjusted the temperature. He stepped into the spray, the dual sets of heads pummeling his body from all sides.

He reached for her, but she shook her head. "Too rough," she said.

"For you? I'm surprised."

She grinned, then leaned past him, turning the ornate lever to shift the water from the side-facing heads to the overhead flow. The ceiling seemed to open up, and they were standing in a soft spring rain. She wrapped her arms around his neck and pressed her body close to his, her crotch nestled against his ready cock. "Now isn't this better?"

"Most definitely," he said, bending down for a long, slow kiss as the water sluiced over their bodies. Hands followed the trail of water, and when she reached past him to one of the many soap dispensers filled with fragrant cleansers, her breasts brushed gently against his skin, sending coils of heat ripping through him.

Her hands were slick, filled with lavender-scented soap, and she rubbed them on his chest, the minimal friction as erotic as a gentle kiss. Too gentle, though. Her touch was driving him crazy, and he pulled her close, crushing his mouth over hers. She responded instantly, and just as eagerly, her legs clinging to his body, then sliding down because of the damnably slick soap.

He grabbed her, lifting her as she hooked her legs around him, pulling her in tight as he slid into her sweet center. Hard and fast, yes, but he couldn't wait any longer, and from the way her breath was coming in desperate gasps, he knew that she couldn't, either.

They writhed together, bodies joined, skin slippery, steam billowing around them. Her hand splayed out, seeking purchase on the cut-stone wall of the shower, even as her back arched and she thrust herself against him. "Yes," she cried. "Oh, please, *yes.*"

He didn't hesitate, didn't answer, simply let his body respond. And soon he felt her tighten around his, watched as a tremor shook her frame. She gasped, her head thrusting back until she was facing the gentle spray of water from above. He thrust again once, one hand clinging to a showerhead for support. He seemed to explode with sensation, and he thrust his own head back, the shower's water seeming to dissolve into steam upon the inferno of heat they were generating.

He held her close, their bodies sinking together to the marble floor. They clung to each other, breath coming hot and fast. After a few moments, when he was sure his body could handle the strain of speech and thought, he shifted a bit. He needed to look into her eyes and see if he saw there the reflection of his own satisfaction. He did, and when she smiled like the cat who'd caught the canary, his heart gave a little leap.

He'd been caught, all right, and he didn't mind in the least.

"We should move," she said, after an eternity of clinging to each other. "We're all wet."

"A small price to pay."

"We'll get all pruney."

"You'll still be beautiful."

"You're a charmer," she said, a smile in her voice.

"And you know it's true," he said, teasing. "You are many things, but modest is not one of them."

That got a real laugh out of her. "Such a short time, and you already know me so well."

"It doesn't feel short to me," he said, then immediately regretted it. He was crossing the line into *date* language. Into *relationship* territory. And that, he knew, was verboten.

"No," she said. "Not to me, either."

The lightness in his heart caused by her words was tempered by the fact that she was physically pulling away. She stood up and pushed the door to the shower stall open, then wrapped herself in a fluffy terry-cloth towel. She leaned against the wall and started to finger-comb her hair.

"Hey," he said. "What about me?"

"You wanted a towel? Too bad for me. I like the view without."

"Yeah?" He strutted forward, doing a convincing imitation of Mr. Nude Universe. "In that case, I'm just fine."

She laughed. "You may be fine—in fact, I'm in complete agreement—but you're also dripping all over the floor."

"So? It's not your floor."

"Good point. Drip away."

He started to go to her. Started to work up the nerve to cancel his flight and tell her he was staying.

He couldn't do it, though. The thought that he'd see nothing in her eyes but irritation—or, worse, disappointment—was too much to bear.

The sharp ring of his cell phone from the bedroom drew his attention, and he hurried toward it, grabbing a towel as he went simply because he happened to know the wholesale cost of the carpet in the bedroom area. He glanced at caller ID, saw his father's name, and seriously considered letting it roll over to voice mail.

He couldn't do it, though. It was the same damn thing that had gotten him to Monte Carlo in the first place. That irritating Pavlov's dog response to His Master's Voice.

He snapped open the cell phone, and barked an irritated, "What?"

"*Ah, bien,*" his father said. "You are still there. I had heard you might be aboard a plane."

"You heard." Dante resisted the urge to bang his head against something hard. "Well, actually you heard right. I'm on my way out this morning. I figure if you don't need to be here, then neither do I."

"*Bien sûr.* But what you don't understand is that I *do* need to be there. And I *must* be there by Friday."

"What's Friday?"

"The opening of the new wing."

"Right." He should have known. Anything for the damn hotel. Nothing for the family.

He shook off the thought. It sounded too damn whiny, and the one thing Dante was absolutely sure of, his father wasn't worth the grief.

"I need you there with me," his father said.

"You've done this stuff dozens of times. I think you can handle it."

"I've never done one with an assassin on the loose."

Okay, *that* caught Dante's attention. "What in hell are you talking about?"

"Just that. Security received a tip. Someone is trying to kill me. *That's* why I called you, Dante. I need your help. Please, son. I can't live in hiding forever. I have to come back for the opening or my reputation will be destroyed. Stay. Stay and help me find this assassin."

Lucia forced herself not to pay attention as her Man of the Moment spoke in urgent tones on the phone. What did she care, after all? Wives and girlfriends cared when their men had tense phone calls with colleagues. But Lucia had never been a wife-or-girlfriend kind of girl.

And she wasn't going to start now.

He was leaving, and that was good. Hell, he was probably getting chewed out right that very moment, his boss wondering why his tail wasn't on the morning's earliest flight. Soon he'd be off to the airport, and the unfamiliar tug around her heart would disappear. That was good. That was what she wanted.

Because what she wanted most was to finish this job.

Her *last* job.

She heard him say something about how he'd handle it, and she forced herself not to smile as she passed by—on her way to retrieve the purse she'd left amid the tumble of clothes by the door. She found her little makeup bag and headed back to the restroom, her thoughts turning to fantasies of making one last use of the bed that he looked so good pacing in front of.

No.

This was over, and that was good. If she was smart, she'd get dressed and leave while he was still on the phone. Direct. To the point. Clean.

But she couldn't quite do it.

Instead, she concentrated on her eyeliner.

After a moment of concentration, she heard him step onto the bathroom tile. She turned, and couldn't help but flash him a smile.

Then she turned quickly back to the mirror and covered the gesture by returning to her makeup. "Your boss?"

"My father," he said. "And my boss. Kind of makes life more interesting, you know?"

"Actually," she said, "I do know." And there was another little tightening of the rope around her heart. That familiarity she'd felt with him was real. They truly did have things in common.

Get a grip, Lucia.

"You work for your dad?"

"Mmmm-hmmm." She kept her face still, her focus on the millimeter-thin line of green liner she was applying.

She expected him to respond with commiseration. An anecdote. Anything but what he actually said.

"Right," he said. "Well, as it turns out, I'm staying here. More work."

The pencil slipped, and she ended up with a green streak marring the soft skin under her left eye.

"Oh." She tried to smile, but couldn't quite manage it. "Oh."

She watched him in the mirror, saw something shift in his face. After a moment, he took a step backward, then disappeared into the bedroom. She moved that way, too, then stopped, unsure of what she should do.

He was staying. And, so help her, even though she knew he'd be the distraction from, well, *hell*, she couldn't deny the fact that she wanted him to.

A little surge of anger burst through her. This was part of the test. That had to be it. It made perfect sense that her father was trying to up the ante.

After all, hadn't her father offered her the keys to his kingdom in exchange for one simple assassination? Never mind that it wasn't nearly as simple as it had been decades, or even centuries, ago. The point was that he'd placed in her lap a test that she couldn't help but win.

And although she might be his favorite, she knew that her father didn't work that way. It simply wasn't in his nature.

Which meant that this man *must* be part of the test. That was the only explanation. Her father knew the kind of man who could distract her, and he'd thrown him directly into her path. *Of course* a simple assassination would be too easy. Hadn't the old devil said he'd tested the boys? And as much as she liked to believe that Jack, Nick, and Marcus had failed because they were incompetent playboys, Lucia knew the truth. They were all *very* competent in their own ways. If they'd failed, it was because they'd been faced with a true test of their worth.

Clearly, that was what was happening here.

Well, that was just fine.

She could handle whatever he threw at her. She was a professional. She could work in the face of distraction.

She leaned in closer to the mirror, inspecting her reflection as she tried to calm herself down. She used the edge of her thumb to fix the stray bit of eyeliner, but really it was all distraction. A delay before she turned back to look at him. At the man that, just hours ago, she'd wanted gone from her life.

Now, she had to admit that she wanted him to stay.

Dear Hades, could her father actually be doing her a favor?

She considered the possibility, then tossed it aside. No. That wasn't like her father at all. For that matter, maybe her father had nothing to do with this man at all.

Maybe, instead, it was a gift. Not from her father, but simply from the universe. Karma. Fate. Whatever you wanted to call it.

So few genuinely nice things had happened to her in her life. And, honestly, she hadn't expected them to. Why would she? Considering her heritage, warm fuzzies were hardly the norm.

But with the man in the other room . . .

She stifled a shiver. Now that she had the chance for affection, no matter how fleeting, she could hardly walk away.

More, she didn't *want* to walk away.

And that, ultimately, was the deciding factor.

Test or gift or simple coincidence, it didn't matter. All that mattered was that she wanted him.

She closed her eyes, taking deep breaths for strength, and then she turned to face the open door to the bedroom. She crossed the threshold in three long strides, then saw him there, standing by the window, nothing more than a towel around those perfect hips.

But although his stance was confident, the face reflected in the glass told a different story. And looking at that expression, she felt both power and shame. Power that she could invoke such a longing in a man. Shame that she had taken so long to make her decision.

He turned around, his expression blank except for the hint of a question in his eyes.

She smiled, hoping that if the simple gesture didn't soothe him, that her words would. "Hi," she said. "My name is Lucia. And you still owe me dinner."

Chapter Six

Lucia. He'd been saying the name all day, albeit quietly to himself. He could still feel the tremor of pure joy that shot through him when she'd smiled, said her name, and tossed their dinner plans into the mix.

She'd had a point; he never had bought her dinner. But that was an oversight he intended to remedy this evening.

They'd parted ways with a kiss and a promise, and although his body had ached for more sex, his heart ached to romance her. Never before had he reacted so strongly to a woman, either physically or emotionally. Had anyone cornered him yesterday and told him that his heart would soon be twisted into knots by a lithe brunette with a devilish gleam in her violet eyes, he would have announced to anyone listening that the speaker was clearly nuts.

Now he was the one who was nuts, and he couldn't have been happier about it. The only downside, in fact, to his newfound infatuation was that he couldn't devote his time to Lucia 24/7.

Because although he'd never expected himself to say it, in these particular circumstances, his father really did come first.

Assassination.

Could it really be true?

He couldn't imagine why his father would lie, and yet at the same time, he couldn't imagine why his father would be at the dangerous end of an assassination threat. Jacques Moreau had offended quite a few people in his time, sure. But in the end, he was nothing more than a businessman. He wasn't destroying rain forests. He wasn't putting people out of work. Just the opposite, in fact. Moreau's hotels and casinos provided jobs and insurance to thousands who'd worked for minimum wage before the Moreau empire had moved into their town. He donated a huge percentage of his profits to charities, putting Moreau's name at the top of most philanthropic charts.

Not exactly the kind of man against whom most people held a grudge. Dante being, perhaps, the sole notable exception.

Even he, however, didn't want his father dead. At most, he wanted to go back in time and teach the man how to be a parent. At worst, he wanted to be left alone to live his own life.

Neither was going to happen, and now he was here, in Monte Carlo, trying to decide if his usually sane father had dipped into paranoia.

The door to the conference room opened, and Linus stepped in. "Find anything?" Dante demanded.

The techie shook his head. "I've got filters searching all the back traffic over the incoming and outgoing servers, and I've got a team watching the actual security footage. I don't see anything related to a threat, and I don't see anybody on the premises that looks suspicious."

"Nobody?"

Linus lifted a shoulder. "A few. But they checked out with Tibor. You want me to pull the tapes for you?"

Dante considered that. Tibor had been his father's chief of security for years, and the man knew his stuff. If Tibor said the suspicious folks weren't suspicious, then they weren't.

Still . . .

Dante wasn't about to let anything get by him on this one. No matter what personal issues might exist between him and his father, there was no way he was going to slack where a death threat was concerned. Even one that he still believed might well be imaginary.

"Yeah," he said. "Pull the tape. And Linus, I want to talk with your team, too. Directly, I mean." He saw the hurt and confusion pass over the tech guru's face. "It's not personal. It's my dad."

A pause, then Linus nodded. "Sure. Of course. You won't find anything, though."

"I know," Dante said. Linus was one of the best computer security geeks in the business, and if he said the communications were clean, then Dante believed him. "But I have to look."

"Anything else you need me to do for you?" Linus asked, everything about his posture and tone of voice suggesting that he understood completely where Dante was coming from. Maybe he'd been offended for a moment, but the moment had passed, and they were on firm ground again.

Dante smiled and shook his head, grateful to the younger man. "No, thanks. Just send in Tibor when you leave."

Linus nodded, then turned to leave the room, snagging a croissant from the buffet Dante had ordered three hours ago. The wares had diminished significantly as the casino's team members had flowed in and out of the room, but Dante had yet to take a bite of anything.

"Linus," Dante called, as the other man's hand closed over the knob. "Everyone is clear on the rules regarding me, right?"

"Same as always, boss. You're our security consultant. Nothing else." His face lit into a mischievous grin. "You're sure not the spoiled son of one of the world's richest men."

"I sure as hell am not," Dante said, but with a smile.

"Don't worry. We know. And under the circumstances, we all know how important it is for you to keep your cover. Mr. *Benton-Smythe*," he added, stressing the name with which Dante had grown up.

Dante nodded acknowledgment, then waved the man out of the room. His cell phone rang, and he checked the ID, then flipped the phone open. "Any word on our missing little ones?"

At the other end of the line, Thomas Murchison let out a low whistle. "I've got my end covered. But you need to bring me up to speed on you. Don't think you can get away with leaving messages as cryptic as that on my office voice mail."

Dante chuckled. "Sorry. Didn't have the time." He brought his partner up to speed on the situation with his father.

"How can I help?"

"Nothing at the moment. I'm going to continue looking at the hotel guests, and I may ask you to run some background checks, just to keep things off book at this end."

"You think it's someone on staff?"

He didn't, but Dante was cautious. "At this point," he said, "I don't know what to think. Give me the scoop on your end."

Thomas did, telling him all about the file of little Megan Anders, kidnapped by her estranged father and taken . . . somewhere.

That was the question of the hour, and Thomas had all their resources on it. "Don't worry about her," he said, apparently sensing the anxiety in Dante's silence. "As soon as we have a lead, you'll be in on the takedown. And there's no reason to believe she'll be harmed. The same isn't true of your father."

"I know," Dante conceded. "So far, I'm coming up dry."

"Go get some dinner and start fresh in the morning. If I know you, you've been going at this without a break for hours."

His buddy knew him well. It was already well past eight, and he hadn't stopped. Now, though, it was time to get cleaned up. He had a date, after all. "As a matter of fact, I'm just about to go grab a bite."

The top was down on the Porsche, and he was racing far too fast for safety along the winding highway that wound like a ribbon through the mountains of Monaco, overlooking the majesty that was Monte Carlo.

He had one hand on the wheel and the other on the door frame. His eyes were on the road, but he could still see her beside him. A scarf covered her hair, but some still blew in the wind. Her lips were slightly parted, as if she were trying to drink in the beauty of their surroundings. And when she turned to him, her smile wide and bright, he just about drove off the road.

"I have to confess that I'd expected to eat in one of the hotel restaurants."

"Good surprise?"

"I think so," she said. "You still haven't told me where we're going. But I'll admit the view's nice."

"That it is." He cocked his head slightly, indicating the crystal blue Mediterranean, breaking in foamy waves on the beach below them, and causing the boats sitting like gems in the water to bob with the surf. The principality of Monaco might be tiny, but it was outrageously beautiful. And while Dante had never been keen on visiting his father for long stretches in the summer, he'd always considered it a gift from heaven that he'd had the town and countryside to explore.

He'd always been drawn to the ocean, and he'd explored the countryside above Monte Carlo and the Côte d'Azur for hours, often staying until the sun disappeared and the sea was illuminated only by the sparkle of the casinos.

All of Monaco encompassed only a few square kilometers, and Dante had picked over every inch during his youth. He'd quickly found two favorites. The oceanographic institute, which sat like a jeweled palace on the coast. And a small turnoff extending from the main road, hundreds of meters above the city. The place was intended to give cars safe haven to pull over and let others pass, but Dante had found it to be so much more than that. He'd discovered a stone staircase that led from the edge of the graveled area down to a rocky plateau. He'd spent many days there, watching and thinking, and simply enjoying the countryside.

He'd never once shared the spot with anyone; now, he was taking Lucia. And despite the fact that he'd been on dozens of dates over the course of his life, he was now actually experiencing first-date jitters.

He glanced over at her, saw her smile in return, and his stomach did a little flip. He gripped the steering wheel tighter, and hoped he was doing the right thing. She was, after all, undoubtedly expecting a restaurant. And the fear of disappointing her was so intense that he almost ignored the turnout altogether and headed on toward a lovely little hideaway he knew about with an excellent menu and wine from a nearby vineyard.

No. He wanted to share this with her, and so he tapped the brakes, turned in front of oncoming traffic, and screeched to a halt on the dusty pullout.

"Something wrong?"

"Welcome to Chez Dante," he said.

Her eyes widened, but not with disappointment or irritation. Instead, he saw curiosity. And since he could live with that, he got out, retrieved the picnic basket he'd stashed behind his seat, then opened the door for her. "Do you trust me?" he asked.

A pause, then a smile that eased into his heart. "Yeah," she said. "I do."

"Then follow me."

He hooked a leg over the guardrail, then held a hand out for her. She hesitated only briefly, then followed him over gingerly, her linen slacks clinging provocatively to her thighs as she moved.

They edged along the cliff for a few meters, then he found the stone staircase. He could only assume it was part of an ancient battlement, and he negotiated the steps carefully, turning back often to make sure Lucia was doing okay.

Considering the nimble way she moved over the weathered stone, he shouldn't have been worried. But it was the expression on her face that truly lifted his heart. Not concentration, but absolute delight and wonder. And when he took the final step, then edged along the narrow path to the stone plateau, her face lit even more, and he heard her quick intake of breath.

"It's not five-star service," he said, "but I like it here." He held his breath, waiting for her response, the picnic basket clutched in his hand like a security blanket. Just hours before, this woman had wanted him gone. Now he'd taken her to the most romantic place he could think of. The place in all the world most special to him.

And he couldn't help but fear that somehow, he'd overstepped his bounds.

But when she smiled, he knew that everything was okay. More than okay, even.

"It's wonderful," she said, her voice thick with emotion. "You couldn't have picked a better place."

Lucia resisted the urge to hug herself. That he would bring her here—to this exact spot—was unbelievable. She'd been here twice before, the years passed too many to count, and the memories too strong to ignore.

At the time, a fortress had stood here. A small watchtower raised from stone with three guards assigned to live and die here, their sole job to look out over the sea and watch for invaders.

She'd known one of the guards, as he'd been a distant cousin of her mother's, and she'd come here twice before in her life. The first was to beg help from that guard, seeking his aid in getting a message to her grandfather that her mother was dying.

She'd been thirteen at the time. A woman, by the day's standards, and she'd been prepared to use whatever womanly gifts were at her disposal in order to ensure cooperation from the unknown relative from whom she'd sought aid.

Her cousin hadn't required that of her. Instead, he'd helped, even going so far as to seek assistance from a local healer. It had been too late, though, and her mother had succumbed.

She'd learned of her heritage, then, when her father had come to claim her and revealed the truth. At first, she'd rallied against him, desperately denying what he'd told her about who she was. But she'd ultimately acknowledged it. How could she not, when all her life she'd felt different? As if the hint of badness she'd felt in her soul had ultimately been responsible for her mother's death. A curse, she'd thought. Punishment from the heavens for being a wild child and thinking impure thoughts.

Her father had swooped in and taken care of her. And in his training she'd found release for all her anger and fear. She had a home. She belonged. And with every assassination, the praise lavished by her father had kept her going, squarely quelling the sense of loss and desperation that screamed out that there had to be more. That she'd somehow lost so much more than a mother.

She'd given in only once to those melancholy thoughts. Once in all these years.

After her first kill.

It had taken her days to travel back to this spot, but travel she had. She'd needed to come here for the strength to face her future. One last glimpse of pure beauty before the lathe of her destiny broke her completely.

She hadn't been back. Primarily because she'd never believed herself worthy to come.

And yet this was where he'd brought her. In all of Monaco, he'd chosen this few square feet of rock as the best place to bring her for a romantic dinner.

"Lucia?"

She jerked her head up, realizing suddenly that she'd been gazing out at the water, lost in her own thoughts. She shook off the melancholy, then took his hand. "It's perfect," she said. *And so,* she thought, *are you.* Even more so than she'd first believed.

Dante was the kind of man she could fall in love with, and that thought was a bit more than she could bear.

So instead of trying to, she took the basket from him and busied herself with spreading out the blanket and uncorking the wine, while he pulled out container after container of fabulous-smelling delicacies.

"You got the restaurant to fix you up with to-go containers?"

"It wasn't that hard," he said. "Best customer service in the world."

She nodded at that, then took the glass of wine he handed to her. They sat for a moment until she could stand it no longer. She had to know. "So how did you know about this place? It's beautiful."

"I'm glad you think so." There was a pause, and for a moment, she feared he wouldn't answer her question. Though why the way in which he found the place would be such a secret she couldn't imagine. "The truth is, I've been coming here for years, simply to get away. I have family here, and I used to come visit during the summers. Believe it or not, the lifestyle here can get old."

"I know."

He looked at her sideways, as if not sure if he believed her. She was serious, though. The glitz and glamour of the life she knew so well had become a yoke around her neck. Escape, however, was not a luxury she had.

After a moment, he cocked his head, indicating the cliff face behind them. "Come here," he said.

"Where? There's nowhere to go."

"Trust me."

And, because she did, she stood up and crossed the two paces to the cliff.

"That stone," he said, pointing to one slightly bigger than the others, and definitely smoother. "Pull it out."

She did, not even worrying about her manicure as she worked the stone free from the ones around it. It came easily, and once removed revealed an inset into the cliff face, at the back of which sat a small wooden box.

"My treasure," he said. "Open it."

She did, revealing a pirate's treasure. Or, at least, the kind of trinkets a child would see as treasure. Chips from the casinos. Paste gemstones. Coins from all over the world worth, tops, five American dollars.

She drew her finger through the contents, smiling as she did. "What is this?"

"I told you. My loot." He chuckled, then reached in for a chip from the Moreau casino. "When I was a kid, I used to play pirate on the beach. I'd spend my days searching for treasure, and that's pretty much what I came up with."

"Impressive."

He chuckled. "Maybe. At any rate, when I was ten, I had a fight with my dad about not being serious enough about my future. I took my moped and headed off, stewing in my own juices. That's when I found this place. I hid the chest behind that stone and never looked back."

"You're serious?" She couldn't believe that he'd pulled out his childhood treasure for her to see.

"Dead serious. I was actually wondering if it would even still be there."

"Thank you," she whispered, touched and a bit distressed to discover that her eyes were actually tearing up. What man had ever pulled her so intimately into his life? What man had ever wanted to?

Because she couldn't look at him without revealing the tears, she examined the box more closely. As she trailed her finger through the treasure she snagged a thin gold chain. She pulled it up, revealing a simple seashell hanging like a charm. "What's this?"

"I found the shell on a walk once. I liked the colors and the perfection."

"It's beautiful," she said.

"Put it on."

And even though she knew she should protest, she found herself working the clasp. "Are you sure?"

"It's treasure fit for a queen," he said. "And I really want you to have it."

She nodded, suddenly afraid that words would spoil the moment. She opened the clasp and handed it to him, then turned so that he could fasten it for her.

The shell settled between her breasts, the simple necklace unlike anything that had adorned her body in centuries of wearing only the finest gems and the purest gold.

But this . . . this really was treasure. More than that, it was a pact. She and Dante were joined now, by more than just sex.

And instead of terrifying her, that realization filled her heart with joy and brought a smile to her lips. And when she turned to kiss him, she found that he was smiling, too.

Chapter Seven

Dante spent the next few days doing everything he could to figure out who could possibly be trying to kill his father . . . and the next few nights doing everything he could to please Lucia. They laughed, dined, and strolled hand in hand through the city, exploring her elaborate retail opportunities, as well as her quiet, flower-lined streets. They even managed to work in a visit to the oceanographic institute, and he'd been thrilled that Lucia seemed as delighted by the aquariums as he was.

But it was outside, on the stone balcony overlooking the sea, that her face really came alive. He reached out and stroked her cheek. "What are you thinking?"

"I'm happy," she said, and he couldn't help but laugh.

"What?" she demanded, obviously offended.

He kissed the tip of her nose. "You sound so surprised."

For just a moment, her face seemed all too serious. But then she smiled, the effect vanishing with the curve of her mouth. "Sorry.

No. Not surprised. Just . . . happy." She took his hand. "I like the way it feels."

"I'm glad. I like it, too. I'm sorry I'm not able to—" He cut himself off, feeling ridiculous for apologizing. After all, a man had to work. Still, most men were able to tell their girlfriends who they were and what they did. He still hadn't even told Lucia his last name.

Of course, she hadn't told him hers, either. For that matter, he had no idea what *she* did during the day.

"Maybe one day I can get away for a few hours," he said. "We could have lunch."

"That would be great," she said. "But you don't have to do that for me. I've got plenty to keep me busy."

"Right." He felt a pull of jealousy at the thought of whatever else she was doing. Or not jealousy so much as a longing. He simply wanted more. He wanted her 24/7. And it made him ache to know that wasn't possible.

Ironic, really. The man who'd waded into espionage and now made a living going after the bad guys couldn't quite work up the courage to ask one beautiful woman if there was a future between them. It wasn't the question he was afraid of, of course. It was the answer.

And although his heart said the answer would make him happy, his head wasn't quite willing to take the plunge.

So he danced around it, offering instead tidbits of himself in an age-old system of barter-dating. *Tell a bit about me, and I'll learn a bit about you.* So far, though, he was the one doing most of the talking. And, he had to admit, he hadn't revealed all that much either.

He took her hand, wondering if now was the time to put a stop to that, but she pulled him close. "Kiss me," she whispered. "Kiss me here, with the wind in our hair and the sunset filling the sky."

How could he argue with a demand like that? He pulled her in close, and he kissed her. And sunset was all but forgotten. Time stopped, and there was nothing in the world but Dante and Lucia. No place but the one under their feet, and no reality but the two of them.

"It *is* a nice view," he said.

"Shut up and take me back to the room."

Dante didn't argue. After all, the view would still be there tomorrow. The woman . . . well, he was still working on that.

Moreau Sur la Mer was only a short walk from the aquarium, and they took it leisurely, hand in hand, enjoying each other's company despite the urgent desire pounding just under the surface.

She broke the silence first, and Dante almost gasped when she asked him what he did back home in New York. When he answered, he was careful not to look at her too directly, because he was afraid of what he might see in her eyes. Did she truly want to know about him? Or was this small talk? A desperate way to keep her mind occupied and her hands off him? Lord knew he'd been thinking along the same lines, almost resorting to singing old childhood tunes in his head simply so he wouldn't jump her and take her, right there in the street.

For the next couple of blocks, he told her about how he'd started the company with Thomas. About how they tried to help the parents of kidnapped children. He even told her about Megan Anders. "We still don't know where she is. That's the hardest part. When you want to do something, but your hands are tied."

"I know what you mean," she said.

"Do you?"

"Not about saving children. Or even about saving people," she added, with a laugh that seemed unduly self-mocking. "But I do understand about frustration. Of wanting to do one thing, but being forced to do something else entirely. Or nothing at all."

He cocked his head, trying to hear the story she wasn't telling him, but it was no use. "What exactly do you do? You work with your father, right?" The question probably crossed some unspoken boundary, but he didn't care. The truth was, he was falling in love with this woman. *There.* He'd let the thought out, and now there was no taking it back.

He let the truth settle into his head, wondering why he should be surprised. True, he barely knew this woman. And, also true, he'd pretty much been smacked upside the head with emotion. But in a way that made perfect sense. After all, he'd fallen into the work he loved, why should it surprise him that he found the woman he loved the same way?

The bottom line was that he *did* love her. And he wanted to know about her.

And their rules be damned.

Thank God she didn't call him on it. Instead she just shrugged and looked a bit irritated. The expression wasn't directed at him, though, but at some faraway paternity figure. He knew; he'd seen that expression reflected back at him at least a thousand times.

"I guess you could say I'm his point person," she said. "He has his fingers in more pies than you can count, but when he has a problem, I'm the gal he calls."

"I can see that," he said. "You're very competent."

He said it with a tease, but she took it seriously. "I'm good at what I do. I'm bored with it, though."

"Maybe you just need a break."

She shook her head. "No. I never really had a taste for the work, but I didn't have options. And I was good at it. I got by simply by knowing I was so damn good."

"And now?"

"I'm tired of it. And that means I'm not as good." She drew in a breath. "I just don't want the job anymore. That's about all there is to it."

"So you've quit?"

She shook her head. "It's my father. It's not that simple."

He nodded, because he understood. "But?"

"But we've come to an understanding. There's one final project in the works and then I'm cut loose."

"And what will you do then?"

A lift of one beautiful shoulder. "I'll stay in the family business."

"You sound like you don't want the job."

"Sometimes I think I don't know what I want."

"Then why take it?"

"Honestly? Because this business defines me. Daddy's *company*," she said, putting an odd emphasis on the word. "What would I do if I didn't do that?"

"I don't know. Maybe—"

She waved her hand. "It was a rhetorical question. Really. I'm just feeling contrite. Of course I want the job. Besides, how could I walk away, knowing it would piss off my sisters to have me step in to run the show?" She looked up at him, mischief in her eyes. "Do you have brothers or sisters?"

He shook his head, and she waved a hand again, as if that explained everything.

"I'm the oldest. I think I never quite got used to not being the only."

"If that's the main reason you're taking the job, you should just pack it in and come work for me." He had no idea where that had come from, but he didn't regret the proposition for a second. Especially not once he saw the warm light of interest in her eyes.

"Do you mean that?"

He considered denying it; after all, he had no idea what she did. But the words wouldn't come. Instead, he uttered an emphatic, "Of course."

It was all fantasy, though, and it was best he remembered that. He might want a future with this woman, but right now, the future extended only into the night. Only into bed.

That wasn't enough for him.

Right then, though, it would have to do.

Once again, they were skipping a meal. But Lucia didn't care. She was full up on Dante, and he on her. At the moment, she was tasting his sweetness, her teeth nibbling at his earlobe as she curled up, languid, against him, her body completely sated and happy.

"You're amazing," he said, his voice low and soft with sex.

"*We're* amazing," she said, and as she spoke, she realized that was true. Together, they seemed to be more than the sum of two individuals. He completed her, and she dared to think that she completed him.

A shiver cut through her, and she squeezed her eyes shut. That was not the direction her thoughts needed to be going. Love and commitment were all well and good . . . just not for her. She had a different kind of life. She knew that. She'd accepted it centuries ago.

And no matter how sad her reality might be, she was in the end a pragmatist. And no matter how appealing it might be to revel in the fantasy that she could chuck it all and go work with him . . . well, a girl had to live in the real world.

"Hey," he said, stroking her cheek. "Where are you?"

"Right here," she promised, pushing the mood aside. "And I'm not going anywhere."

To prove the point, she covered his mouth with hers, tasting his sweetness. Beneath her, she could feel the press of his erection, rock hard again despite having satisfied her so thoroughly only minutes before.

She reached down and stroked it, her body tingling with emotion and need. He felt like velvet and steel. Most of all, he felt like *hers*.

"I want you," she said.

"You've got me."

"*Now.*" And as if to prove it, she straddled him, then took him, demanding with her body that he never leave her, and that she never leave him. It was a lie, of course, an illusion. But what a sweet, sweet fantasy.

And as they rocked together, their bodies throbbing with heat and lust, she forgot who she was and what she had to do. And for those few minutes, it was good.

"You're beautiful," he whispered sleepily, his breath tickling her ear.

Lucia snuggled closer. They'd made love all night, and she'd willingly lost herself over and over to the fantasy that her time with Dante was the reality, and everything else was somehow just a dream.

It wasn't, though, and in moments of clarity, she had to acknowledge that. After all, each day she'd been scoping out the hotel, planning the assassination. Her investigation had made it clear that her usual plan of getting close to a subject wasn't going to work here. The time frame her father had given her had almost expired, and the man still wasn't on the premises. That meant that she'd have to go the old-fashioned way, abandoning a syringe for the messier approach of a sniper's bullet.

Not a big deal, really. After all, she'd taken out many subjects that way.

Still, there were risks. She lived in the mortal world, and murders were investigated.

This time, however, that didn't matter. Once the deed was done, she'd be abandoning her old life and taking over her father's empire. Things like pesky police investigations would never bother her again (and, really, such things had only ever been an annoyance, not a true threat).

She was only a day away from finally being done with this life, this career. And yet instead of being happy, she was drowning in melancholy.

Beside her, Dante had fallen asleep, oblivious to her turmoil. But Lucia couldn't sleep. Instead she lay there, her head on the pillow, Dante's arm possessive across her chest. Between her fingers, she held the necklace, her thumb idly rubbing the ridges on the seashell.

She wasn't used to feeling so out of sorts. So lost. So . . . *emotional.*

And the truth was, it wasn't just Dante. These thoughts had started long ago. When she'd begun to lose her taste for her job. The kill and the hunt didn't satisfy. And yet without them, what purpose did she have? What was she without that one thing to define her?

She didn't know, and the future seemed to loom before her like an abyss.

She knew she wanted more; she just didn't know what. And the warm fuzzy feelings she'd been having weren't just limited to sex and cuddling. She'd felt a tug of something warm and compassionate when the baron had pulled out all those family photos . . . and completely decimated her ability to inject him with the poison.

She was losing her edge, and that terrified her.

Especially since she knew, deep down, that the man beside her could be her perfect mate. She loved him. No matter how terrifying it was to utter those words, even in her own head, she had to acknowledge the truth.

She loved Dante. And once she was free of the yoke of her profession and had control over her destiny—and her father's kingdom—perhaps she could find a way to make that love last.

The thought satisfied her, and she snuggled closer, managing in the process to wake Dante up. "Hey," he whispered, "you can't sleep?"

"Thinking," she said, secretly happy he'd awakened. She loved talking with him. Loved holding him. Loved everything about him.

"Lucia?"

"Mmmm?"

His gaze met hers, and she saw both strength and fear. "You're going to think I'm crazy, but I'm falling in love with you."

She gasped, and then she smiled, the slow sweetness spreading through her and lighting her from within. *He loved her, too.* In all her years had she ever heard anything so wonderful?

She wanted to repeat the words back to him, but they were too foreign. She'd never said such things aloud—not in earnest, anyway. And so instead she tried to show him, cuddling closer, stroking his skin with soft touches, hoping that he could see in her eyes what she felt in her heart.

Maybe soon she could work up the courage to speak, but until then she said the only thing that came into her head. In retrospect, she wasn't sure where the question came from. Perhaps it was innocent; she simply wanted commiseration from someone else stuck working for their father. Or perhaps deep in her heart she knew that his love was too good to be true. And her reality was too bad to overcome.

Whatever the reason, she asked the question: "You never did tell me. What does your dad have to do with your business rescuing kids? Is one of the kids here?" She almost hoped the answer was yes. That insidious beast of compassion was working on her, and she would happily help Dante look for the child. Penance, she thought, for the life she'd led and the kingdom she would inherit.

"He doesn't have a thing to do with it," Dante said. "I used to work for him, but I cut myself loose."

"But you said—"

"I know. I'm temporarily working for him again. He found the one way to bring me back."

"I don't understand."

He hesitated, and for a moment, she thought he wouldn't say. Then he propped himself up on his elbow. "My father is Jacques Moreau. And someone is out to kill him."

Chapter Eight

Jacques Moreau. Hell and damnation, Lucia still couldn't believe it. The man she'd fallen in love with was the son of her target.

Her father had well and truly screwed her this time.

She paced, agitated, back and forth in her suite. She'd managed to hold it together in the room with Dante, centuries of acting and self-control coming to her rescue in the face of a horrific snowfall of information. But he had to know something was up. Not only had she never told him that she loved him, but as soon as he'd spoken of his father, she'd started easing away. His words were the harshest reminder of what she was here for. Of who she was.

And of what she had to do.

Except, damn it all, she didn't know *what* to do.

"I like the approach you're taking."

Startled, she whirled around, finding her father standing beside her, his Armani suit crisp and perfect.

"It's brilliant." He stepped closer and kissed her cheek. "I always knew you were the cleverest of my children."

She knew he was lying, but it was a nice lie, and she wanted to cry on his shoulder, but her father had never been *that* kind of a father. So instead, she stood a bit taller, held her chin high, and looked him in the eye. "I've been researching Moreau," she said. "I can't imagine why he's important to you."

"Hmmm." Her father tapped his fingers together. "Yes, I've been keeping tabs on your progress. Your days have been productive, though the nights less so than I would have hoped."

"He's not here," she spat. "I can hardly assassinate an absent man."

"And yet you haven't run off to find him elsewhere."

No, she thought. *I haven't.*

"No matter," he said. "As I said, your reason is clear. Get close to the son, get close to the father."

"I'm not using Dante for this." The idea was unthinkable.

"No?" Her father's voice rose, the epitome of innocent curiosity. "Then you have a plan?"

She let out a slow breath, then nodded. "The roof of the main casino tower. It overlooks the west wing garden. He's coming in tomorrow for a dedication ceremony. I'll have a direct shot. A single bullet. And then I'm done."

Her voice broke a bit on the last. Because being done in Monte Carlo meant being done with Dante, too. But she couldn't dwell on that. Couldn't let her father see weakness in her eyes.

And she *wasn't* weak. She was simply bound by the inevitable. There was no future with Dante. Even if she weren't about to kill his father, there could be no future. It wasn't as if she could be with him forever. She was immortal. He was not.

This was a fling. An interlude. A delicious vacation before she got down to the serious business of running her father's very vast empire.

And she was fine with that.

Really.

In front of her, her father smiled. "Good. Very good. I'm glad to see that my darling Lucia hasn't lost her touch."

"Tell me why, Daddy." She had to know. There had to be a reason. Something large that she could cling to and say, *yes, this was worth losing out on love.*

But he waved the question away as if it were nothing. "Competition. I told you. I'm looking to expand my gaming interests. And Moreau has always been a thorn in my side." A gentle caress to her cheek. "But what does it matter to you? Once he's gone, you're in the catbird seat. And I would think you would do anything to get there, now wouldn't you, my dear?"

She hesitated, wishing she could deny it. But she couldn't. She was desperate to leave her life as an assassin, and this was her way out. Her one last job, and then freedom.

Freedom. That had a price, too. Because once she was free of the shackles of her profession, then what was she if she didn't take her father's offer? Simply some immortal girl spinning her wheels. She could have Dante, true, but to what end? To watch him grow old, then die? She couldn't even bear the thought.

She was who she was, and that was a sad fact that she had to live with. More than that, she had to live with it for eternity.

She was the devil's firstborn. And his kingdom was hers to inherit.

She straightened her shoulders and drew in a breath. "Yes, Daddy," she said, the words so simple and yet meaning so much.

"Good girl." And then he was gone in a puff of smoke. And Lucia could do nothing except fall on her bed and cry, just as she had when her mother had died and, like now, her entire world had been lost.

Dante held her close, the night tight around them, and his body trembling with the aftershocks of a powerful orgasm. He'd been well and truly sated . . . and yet that wasn't enough. Something wasn't quite right, and as he traced his fingers up and down on Lucia's bare arm, he wondered if he had a right to ask. Especially since he feared that he already knew the answer. After all, he'd confessed to loving her. But she hadn't spoken the words back to him.

"Sweetheart," he whispered, "you're so far away."

She rolled over to face him, a smile on her face, but something distant in her eyes. "I'm right here."

"You are. And you're not." He pushed a lock of hair away from her eyes. "Can you tell me what's wrong?"

She flashed a sad smile, then got out of bed and started pulling on her clothes. "I'm just tired. That's all. Really. And now's not the time to talk about it. Your father will be here soon. You have work to do."

His heart twisted, but he had to ask. "Are you upset because of what I said? That I love you? I would never try to—"

"*No.*" She whipped around to face him, her words spoken with such ferocity, that he had no doubt as to their veracity. "No, please don't take it back. You have no idea how much that means to me."

He waited, hoping that she'd say the words back to him, but all she did was stand there, her lips together and her eyes sad. But she held her body rigid and proud, her fingers stroking the shell necklace he'd given her. That one fact gave him hope. Since that day on the rocks overlooking the ocean, she'd never taken it off. He hoped she never would.

A second passed, then another. "I . . . I have to go."

She bent down then and kissed him quick, before he could get out a protest. And then she was gone, ducking out the door and disappearing down the hallway.

Dante stood, frustrated. He had no idea what he'd done wrong. He'd had few serious relationships, of course, but the workings of the female mind baffled him. She'd said his confession of love hadn't bothered her, but he didn't know if he should believe her.

Something was bothering her, and he hated the impotent feeling of not knowing how to make it better for her.

His cell phone rang, and he realized that he'd been pacing, trying to find the answers in some sort of rhythmic trance. With a curse, he snatched the phone up, then barked out a curt "What?"

"Don't shoot the messenger."

Thomas. "What have you got for me?" Dante demanded. He'd struck out on getting wind of any plot to kill his father, but he knew that something had to be in the works. And if someone were going to pull off an assassination, this evening at the dedication of the new wing would be the perfect opportunity. He'd tried to get his father to cancel the damn ceremony, or at least move it inside, but the man was deaf to rational suggestions.

Instead, Dante had upped the security force for the property, ensured that his father was under guard at all times, including during his flight to Monaco from Paris, and overseen the installation of video cameras on the grounds.

Still, that wasn't enough. Somehow, he just knew it wasn't enough.

"If I were there," Thomas said, "you'd kiss me."

"Tell me why," Dante said. All hotel guests were required to have their passports scanned upon arrival, pursuant to a procedure Dante had implemented years ago. He'd had Linus send Thomas all of the images—an unreasonable amount of data—along with a request that Thomas see what kind of magic their connections in the States could work on the facial images.

It had been a hell of a long shot, and not one that Dante had expected to pay off. Not unless hell froze over, anyway.

Apparently, today was pretty damn chilly.

"I got one hit," Thomas said. "And it was a doozy."

"What do you mean?"

"It's weird, man. This gal's never been implicated in any crime, but she's been nearby when a lot of society folks have bought it."

"Sounds like a good lead," he said as the fax machine in the suite started to ring. "What's odd?"

"We cross-referenced with a new project. One of the universities is inputting older photographic material."

"And?"

"And the same gal showed up."

"Not following you."

"The photo is fifteen years old, Dante. And she's right there. Looking exactly the same, like she hadn't aged a day."

"So she was thirty-five in one photo, then fifty in the next. Some women age well. You should see some of the women who come here to my dad's casin—" He cut himself off, because the fax had finished. He'd grabbed the paper, and found himself looking at a crystal clear image of Lucia—just as she looked that morning. *Impossible.*

"Fifteen years ago, she would have been only ten years old," he said softly, the picture he was holding baffling him. "Twelve or thirteen at the most."

"That's what I'm saying," Thomas said. "Hinky. But one thing isn't hinky."

"What's that?" Dante asked, amazed his voice still worked.

"She's your gal, buddy. She's got to be."

The flu.

That had to be why Lucia felt so hot. So nauseous. And so completely miserable.

The flu. The plague. Some hideous malady. That was, of course, the only explanation.

Except, of course, that she'd never been sick a day in her very long life. And except, of course, that she knew exactly what her problem was.

She was sick all right. She was lovesick.

Get a grip, Lucia.

She concentrated on setting up the scope on her rifle. She'd done it well over a thousand times, on assignments and during the drills she'd forced on herself, just so she could stay in practice. Hell, she could assemble a rifle in her sleep.

Today, though, she would have been better off playing with Tinkertoys. Her concentration was all shot to, well, *hell.*

She needed to do the job, finish the job, and leave. There really was no other way. She already knew that she'd lost her edge, so continuing in her current profession wasn't an option.

And while Dante may have been serious when he'd said she could come work for him, she knew he'd retract that offer in a heartbeat if he knew who she really was. He didn't love her. He loved an illusion. An imaginary woman who hadn't been sired by the devil himself. A mortal woman he could grow old with.

Not a woman who would stay twenty-eight for the rest of

eternity. Not a woman who would stand there as he grew older and, eventually, died.

The thought of losing Dante that way ripped her heart out. The truth was, she wanted to grow old with him. Wanted a normal, mortal life with him. Wanted children, a picket fence, and the whole sappy, ridiculous life. Well, maybe not the picket fence, but the *life*—that she wanted desperately.

She couldn't have it, though. She knew that.

The simple, painful truth was that she couldn't have the life she wanted, and she didn't want the life she had. There was only one way out for her—her father's offer. Take over his kingdom and then, maybe, she could find some kind of peace.

Determined, she focused again on her task, this time completing the assembly of the rifle. She'd poked around enough that she'd heard what Dante had done to beef up security, and she had to commend him on his thoroughness. But she was thorough, too. She was also a hell of a shot, and could hit a stationary target from almost a mile away.

Comparatively speaking, this time would be easy.

True, she'd abandoned her plan to camp on the casino's roof. But Monte Carlo was crowded, and filled with hotels. The competition had proved quite accommodating, the balcony of a nearby penthouse providing a perfect angle into the garden of the new wing. And the penthouse's occupant, Charles Wellington, the retired film star, had been easily subdued by a kind word and an extra-strong sleeping pill slipped into his cocktail.

She had the balcony all to herself.

Now all she had to do was wait. And try not to think about Dante.

"Eagle's Nest to command: all clear."

The voice crackled into Dante's earpiece, and he answered into the microphone wired into his sleeve. "Copy."

That was the final check-in. Everything was ready. Nothing was amiss.

Perhaps it had all been rumor. A horrible coincidence.

A sick joke that Thomas was playing on him, making him think that Lucia was out to kill his father. Making him think that she'd gotten close to him only because it was part of a job.

You're the one who saw her that first day. You sought her out.

Maybe so, but that was slim consolation.

Damn it! He'd fallen in love with a woman who wanted nothing—and everything—from him. In truth, he had no doubt that she was the assassin, and for that he hated himself. At the same time, he couldn't escape the obvious. Her refusal to tell him her name. The way she carried herself. Her intense examination of the casino catwalk that first day they'd walked the floor together.

She'd played him for a fool and, like a fool, he'd fallen for her.

God, she must be having a big laugh now.

The only question was *where*. Where was she laughing?

Because this wasn't the time to bemoan his own stupidity. No, he could do that when his father was off the premises. Now was the time to find her, and to stop her.

Once he had her in custody—once it was over—then he could look into her eyes. See the flatness there. And know that she had never really loved him. No matter how much he'd wanted to believe.

The Rolls-Royce pulled up in front of Moreau Sur la Mer, and from her angle, Lucia could see the doors open. Bellmen and security guards quickly surrounded Jacques Moreau, ushering him into the casino and away from her view.

No matter. She knew what would happen next. Despite all of Dante's urging, Jacques would do exactly what he wanted. Because that was what fathers did. They didn't listen to their children, they just moved forward, fulfilling their own needs.

And Jacques Moreau needed the press. Needed the spectacle.

Dante might want the ceremony to take place inside, but at a cost of over one million American dollars, Jacques wasn't going to ignore the fabulous garden that was the jewel of the new west wing. The ceremony had been scheduled to take place there, and it would.

Lucia was betting her future on it.

Sure enough, minutes later he emerged in the garden, the press entourage and invited guests following at heel. The security was still tight, but by necessity they had to loosen the noose. How else could the camera crews get good footage? And how else could Lucia get a shot?

Except . . .

Except she couldn't get a shot.

Her finger wouldn't pull the trigger no matter how much her head told it to.

Damn it, damn it, damn it!

No. This wasn't happening. She wasn't going to lose this time. She didn't know exactly how this would play out, but she did know one thing—she was going to fire that damn rifle.

The heat in her blood had long since faded, replaced with ice. She positioned herself, checked the scope, calculated the distance, factored in the wind, and then—when there were no more preparations to be made—she pulled the trigger.

Chapter Nine

The bullet slammed into the brick just shy of a second-story window, sending everyone at the ceremony crashing to the ground in terror, but injuring no one. The security team scurried to action, all but Dante. He merely stood there, his mind replaying the incident, trying to calculate from where the shot had come.

He turned toward the east, and looked up, noting the penthouse balcony of the reclusive Charles Wellington and the slim figure standing there.

And then the assassin was gone, and Dante was racing that direction, his heart desperate to believe it wasn't her. His head just as sure that it was.

By the time he reached the balcony, it was empty. The gun was long gone as well, though the marks it had made on the marble flooring made it clear that forensics could figure out the exact type and weight. Dante knew they'd be up soon to do just that.

And that's why he reached down and pocketed the necklace. A single seashell on a golden chain.

He'd been right. Lucia was the assassin.

He didn't know why she'd missed, though. Maybe she'd been surprised by something that fouled her aim. Maybe she was toying with his father.

Maybe she loved him.

The last thought came unbidden, and he pushed it away. She was an *assassin*. She'd come to Monte Carlo with one purpose: to kill his father. She didn't love him. She'd used him.

Damn her to hell for breaking his heart. *And,* he thought, swinging the necklace that no professional would ever leave behind, *damn her for laughing at him now.*

She was waiting for him when he arrived. Tucked away in her suite, registered in her own name.

She'd known he would find her, and she was impressed that it had taken him barely half an hour.

"Why?" he demanded.

"Why what?" she asked, desperate for him to ask the right question, but so afraid that he wouldn't.

"Why did you try to kill my father? Why did you use me? *Why are you here?*"

She closed her eyes. Those were the wrong questions, but at least she had her answer. And, soon, she'd be gone. Out of his life forever.

What she would do then, though, she didn't know.

"Damn it, Lucia, answer me! And while you're at it, tell me who the hell you are!"

"You're close with that one," she said, unable to keep the hard edge out of her voice.

He must have heard the truth, though, because he took a step back, his eyes wary. "What are you talking about?"

"Hell, Dante. It's just a little slice of home."

"You're . . . *what*?"

"The devil's daughter." She laughed. She couldn't help it. "And you thought your dad was bad."

"Lucia, you can't be serious. You—"

"Haven't aged. The pictures that Thomas sent you. Didn't you wonder?"

"Of course, but . . ." He frowned. "That can't be. It's—"

"It's true," she said, never taking her eyes off his, and silently willing him to believe.

He cocked his head, studying her. "How do you know about the pictures? Do you have some sort of powers?"

She shook her head. She did have a few, but they were hardly worth mentioning. "I have money and resources. And I'm good at getting information."

She saw him file that tidbit away. A leak in his perfect security. But there were always leaks. He knew that. For that matter, his entire business with Thomas depended on it.

"I'm good at what I do, Dante. And I've been doing it for a long time."

"A long time," he repeated, his voice soft. He was, she knew, starting to believe.

She waited for him to ask the one question. The one question that could open the door to a future and whisk them beyond her past. But there was no future. She could see that in his eyes. He was too stunned, too baffled. And certainly not willing to bring the devil's daughter into his life, or his heart.

"Go away, Dante," she finally said, standing up and using her most regal glare. "Your father's alive. You've got nothing on me."

"I have proof you were there," he said. "I have the necklace."

"Then arrest me," she said.

He didn't, though. He simply looked through her, his face pale with pain. And then he left.

He still didn't know the answer, though, and the question hung unasked in the still air of the room. *Why? Why had she missed?*

But it didn't matter now. He was gone.

And, with him, hope.

Three weeks had passed. Three long weeks. And Dante had slogged through them, trying to bury himself in work. In the thrum of daily life in Manhattan. In the search for little Megan Anders.

None of it was working. His sources had dried up. And, for that matter, so had his heart.

Part of him didn't want to believe she was who she said she was. And another part of him didn't give a damn. He *should* give a damn, of course. But then he had to ask himself why. She had no control over who her father was. And she obviously wanted out. Hadn't they spent hours commiserating over their paternal situations?

True, she'd come to kill his father, but she hadn't managed to do that.

He frowned, that one fact still bugging him. He'd followed up on Thomas's information, and from what he could tell, Lucia was an expert. Exactly as he'd suspected: if she missed, it was because she wanted to miss.

He held the necklace in front of him, the seashell moving back and forth like a hypnotist's watch. Even now, he could picture it so clearly on her neck. She'd never once taken it off. She'd stroked it after they'd made love. And she'd worn it instead of diamonds or pearls when they'd dressed for dinner.

She'd left it for him that day as a message, but all this time, he'd misunderstood the text. Now, with time away from anger and shock, he saw it all so clearly: she'd missed because she loved him.

And he'd been too much of a fool to believe that at the time.

Now he was even more the fool, because he was in love with her as well. He was in love with a damned assassin. Him. A man who'd dedicated his life to finding missing children. Him . . . with an assassin.

Could the universe really be so cruel as to fill his heart with the one woman he could never truly be with?

No.

He couldn't believe it. He was too full up on her. She'd been his everything since the moment they'd met. They'd laughed over stupid things and bonded over their miserable fathers.

He fought a laugh. As for *that* she really did win the prize. But it was more than just having the father from, literally, *hell*. He could remember now so clearly the way she'd clung desperately to the fact that she was there for one last job. One final job, and then she'd be free of a job that had bound her.

His father had been that job.

Which meant that she'd defied the devil. And she'd done it for him.

Dear God, he really had been a fool. She'd done everything but shout from the rooftop that she wanted to be free—wanted to be with him—and didn't want to be an assassin anymore. He hadn't heard her, though. All he'd seen was the gun and the bullet, the message lost in the packaging.

He'd pushed her away, and in doing that, he'd screwed things up for both of them. Because how did you go about finding a woman who didn't want to be found?

He drew in a determined breath. This wasn't over. Not yet. Because fortunately for Dante, that was the business he was in. And he intended to put all his effort into the task.

Lucia paced on the beach in front of her father, trying to ignore his glare.

"I had hoped this would be my permanent situation by now," he said, holding a drink topped by a little umbrella. "How disappointing."

"Just tell me, Daddy."

"Tell you? Tell you that you failed me?"

"No," she said. "*That* you've been telling me for weeks."

"Perhaps I still can't believe it's true." He cocked his head. "It doesn't have to be. Go back and finish the job and my kingdom is yours. You can't honestly want it to go to Jessie."

"She can have it with my compliments."

Her father put a hand to his heart. "You wound me."

She closed her eyes, counted to ten. She needed to get what she wanted from the old goat, but she needed to do it without arousing that famous temper. Fortunately, the fruity beverage seemed to be helping in that regard.

She'd thought she could live without Dante, but so far she was doing a miserable job. And so she'd made up her mind. She was getting him back.

She just wasn't sure how. And so she figured groveling and the bearing of gifts seemed like a good plan. Unfortunately, she could only think of one gift that would mean anything to him.

"Megan Anders," Lucia said. "Do you know where her father is?"

The old devil peered at her, and for the first time ever, she saw real bafflement on his face. "My dear child," he finally said, "are you asking me a favor? After turning your back on me? On your heritage? Do you really have the nerve?"

She almost cowered, almost backed down. She didn't, though. Instead, she took a step closer and lifted her chin. "Yes. I am. It's important to Dante. And Dante is important to me."

For just an instant, she saw a flicker of something that might have been pride shine in her father's eyes. Then it passed, and the eyes turned flat. But flat, at least, was better than furious. "I'm not in the habit of doing good deeds."

"And I'm not asking you to," she said. "Merely a means to an end."

"And what end might that be?"

"Surely the father's anger and frustration when he loses his daughter is worth something to you. He might even try to retaliate."

"And your man would be there to stop him," her father said. Lucia just lifted a shoulder.

No response.

Lucia held her breath. And then her father looked at her, his eyes hard. "Go," he said, his voice rippling with emotion. "You disappoint me. And now you will know the price for failure."

She shivered, her body quaking from a tremor she'd never

experienced before. She knew the cause with certainty, however—her immortality leaving her.

She closed her eyes, sighing, but calm. She'd made the right decision, she knew that. And she had no regrets about leaving her family behind.

She only hoped that Dante would take her back. About that, she had no certainty at all. None, except that she loved him. And that she was going to do everything she could to prove that to him.

She turned to go. There was, after all, no reason to stay.

"Stop!"

The command in her father's voice froze her, and she looked at him over her shoulder.

"Nepal," he said. And then he was gone, Lucia's whispered thanks buried in a maelstrom of fire and brimstone.

Dante slogged across the beach, hoping he wasn't too late. It had taken all of his resources, but he'd finally found her, here on this island.

He'd arrived after traveling fifteen straight hours, and she was no longer in the hotel. A bartender had thought he'd seen her on the beach, and that's where he was heading, hope held tight in his hand.

And then suddenly hope turned to reality. She was there, right in front of him, looking surprised—but pleased—to see him.

"Hey," he said, because he hadn't yet rehearsed anything better. He glanced at the scorch mark in the sand in front of her, then decided it was best not to ask.

"Hey yourself." She licked her lips. "How did you find me?"

"That's what I do."

She tilted her head, looking at him a little shyly. "Fair enough. *Why* did you find me?"

He drew in a breath, and said the one thing that was true above all others: "Because I love you."

Lucia's heart leaped in her chest, his words filling her with joy. "But what about—"

"Your dad? How about we just not invite him to the wedding, okay?"

She grinned, the word *wedding* doing a little jig in her head. "Fair enough. He and I aren't exactly speaking these days anyway. He's a little ticked off at me about—"

"*My* dad," Dante said, neatly filling in the blank.

"I was supposed to kill him." She made the statement matter-of-factly, but her palms were sweating as she waited for him to respond. "That was my job."

He nodded. "I know. And from what I've read, you were damn good at it."

"I was."

"But you missed."

"I did." She held her breath, wondering if he'd finally asked himself the key question. More, wondering if he'd truly figured out the answer.

"You don't seem like the kind of woman who'd miss. Not by accident, anyway. And you certainly don't seem like the kind of woman who's sloppy."

"Sloppy?"

He held up the necklace. "You love me, Lucia," he said,

answering that ultimate question. "And I've got the proof right here." He met her eyes. "Don't I?"

She couldn't deny it. Wouldn't ever deny it. "Yeah," she said. "You do."

He pulled her close, then kissed her soundly before tilting his head back to look deep in her eyes. "Say it," he demanded.

She complied happily. "I love you, Dante." She smacked him softly in the shoulder. "It took you long enough to realize that."

"I know. I'm sorry. But I finally got with the program." His slow smile seemed to fill her. "So what do we do now?"

It was her turn to smile. "Actually, I was thinking that maybe we should leave on a romantic little getaway. Someplace out of the way. Like, say, Nepal . . ."

JEZEBEL'S STORY

Dee Davis

Chapter One

Jezebel Wyatt stood at the corner watching the *Strassenbahn* go by. It rumbled against the pitted pavement, the reverberation loud enough to interrupt the cell phone conversation of the man she was watching.

She pulled tighter into the shadows of the tobacco shop's awning. It was tempting to move closer, to try to listen in on the conversation. But caution overrode her need to move. Better to wait, to follow at a distance. Herr Schaufberg had access to the formula. And she had a buyer who needed it.

All she had to do now was bide her time and follow the scientist. A simple enough game. She'd certainly had more formidable quarries. Schaufberg was pushing sixty and not in the best of health. A lifetime of *Weissbier* and *Bratwurst* expanding his girth until he threatened to explode from his carefully tailored suit.

But it wasn't Schaufberg that kept her at a distance. It was the man standing on the corner, pretending to be engrossed in the latest issue of *Der Spiegel*. A bodyguard maybe. Or another player targeting Schaufberg. Hard to say for certain. Jessie had never seen him before. Despite being spread over several continents, there weren't that many information brokers and Jessie made it a point to keep an eye on the competition. So either he was new, or he was after the old man for another reason.

Either way his presence intrigued her. These days it was overly easy to obtain information. With only a few clicks of a computer she could gain access to almost anything a client desired. In and out in a matter of seconds. It made for a nice paycheck, but the adventure was gone.

Jessie wasn't one to dwell on the past, but if she were honest with herself, she'd have to admit that she missed the old days. Seducing a slip of the tongue or enticing an emperor or king into trusting her beat the hell out of keystrokes and cyberspace.

Schaufberg closed his phone and headed toward Potsdamerplatz, away from Jessie and the man on the corner. She waited until he, too, had begun to move, watching as he passed her, then pushed off the wall of the *Tabak* to follow them both as they made their way up the busy street.

Potsdamerplatz sat almost at the center of Berlin, the remnant of what had once been the border between the British, American, and Soviet sectors. Checkpoint Charlie was nearby, the famous gateway now no more than a muddled museum. A reminder that life was constantly changing—evolving.

At least for most of the world.

But not for her. Never for her.

Shaking off her lethargy, she rounded the corner, scanning the sidewalks for Schaufberg and his stalker. Both men were still in plain sight, Schaufberg still clutching his cell phone, the stranger now carrying the rolled-up newspaper under his arm. The perfect disguise for a drawn weapon.

Jessie patted her jacket, tracing the lines of the Beretta hidden beneath the soft leather. At least if push came to shove, she'd be ready. Whatever the man with the newspaper was after, she was fairly certain he was an operative of some kind. It was evident from the way he carried himself, a subtle confidence that couldn't completely be disguised.

She'd met his type before. A man's man—and a woman's nightmare. The kind who stormed a woman's heart and then destroyed it without even stopping to assess the damage. She'd thought herself immune to that kind of manipulation. But she'd been wrong.

Twice.

Twice in a very long lifetime, she allowed emotion to challenge her better instincts. Once she'd come out of the encounter unscathed. And once she'd lost more than she cared to admit. But it wasn't going to happen again.

Not ever.

Narrowing her eyes against the glare of the afternoon sun, she watched as Schaufberg disappeared into an unmarked door in the Sony Building, the monolith of glass and steel a monument to the new Berlin—the new Germany.

Jessie wasn't impressed.

The second man stopped in front of the door, the crowds of tourists billowing out as they surged around him. For a moment she lost sight of him, but then the crowd thinned and she saw him check right and then left before ducking inside, following Schaufberg, the newspaper still tucked under his arm.

She considered abandoning her quarry. If the newspaper man

was an operative she might be stepping into a situation she couldn't handle. But even as she had the thought she abandoned it. The hunt was half the fun, and her mystery man only made it that much more interesting. The unmarked door swung open silently, the corridor beyond seeming overly dark, a stark contrast to the bright street outside.

Counting silently to ten, she waited for her eyes to adjust, her back to the wall, her hand resting on the butt of her gun. The corridor was clear, no sign of Schaufberg or the mystery man, but a stairwell to her right yawned black and inviting.

Farther down the hall, an open doorway spilled light across the corridor, laughter punctuating the sounds of conversation. Unless she was off her game, they hadn't gone that way. At least not Mystery Man. It was too damn public.

And considering Schaufberg's recent behavior, she doubted he was in a laughing mood. Secrets tended to isolate a man, and Schaufberg had more secrets than most. Centuries of experience told her that both her quarry and his hunter were downstairs in the basement.

Which meant there was no time to waste. Mystery Man had a bit of a lead. But then, she had the advantage. Containing a smile, she started down the stairs, this time with her gun drawn. She'd always made it a point to try to attain the information she needed without violence. Not because she abhorred it, but because it lessened the victory in the end. And after all, winning was the only thing left that gave her pleasure.

A pitiful admission, but nevertheless, the truth.

Given enough time, even the basest of pleasures become mundane, if only from repetition. Jessie hit the bottom of the stairs, and quickly moved back into the stairwell. Mystery Man was straight ahead. Schaufberg was nowhere in sight, but based on the faint light spilling into the corridor from a room to her left, she'd take odds he'd gone inside.

Like her, Mystery Man had his weapon drawn, but unlike her, he was not aware that he had company. Moving with seasoned silence, Jessie covered the distance between them in seconds, the butt of her gun cracking hard against the stranger's head.

He went out like a light, with nothing more than a muffled thud. Seconds passed; the corridor remaining silent. Satisfied that she was still alone, Jessie checked the man's pulse, and almost laughed. Lucia would never check. But then, her sister would have shot to kill.

To each her own.

Reaching inside the man's jacket, Jessie retrieved his wallet, flipping quickly through his identification. Nothing out of the ordinary. A driver's license and a couple hundred in euros. She searched his other pockets and was finally rewarded with a small leather billfold. This one containing a different kind of ID.

Interpol.

It was tempting to take the bastard out. Interpol had been a constant headache since its inception in 1923. But Dieter Von Keismann had no idea she was here. Better to let him wake up with a headache long after she was gone.

After checking the corridor again, she reached down, grasping the man under his arms. Despite the deadweight, it took only a few minutes to pull him into a nearby service closet. After securing his hands and mouth, she pulled the door closed and inched toward the open doorway.

The outer office was empty, the only furniture a desk and some discarded boxes. It was almost as if the last tenant had left in a hurry—or maybe that was just what people were meant to think.

There was no sign of Schaufberg, but Jessie knew he was nearby. She could smell his aftershave. Like many men of a certain age, he tended to overdo a good thing—or in his case, a bad one. Moving over to the doorway leading to an inner office, she bent to peer through a crack in the door.

The room was empty.

She yanked open the door, mindless of the ensuing rattle. Damn it all to hell, she'd wasted precious time on the international policeman and now Schaufberg was gone. A quick visual search of the room yielded no answers. Like its predecessor, there was a smattering of furniture. All of it clearly abandoned. And more important, there were no additional doors or windows.

Which meant one of two things. Either she'd been mistaken about Schaufberg's destination or there was something more to the room. Experience pointed toward the latter. That and the fact that Mystery Man had clearly had the same idea.

Pushing her anger aside, Jessie began a methodical search of the room and its furnishings, her fingers reaching into every nook and cranny, feeling for a latch or a handle. Something that triggered another doorway—the opening to some secret room.

Her first attempt yielded nothing except the decaying remains of a rodent of some kind, and a thick layer of dust and grime. If Schaufberg had gone this way, he'd have left evidence of the fact.

She turned slowly, letting her eyes travel the length and breadth of the room. A decrepit old bookcase looked as though it might topple if one touched it. A desk in the corner was mockingly empty, and a stack of crates proved to be exactly what they seemed. Still, every instinct told her Schaufberg had come this way.

She stopped in front of the bookcase. Like the rest of the room it was coated with dust, and like everything else it showed no signs of having been disturbed. Blowing out a breath, she ran a hand through her hair, frustration cresting as she stared down at the floor. And then she smiled, all of her nerve endings firing at once. There was no dust in the corner where one end of the bookcase sat, the cleared floor making a perfect triangle. Like the arc of a door.

With new determination she studied the bookshelf. It was as old as the rest of the furniture, but that was where the similarity ended. Unlike its fellow roommates, the bookshelf was ornate. Carved indentations decorated the pediment on each side, a sculptured flower marking the center.

Certain she'd found the answer, she reached upward, her fingers brushing against the flower. Pushing harder, she felt the wood give way, and stepped back as the bookcase slid silently open, harsh fluorescent light spilling out into the vacant room.

Her gun at the ready, Jessie moved into the light, her gaze resting on Schaufberg. He was hunched over a microscope, his attention on the slides he was examining, totally oblivious to the fact that he was no longer alone.

"Herr Schaufberg," she said, her voice splintering the silence.

The old man jerked around, a slide skittering to the floor with the movement. His hand rose to his throat, almost as if he were willing himself to scream, but instead he was silent, his eyes wide with fear.

Jessie fought against her smile. It seemed cruel to frighten the man to death. "There's nothing to fear." She shifted her stance, the gun now pointed over the man's left shoulder. "I've no interest in hurting you. I just need the formula."

Schaufberg sputtered, his eyes if possible growing even wider. *"Ich spreche Englisch nicht,"* his voice was steady, but his shaking hands told another story.

"No problem," Jessie said over the barrel of her gun. *"Mein Deutsch ist gut."* Truth was she was fluent in something like sixteen languages, six of them long dead. "So," she continued in German, moving the barrel of her gun so that it was again pointed at his chest, "if you'll give me the formula, I'll get out of your hair."

Schaufberg blinked twice, clearly trying to come up with some way out of his present situation.

"Look, I'll make it simple. You can copy it onto a disc and I'll be on my merry way."

"And if I don't give it to you?" the old man asked, in perfectly accented English.

Jessie smiled. "I'll have to kill you"—she waved the gun for emphasis—"or better yet, I could wake up the fellow I disabled outside, and let Interpol have its way with you."

At the latter, whatever bluster the man had managed dissipated on a sigh. "If I give you the formula they're sure to kill me."

They, meaning the cartel developing the weapon. Jessie preferred to keep it on a need-to-know basis, but she knew enough to know that the formula would yield a chemical that made sarin seem safe by comparison.

"There's no reason for them to know it was you. Hell, there's no reason for them to know at all."

"And if I tell them that it was you?"

Her lips curled, welcoming her cynicism like an old friend. "Then we'll both be dead. Doesn't seem like a winning equation." She reached into her pocket and produced an envelope. "I've brought along a few friends for persuasion." She held out the envelope and, despite his fear, Schaufberg grabbed for it.

It was an old lesson. Greed always outweighed fear.

"And no one will know I was involved?"

"Only if you tell them."

The man held her gaze for a moment, and then he nodded. "It'll take a minute or two to copy the files."

"I'll need the key."

"The key?" He cocked his head with a frown, but not before she saw the flicker of fear.

She lifted the Beretta. "For the encryption?" She waited, the silence growing louder with each passing second.

Finally with a shiver, he sighed. "I've got it in a separate file." She watched as he loaded both the formula and the encryption onto a DVD.

"If this is a trick, I'll find you. Or failing that, I'll make sure they know you're a traitor. Am I making myself clear?"

His Adam's apple bobbed as he handed her the disc. "It's for real."

She watched for any sign that he was lying, but saw nothing more than a scared old man trying not to piss his pants—an overreaction, considering the amount of money in the envelope.

"Then our business is done." She pocketed the disc and walked back through the bookcase without bothering to look behind her. Schaufberg was a predictable sort. Quick to follow the money and too spineless to do anything that might jeopardize his life.

He'd never tell. And the man in the closet would never even know she'd been there.

Mission accomplished. Now all that was left was to get the package to her client and collect the money. She stepped out into the now fading sunshine and turned toward Wilhelmstrasse.

"You should have killed him." The voice came from just behind her and she whirled around to face her father.

"What in the hell are you doing here?" She hadn't meant to

sound so angry but he pissed her off with his popping in and out at will. "I don't have time for any of your games."

"I still think you should have killed the old fart."

"Let me remind you, that old fart is a hell of a lot younger than either of us."

"I'm just saying . . ." Her father shrugged his Armani-clad shoulders, twirling a silver-headed cane with one hand. Leave it to Daddy Dearest to dress to the nines.

She started walking again. Maybe if she moved fast enough the old goat would disappear. His long stride easily matched hers. So much for the easy way out. "Why are you here?" she asked. "Surely you've got something more interesting to do than to interfere in my business."

"It's a ridiculous business if you ask me. You're almost as bad as Marc—" He cut himself off before he had the chance to speak her brother's name.

"Marcus—Daddy, his name is Marcus."

"I know what his name is." Her father's tone forbade further discussion. Clearly, Marcus and her father had had a falling-out, a serious one at that, but neither of them would talk about it, so she'd had no choice but to let it go. "But that's not why I'm here."

"No, you're here to annoy me. How long were you watching?" It was an old trick, her father zipping in just to check on her, but while his invisible antics had been humorous when she was a child, as an adult she found them trying.

"I came in at the part where you were threatening Whale Gut." It was an apt description and Jessie fought against laughter.

"Ah, come on, you know you can't stay mad at your father." It really was easier than he thought, but to some degree he was right. Not that she'd admit it. "You never pop in without a rea-son." *Pop* being the operative word.

"Can't a father check up on his little girl?" If it was possible for the devil to look innocent, her father was doing a bang-up job.

"What do you want?" She spat the words out, pulling him into an alley out of sight. One never knew when he'd get the urge to torment someone.

"I need a favor." His face hardened, and she knew he'd finally come to the point.

"From me?" The words were out before she could stop them. Her father had never asked anything of her before. Choosing in-stead to flit into and out of her life on a whim.

"There's something I need. And I think you can procure it for me."

"Information?" She was the best when it came to securing the intellectual tidbits that others desired.

"An object, actually."

"I don't do that. Call Marcus." She'd only meant it as a joke. A small dig. But his eyes flashed with fire, and she took a step back-ward. Sometimes she forgot exactly what he was. "I'm sorry. That was out of line. What are you looking for?"

"A religious relic."

"Religion. That's not your usual shtick." She laughed, her sur-prise genuine.

"And this isn't just any religious relic. It's something special. A box." He paused, flexing his long fingers over the head of his cane. "A golden box."

"That's it? A box?" She shook her head, trying to fill in the missing blanks.

"It's part of the treasure."

That made a little more sense. There was only one treasure, at least where her father was concerned. "The Knights Templar?"

"Exactly. Only this is the prize of all prizes. Something that has been kept hidden, but by happenstance was liberated. And now rumor has it that it's on the move, which means that for the first time in eons, I have a chance to obtain it."

"So why don't you just get it yourself?" She swallowed a tingle of curiosity—she'd learned a long time ago to stay out of her father's business. The repercussions simply weren't worth the effort.

"I can't." It was unusual for her father to admit he was incapable of something.

"Why?" She frowned up at him.

"Let's just blame it on infernal rules, shall we? The point is that I need that box, and you have the ability to get it for me."

"I thought you didn't approve of my endeavors."

"I don't. But that doesn't mean they can't be useful. And I promise you there'll be ample reward if you succeed."

"I've got everything I need."

"But I can offer you more than everything."

"Stop talking in riddles."

"Fine." Her father blew out a frustrated breath and she couldn't tell if he was disappointed in her or just exasperated. Probably both. "The box is a part of the Templars' treasure. But it's been kept separately from all the rest. And as such it's infinitely more important. In the ancient scripts it's referred to as the Reliquary of the Four Horsemen."

She stared at her father, not bothering to conceal her amazement. She'd only heard one other person speak of it that way. "You're talking about the Protector of Armageddon."

"You've heard of it." Her father seemed pleased.

"Only in passing. It was important to someone I . . ." She stumbled, trying for the right words. "Someone I knew."

"David Bishop." Her father's eyes flashed with anger. "I thought you were finished with him."

"I am." She met and held her father's gaze, keeping her own steady. "But that doesn't mean he can't be useful."

"As long as you wind up with the Protector, I guess I can't argue about the methodology." As usual her father skipped right over the touchy-feely parts.

"Maybe I won't need him." She shrugged, not really certain she was willing to take the chance on seeing him again. "Anyway," she said, shaking off her roiling emotions, "I haven't agreed to find it yet. What am I playing for?"

Her father smiled, her question distracting him just as she'd known it would. Never let an opponent see a weak spot. She'd learned it from the master. "My kingdom."

"Say what?" It wasn't a brilliant response but it was the best she could come up with. "Your kingdom?" she repeated, apparently losing all ability for cognizant thinking.

"Lock, stock, and barrel."

"You want me to take over for you?"

"Well, I offered it to your brothers, and to Lucia. But they failed me."

The idea was ludicrous. But maybe this was the answer she'd been looking for. Taking over for her father would mean an end to her life here. A way out of the endless yearning for the simple joys that came with mortality.

"So all I have to do is find this box?"

"Well, not exactly." Her father smiled, his ebony eyes remaining deadly serious. "What I want you to do . . . is steal it."

Chapter Two

"You're a hard man to track down." David Bishop studied the man in the chair opposite him. If he hadn't known better, he'd have dismissed the prick without a second glance. But sources confirmed that Elliot Iverson was a master at hiding behind the innocuous.

It had taken almost six months of digging to uncover the bastard, and now that David had him in his sights he wasn't about to let Iverson slip away.

"I don't make a practice of hiding." Iverson shrugged, his eyes fixed on a point just beyond David's shoulder.

"Maybe hiding is overstating it, but the fact remains that I've spent more time than I care to admit tracking you down."

"So, you have my attention. Make the most of it." Iverson's upper-class English was as fake as the diamond in his pinky ring, and David fought to control his temper. It was almost as if Iverson wanted to be caught. But David had dealt with men far more idiotic, and so he wasn't about to let the stupid act deter him from the prize.

"I want the Protector of Armageddon. Or more important, I want the men who have it."

"The protector of what?" Iverson frowned, the expression making him look more simian than human.

"Don't pretend you don't know what I'm talking about. You brokered the deal." David fingered his pocket, resisting the urge to pull his gun.

"I honestly haven't got a clue."

With a speed born of years of practice, David closed the distance between them, the man's eyes widening as David slammed him against the wall. "There's no point in pretending, Iverson. I know you've brokered a sale. What I need is information about the seller."

"Everything I do is confidential. And if you're as knowledgeable as you say you are, you'd know that there's no way I can reveal a client."

"In your business, the word *client* is an overstatement. Scum protecting scum is more like it." David tightened his hold on the little man. "Tell me who the seller is."

"Seems to me that you've got the wrong end of the stick, old man. The important information here is the item being brokered, not the seller." Iverson frowned, his confusion laughable in any other situation, but David had been searching too long to see the humor. Hell, it was all he could do not to kill the man on the spot.

"From where I'm sitting," David said, "I don't see that you're in a position to call the shots. Tell me who you're representing."

Iverson eyed him for a moment, calculating his chances, and

then with a sigh he deflated, all bravado vanishing. "I honestly don't know. Everything is done with blind e-mails and anonymous post boxes."

David studied him for a moment, frustration cresting. It was the first hint of truth he'd heard from the man, and the reality was bitter. "Come on"—he shook Iverson, watching dispassionately as he winced—"you have to know something."

"I swear to God." Iverson raised a hand. "I just helped arrange the details of the sale. I don't know the buyer or the seller. I'm just the go-between." His eyes pleaded for understanding, but David had come too far to give a shit.

"If you arranged it, you've got to know more than you're telling me." He waited a beat, then produced his gun. A sweet little Sig-Sauer that had seen more action than most government-issued weapons.

Iverson blanched at the sight of the gun. "I'm telling you everything I know."

"Bullshit." He leveled the gun.

The man's gaze shot over David's shoulder again, the importance of the gesture coming about two seconds too late.

"You son of a bitch . . ." David hit the ground on a roll just as a bullet whizzed by his left shoulder.

Iverson squealed and made an awkward dive for the protection of a table in the corner.

Swiveling to try to spot his opponent, David rose to one knee, his gaze sweeping across the seemingly empty hotel room.

For three counts the only sound was the rasping of Iverson's breathing, and then, almost predictably, gunfire exploded as a man rounded the entryway corner, his handgun spraying bullets into the room.

Iverson peeked over the top of the table, and then with a yelp disappeared again.

David checked the magazine of the Sig, cursing himself for not bringing additional ammo. But then he hadn't been expecting an ambush.

Behind him, a drawer scraped, the sound abnormally loud in the silence. Damn it all to hell. Iverson was going for a gun. Popping up from behind an overstuffed armchair, David shot in Iverson's direction. It was a waste of a bullet, but in response, the little man hit the floor in terror.

Score one for the away team.

"Don't move, Bishop," a voice rang out from the entry hall.

"Like hell," the reply came even before David had the chance to think it through. Truth was, he hated being told what to do.

He popped up again and fired a couple more rounds. At least he wasn't going to go down easy.

Of course it was a last cry and it was coming too late. Without a balcony or easy access to even the window, he wasn't exactly in a position of power. A part of him cursed the stupidity that had allowed him to wind up in such a situation, but another part of him, the part that loved his brother, accepted that there hadn't been a choice.

Besides, if he'd learned one lesson in life it was the fact that it was never over until it was—well, *over*. The best way to go out was with a decided bang, and so, with a silent count of three, David launched himself out from behind the chair, firing alternately toward the front door and toward the table that sheltered Iverson. A couple more shots and he'd be dead in the water. Not the way he'd planned to go, but, goddamn it, if he was going, he'd take a least one of these bastards with him.

Return gunfire exploded all around him, and instinctively he hit the floor on a roll, eyes scanning the room for location and condition of his enemies. There was nothing from the entry hall. And from his current position, he couldn't see Iverson.

So instead he waited, his gaze moving from the entry hall to the table and then back again. Silence filled the room, its heavy presence almost more powerful than the staccato of bullet fire. David figured he had two options. Fake the shooter out and try to cut his losses by climbing out the window or come up shooting and pray that he'd manage to take out his opponents before they could kill him.

Not the best of odds. But then David had never been one for playing from the strong hand. It was much more fun to beat the players at their own game.

"Bishop?" Iverson's voice was shaky but audible. "Can you hear me?"

David considered not answering but rejected the idea almost immediately. He was cornered, no sense in denying the fact. "I'm here."

"Well, unless you've got a death wish, I suggest that you throw your gun out here so that I can see it."

"Come on, Iverson, why would I do that?" The question was rhetorical but David didn't push the point. After all, for the moment at least, Iverson and his crony were calling the shots.

"Because you're not a stupid man." The son of a bitch sounded so confident David almost laughed. When it came to avenging his brother—stupidity seemed to be ruling the day.

"Stop trying to read me, asshole," David hissed, shifting so that he had a better shot should the opportunity arise.

"Yes, well, I really think we ought to talk about your attitude,"

Iverson said, all remnants of his fear dissipating in the wake of his colleague's gun power.

David sighed, cursing himself for allowing himself to be trapped. "If anyone's got a problem, Iverson, it's you. Tell me where the fucking box is."

"Considering the circumstances, I don't think that's going to happen." The man actually sounded smug. "Maybe it's time to let go of your obsession."

"I'm not obsessed." The word grated. The last time it had been hurled at him, the impact had hurt—a hell of a lot more than he cared to admit. Not that any of it mattered now.

"Right, you're just hunting me down for the pure hell of it." Iverson's cockiness had definitely returned, and David clenched his fist, resisting the urge to stand up and shoot the bastard, shutting him up once and for all.

Better to concentrate on the gunman. The voice had been familiar. He struggled to place it, even as he popped up to take a shot in the direction of the entry hall, the responding gunfire indicating he hadn't managed to hit the mark. But his brain had finally identified the man.

Gaston Renauld. A cocksucker if ever there was one.

"Give it up, Bishop. It's over," Renauld called from the safety of the foyer.

"What the hell are you doing here?" The words were out before he could stop them, and immediately he regretted his lack of control. He only had two more shots and they'd goddamned well better be on target.

"Stalking you," Renauld said, the sarcasm in his voice making it clear that he wasn't feeling overly taxed with effort.

One beat passed, and then another—and then all hell broke

loose, gunfire seeming to come from every direction at once. David got off his last two shots and then ducked back behind the relative safety of the overstuffed chair.

There was a moment of silence and then another bullet pierced the air. Iverson gasped audibly and then fell to the floor, a cauliflower burst of blood staining his forehead. Two more shots and Renauld's body fell into view.

David edged around the chair, eyes scanning the room for the new source of danger.

"Cat got your tongue?" Jessie Wyatt emerged from the entry hall, her hands raised slightly, the gesture doing nothing to negate the cold superiority of the Beretta in her hand.

"What the bloody hell are you doing here?" David stood up and crossed over to Iverson's body, feeling for a pulse. There wasn't one, but then he'd already known that.

"Saving your life." Jessie shrugged, her gaze falling to Renauld. "Among other things."

"Right, you just happened to be in the neighborhood." Last he'd heard, she was holed up in Italy. Not exactly walking distance to London.

"No. I was looking for you. And so was Renauld. So from there it was an easy jump from following him to finding you. Although I hadn't any idea you'd be in such dire need."

"I was doing fine on my own."

Jessie stared pointedly at the two dead men, both still holding their guns. "I could see that."

"Damn it, Jessie," Saying her name brought a flurry of memories. Feelings he didn't want to acknowledge, let alone remember. "I needed Iverson alive."

"Well, it's not as if I got off on killing the man." Her eyes sparked with anger. "I didn't have a choice. It was you or him. And given the thanks I'm getting, it looks like I may have picked the wrong man."

"We'll talk about it later. Right now we need to get the hell out of here." David leaned down and picked up a couple of spent casings. "If we're lucky the police will assume the bastards killed each other."

"It's possible"—Jessie shrugged—"if they don't look too closely."

"Either way, I vote we're long gone." He started for the door, but she lifted her gun.

"First I want you to promise you won't try and give me the slip."

He swallowed a retort; there was no point in antagonizing her. She was tenacious enough without giving her further motivation. "Fine. I'm all yours."

"Well, aren't I the lucky one." There was an edge to her voice, a hint of bitterness. He cringed at the thought that he'd been responsible for it.

He started to walk past her, then stopped, his gaze locking with hers. He could smell her, feel the rhythm of her breathing, and suddenly, he wished it could have ended differently between them.

"Jessie . . . ," he started, reaching up to cup her chin.

For a moment they were connected, and he held his breath, savoring the contact. Her skin was soft, her eyes full of regret. But then with a flash of anger, she twisted away.

"Right, then, what do you say we get the hell out of here?" He stepped over Renauld's body, reminding himself that she deserved more than he could ever give her.

It was as simple as that.

Jessie cursed her own vulnerability. If time had taught her anything at all, it was that nothing was worth opening her heart. And even if there were something out there—it wasn't David Bishop. She'd already been on that ride and the thrill was overrated. The cost too damn high. She'd spent the last couple of years trying to exorcise him from her system. Apparently without any success at all.

She told herself that it was just proximity. Sensory memory or something equally inane. Pheromones always seemed to have a mind of their own. But it was hard to ignore the real fear she'd felt when she'd found him cornered in Lewisham.

In all truth, it was a new and powerful emotion. An immortal didn't really experience a whole lot of fear—and considering she'd been hung, poisoned, and shot to death on three separate occasions, she was more immune to the feeling than most. Basically, from her point of view, death was a less than frightening experience.

Except when it was happening to David.

Even with Henri, the only other man who'd managed to penetrate her shell, she'd never felt such raw, physical anguish. And she'd watched him die. At the time she'd mourned Henri's loss, her pain real, but it had been nothing like the stark desperation she'd felt upon seeing David in Iverson's hotel room.

She glanced over at him, sitting in the plane seat next to her. His eyes were closed, his breathing even. Obviously he'd taken the adventure in stride. In fact, he'd managed to act as if nothing of importance had happened at all.

Of course there was the little fact that Iverson had quite possibly known the location of the Protector. Her father wouldn't be too happy when he discovered she'd saved a mortal and in doing so had lost the key to the quest. But then she didn't have to tell her father.

"Having a little bit of trouble, are you?" The monitor embedded in the seatback sprang to life, her father's head sort of bobbing in place against the dark blue background.

"What are you doing here?" Jessie whispered, shooting a sideways glance at David and the passengers across the way. Thank God for first class—she'd learned a long time ago that people with money tend to tune out everything around them. The epitome of turning a blind eye.

"Just checking on your progress." Her father's smile was jaunty, but his black eyes were not amused. "I see you've picked up the garbage." For reasons Jessie had never really understood, her father had reacted almost as violently to her liaison with David Bishop as she had. Practically ordering her to stop seeing the man.

But Jessie had never listened to anyone. Particularly her father. And of course the irony was, he'd been absolutely right.

"I told you I need his help."

"Blast and damn, girl. You don't need anyone's help," her father thundered. Fortunately, no one but her could hear him. "Especially not a mortal. What do they know?"

"Well, this one is an expert on the Protector of Armageddon, remember? And if you want me to find the damn thing, I'm going to need his help."

"I assumed you'd simply use your *gift*—after all, that's what gives you the upper hand in finding things, am I right?" His smile this time was genuine. Her father liked it when she played by his rules.

"I tried. More than once, as a matter of fact." Since she was a tiny girl, Jessie had been able to *see* things, visualize who exactly held the information she needed. Sometimes it was quick and to the point, sometimes it was so vague it took her weeks to work it out, but always it was ultimately on target.

Except with the Protector. She'd tried to find it years ago—for David. And she'd been trying now—for her father. With absolutely no success at all—except that'd she'd managed to locate David, and stop him from being killed.

"I'm blocked. Or the box is protected in some way. Long and short of it is that if I'm going to find it, I'm going to need help, and David's been hunting the thing for years. He's my best shot."

"Well, I'd think the very fact that he hasn't found it would mean just the opposite, but who am I to question your choices. I'll just believe in your resourcefulness, and remind you how much is hanging in the balance here, for you—and for me." Leave it to her father to make it all about him.

"I'll get the box, Daddy. I promise. But no more popping in to see how I'm doing. You owe me that much."

For a moment, her father's frown seemed to reach out from the monitor, his eyes shooting flames, but then with a sigh, he capitulated. "Fine. Have it your way."

It was an old battle. "I don't need your help. I'm perfectly capable of taking care of myself. I'd think the last few centuries would have more than proved the fact."

"What can I say?" Her father's head bobbed. "I'm your father. I worry."

"And the moon is made of green cheese." She started to laugh, but swallowed it, worried that David would wake to find her father ensconced in the little monitor. "Look, Daddy, I learned my lesson.

Relationships can't work. Not for someone like me. So I'll handle this—without your interference."

She waited as her father digested the information.

"I'll have your word." He opened his mouth to argue, but she shook her head. "If you can't give me that, then I won't even try to find the box. You can take your request to Lola." She knew he couldn't. Her little sister was capable of a lot—wrecking havoc among men being chief of the list—but she wouldn't be able to find the Protector.

"I gave you the quest. And I guess I'll just have to trust that you know how best to find the box."

It wasn't a glowing endorsement, but considering this was the devil, she'd take it.

"Who are you talking to?" David's eyes were open and watchful.

Jessie stole a quick look at the monitor, which thankfully was blank. "No one. I was just thinking out loud. Bad habit."

"If that's the worst you've got, I wouldn't be overly worried." He reached over to cover her hand with his, his dark eyes sparking with something she was afraid to put a name to. "I didn't say thank you. For saving me. I might have gotten out of it all right. But I'll admit the odds weren't in my favor."

"I'm just glad I could help." She pulled her hand away and gave him what she hoped was an empty smile.

"So what exactly were you doing in Iverson's hotel room?"

In the rush to get out of London and to the airport, there hadn't been time for anything but perfunctory talk. And it wasn't as if she could tell David that she'd known he was going to Iverson's room— that she'd "seen" him cornered there. "I told you, I followed

Renauld. He's never been particularly good at covert." Gaston Renauld was a competitor of sorts. A broker for almost anything someone wanted to buy—information, art, and jewelry—even weapons. Only, Renauld had never perfected the art of covering his tracks. She hadn't needed to follow him, but the story would be plausible, and she wasn't about to let David know how much they were still connected.

He studied her for a moment more, as if trying to discover her secrets, and then shrugged. "So you want to tell me why you were looking for me?"

"It's about the Protector."

Disappointment flashed in his eyes, but was gone almost before she was certain that she'd seen it. "I thought you weren't interested in the box."

"I'm not. But I have a client who is."

"I should have known. This has nothing to do with me."

"Why would it?" It was her turn for anger. "In case you've forgotten, you're the one who ended things between us. Not the other way around."

"As I recall you didn't fight very hard to make me stay."

It was true; she hadn't fought at all actually, knowing that if he stayed it was only going to prolong the inevitable. Eventually, he'd have recognized the truth. Noticed the gray in his hair, the wrinkles at the corners of his eyes, and the disquieting fact that she never changed at all. It was an impossible situation. So she'd let him go. To hell with the fact that it had ripped her apart.

"You made it pretty clear that your priority was Jason."

"He's my brother. And he was murdered on my watch. He deserves vengeance."

"Not if it destroys you in the process." She'd said it all before, and knew that he wasn't going to change. Even if she hadn't been immortal, they wouldn't have had a chance. David's need to avenge his brother had all but consumed him. And nothing, not even love, could survive that.

"Obviously you're not too worried," he said, eyes narrowing. "After all, you're asking for my help. And in doing so, you're feeding right into my so-called obsession." She opened her mouth to protest but he waved her silent. "We've covered this ground before. I haven't changed, Jessie. I still live to destroy the people who killed my brother. So if this is an attempt to save me from myself, you can forget about it."

"I'm not here to rescue anyone. I just need your help. You know as much about the Protector as anyone does. And thanks to all those years in black ops, when we find it, I have every confidence that you'll be able to get me in and out in one piece. That's it. That's all I want. No entanglements. No walking down memory lane. No distractions at all." She glared at him, letting her anger push away all other emotion. "We pool our resources, find the box, and everyone gets what they want."

"So what if I don't want to work with you?"

"Then you have a funny way of showing it, considering we're trapped together in a first-class torpedo, skimming the earth at something like thirty-two thousand feet." She glanced at her watch. "I'd say we're almost halfway home."

"I live in London."

"Yes, you do. Which again begs the question as to why you agreed to fly to Italy with me, if you have no intention of helping me."

"Maybe I thought it would be a good idea to disappear for a while. No one is going to miss Iverson, but Renauld has some pretty powerful friends."

"Allies, maybe"—she shrugged—"but not friends. People like Renauld don't make friends."

"You're in the same business."

"And I meant what I said." They stared at each other, the silence punctuated by the hum of the airplane's engines.

"All right, so Renauld's death isn't going to cause much of a ripple. It's still not a bad idea for me to lie low. And maybe if—just to the pass the time—I decided to help you with your goal—"

"Our *mutual* goal," she corrected.

"Right," he admitted, albeit grudgingly. "You get the box and I get Jason's killers. Mutual satisfaction. But that's it—we work together to find the Protector. As you so cleverly put it, no distractions."

"Absolutely not." She shivered, her body already negating the promise she was making. "It'll be business. Just business."

"So where exactly are we going?" he asked, his dark eyes hooded. "I'd heard you were in Italy. But not where."

She sucked in a breath—her heart pounding in her ears. "Stresa. I live in Stresa." Maybe he'd miss the significance.

"Interesting choice." His eyebrows rose, the hint of a smile playing on his lips. He never missed a goddamned beat.

"Don't make it more than it is," she snapped. "I fell in love with the place."

And the man, but that wasn't something she liked admitting—even to herself.

Chapter Three

David stood at the window of Jessie's villa, the lake lapping peace-fully at the far edge of the lawn. Delphiniums and poppies fought with one another for superiority in a garden long ago abandoned, the riotous color better than anything someone could have planned.

The villa had an oddly dilapidated charm, as if it were stuck in time somehow, unable to shake off its past. Kind of like Jessie. Al-though the analogy was admittedly an odd one.

She hadn't changed. Which shouldn't have surprised him really. She had the kind of classic beauty that defied even the passing of time. Or maybe he just saw what he wanted to see.

He shook his head and turned to face her, banishing his senti-mentality. He already knew how easy it was to lose himself in her and forget everything that was important, and he wasn't about to let it happen again. "So what do you suggest we do? You've killed the only man who might have been able to tell us where the Protector is."

"I didn't have a choice." She was sitting in a tapestry-covered armchair. The kind Sotheby's coveted. Flanking the chair was a pair of tables—original Chippendales. A Ming Dynasty vase sat on one, a Tiffany lamp on the other.

With no consideration for style or design, Jessie had filled the room with a myriad of treasures, a collection that was no doubt worth a fortune. His mother would have been in seventh heaven, despite the fact that there had been no effort to conserve any of it. In point of fact, Jessie managed to make it look as if they were nothing more than favorite pieces. The arrangement careless—without any thought to display or preservation.

He suppressed a smile.

"What?" she asked, raising an eyebrow.

"Nothing. I was just admiring the room."

"If I remember correctly, you once referred to it as a backwater Louvre. And since the two words don't normally go together, I'm fairly sure you didn't mean it as a compliment."

"Well, it suits you."

"I'm not sure what to make of that."

"I was actually thinking my mother would love your collection."

She frowned. "She was a curator for the Met, right?"

"For fifteen years. That's where my brother developed his love of antiquities." Just the thought of Jason brought pain. If only he'd shown more interest in his brother's passion, maybe his brother would still be alive.

"You're doing everything you can." She'd always had an uncanny knack of reading his mind. At first it had been a bit disarming, but now it actually felt comforting—familiar. "And right now, we need to concentrate on finding the Protector. If it is on the move, this could be our best chance. So what do you say we go over it again?"

"Nothing like a little repetition." His response was flip, but he knew she wasn't fooled.

She walked over to the drinks table and poured a healthy measure of scotch. "Drink?" she asked, holding out the glass.

"Just what the doctor ordered." He reached for the glass, his fingers lingering on hers just a moment too long. Fortunately, if she noticed she kept it to herself, instead pouring herself a drink.

"So you think Iverson was brokering the sale of the box?"

"I know he was. And I've got sources to back it up. Unfortunately, what I don't have is a location or the identity of the buyer and the seller."

"But the deal is supposed to go down soon, right?" She crossed over to sit in the chair again, and he dropped down onto the sofa.

"Yes. If I had to call it, I'd say in the next couple of weeks."

"So that means it's got to surface long enough for the transfer to be made."

"Exactly. And I was hoping that Iverson could be convinced to share information."

"Except that I took him out." She frowned down at her scotch. "We seem to keep coming back to the same place."

"No." He shook his head, containing a sigh. "The truth is I don't think he knew any more than he'd already admitted."

"That he was brokering the deal."

"Right, and unfortunately, that's all we've got."

"Well, at least we know for certain that there had to be a buyer. And there are only a limited number of people that would be interested in something like the Protector of Armageddon."

"Evil mad scientists who want to bring about the end of the world?" David quipped.

"If you believe the stories, I suppose you could count them in. But I was thinking more along the lines of collectors who specialize in religious artifacts. Maybe we can start there and work backward."

"It's worth a try." David reached for his glass, then paused as a tiny sound punctured his consciousness, something out of place. He held up a hand, glancing over at Jessie. She nodded, her eyes on the doorway from the study out into the hall.

Silence filled the room, unbroken except for the ticking of a grandfather clock. David moved over to the doorway, Jessie right behind him, her Beretta already drawn. He followed suit with the Sig and edged out into the hall.

Dappled sunlight filtered through the window by the door, shifting with the wind in the trees. The doors to the dining room stood open, most of the room in plain sight. David shook his head and motioned toward the closed kitchen door. As if in answer, another sound emanated from the kitchen, this one louder. A bang, followed by a muffled curse.

Frowning, Jessie moved past him, her back to the wall. She stopped at the door and reached for the handle, waiting until David was in place on the opposite wall. She held up three fingers, and he nodded, watching as she silently counted—one, two, three . . .

David swung into the room, gun leveled. "Move and I'll shoot."

"Try not to hit the teacup." The man standing at the sink was indeed holding a cup, the delicate kind that gave a man the sweats just thinking about breaking it. "Eighteenth-century Limoges. The Empress Josephine. Am I right?"

Despite the fact that there were two guns pointing at him, the man actually had a twinkle in his eye.

"Faust." There was a strange mixture of emotion in Jessie's voice. Chagrin competing with what sounded like delight.

"I take it you know him?" David said, lowering his gun.

"A friend of my brother's." She holstered hers, her eyes never leaving Faust's. "Is Marcus with you?" She sounded like a child at Christmas. He felt as if he'd been dropped into some alternative world. Jessie had never seemed like the family connections type. More of a loner.

Like him.

"No." The man called Faust shook his head. "But he sends his love."

Faust was hard to describe. Solidly built, with the hands of a laborer, he was one of those men who blended into the background, always there and yet one never really saw him. His face was craggy, but there was a keen intelligence reflected in his eyes. If pressed, David wouldn't want to guess his age. Fifty—fifty-five, maybe. But he could be off a decade either way.

When David had worked for the CIA and its various nonentities, he'd been an expert in tagging people. In figuring out what they wanted even before they were sure of it themselves. And despite the fact that he was no longer working covert ops, he still trusted his gut. But Faust was one of those men who was difficult to get a handle on.

"I can't believe you're here." Jessie had thrown an arm around the man's waist, the two of them walking back toward the study. For the moment they'd forgotten all about him. A fact that was oddly unsettling—at least where Jessie was concerned.

David shook his head, clearing his thoughts. What he needed

now was to keep his wits about him. Emotions only got in the way of truth. He'd learned that a hell of a long time ago. Even before he'd lost his brother. And the notion always served him well.

"So, tell me the truth, what brings you here?" Jessie asked, sitting next to Faust on the sofa. "You never leave Marcus's side."

David refilled his drink, then settled back into the armchair, watching the two of them.

"Before we go any further, don't you think it would be a good idea to introduce me to your friend?" Faust smiled and sipped his tea.

"God, I'm sorry. I was just so surprised to see you."

It was as if Faust had freed her from some dark place where she'd chosen to exist. David had only heard her laugh like that one other time. With him. In bed. But the memory was hardly relevant to the conversation at hand.

He put down his drink and leaned forward to offer a hand. "David Bishop."

"Ah, yes, I remember hearing your name." The older man's handshake was firm and strong. "The two of you worked on a project together, right?"

"You shouldn't eavesdrop, Faust," Jessie said, her frown forgiving. "Marcus and I were having a private conversation."

"About me?" David asked, the conversation taking an interesting turn. "I trust you weren't too disparaging."

"Oh, quite the contrary," Faust started, only to have Jessie angrily shush him up.

"I was just telling my brother about the Protector. So of course your name came up."

David smiled, knowing damn well that it had been more than that.

"I'm Faust," the other man said, cutting through the rising tension. "I've come to help."

"With the Protector?" David tried but couldn't keep the suspicion out of his voice. "How did you know we were looking for it?"

"Well, the whole world knows *you're* looking for it," Faust said with a shrug. "At least in my world they do."

"Faust is a thief," Jessie said, by way of explanation. "So is my brother. And for that matter—if you look at it the right way—so am I. Guess it kind of runs in the family."

"Actually, to be honest," Faust said, "Marcus is the thief—although he prefers to think of himself as a pirate. I'm more a logistics man."

David wasn't sure which was more interesting, imagining Faust as a pirate or realizing that Jessie actually had family. Come to think of it, despite all the passion, they hadn't really shared that kind of intimacy. Surface details, but not the ones that really mattered. But then again maybe there were some things not meant to be talked about.

"Yes, but you said my brother was well known among those of your profession. Jason wasn't a thief so I don't really see where the parallel comes in."

"I never mentioned your brother. I said that your quest for vengeance is well known. And you know as well as I do that your chosen path has crossed into my world on more than one occasion. Most recently in the rather reprehensible form of Elliot Iverson."

"Iverson's dead," Jessie said, eyeing Faust skeptically.

"I'm aware of that fact. You'll be delighted to know that despite rumors to the contrary, the authorities believe he and that sleezeball Renauld murdered each other in a fit of pique. Nice of them to leave the two of you out of it."

"How the hell did you know we were there?" Jessie asked.

"I haven't survived this long without keeping an ear to the ground. Besides, Marcus likes to keep tabs."

"Marcus has been otherwise occupied of late." She shot back.

"So let's just say I'm filling in."

"I don't need a watchdog, Faust," she said, her eyes sparking with anger.

"Don't you?" His answer was fuel for the fire. Not that it made a bit of difference to Faust. The man just sat there drinking his tea as if everything were right as rain.

"So what is it you think you have to offer us?" David said. "I mean, you said you want to help. How exactly do you plan to do that? Between the two of us, Jessie and I have the experience necessary to break in and steal the box."

"Yes, but there's a little problem. You don't know where it is."

"And you think you can find it?" David crossed his arms, trying to size up the other man's motives.

"Possibly. But first I need to understand what happened out there in the Sudan." He sat back, waiting.

"Why? What difference can it make to you?"

"If I'm going to help you, I need the whole story. All the little details."

"So what? This is a test of some kind?" David had had pissing matches with tougher customers than Faust. And he wasn't about to dredge up the pain just so some friend of Jessie's could satisfy his morbid curiosity.

"I think it's a good idea if we all lay our cards on the table. Motivation is an important thing. I want to understand why you want to find the Protector."

"You first."

"I don't want it at all. I just want to help Jessie."

"So you say," David said, his gaze locking with the older man's.

"Oh, for God's sake, David. Faust is always trying to protect someone. It's what he does. And when Marcus doesn't cooperate he comes and finds me. And since we're apparently playing true confession, I don't want the box either. I just promised to get it for a client."

"A very special one," Faust said, not bothering to hide his sarcasm.

"Look, I broker information, and when the situation warrants I broker things. This was an offer I couldn't refuse. A chance to attain something I've always wanted."

"And that would be . . . ?" David asked, surprised that he'd voiced the question.

"Peace. But I don't expect you to understand that."

Considering the way Jessie lived her life, peace seemed the last thing she'd want. Hell, she was as much of an adrenaline junkie as he was.

"Right, then," Faust said, his expression purposefully blank. "I want to watch out for Jessie, and she wants the box for a client. That leaves you."

"You know the answer. I want to find the box so that it can lead me to my brother's killers."

"A noble cause. But I want to know why."

"I think it's pretty goddamned clear. The bastards blew my brother's brains out and left him to rot in the sun."

"Yes. It's pretty straightforward. But there's more, isn't there?"

He wasn't sure why Faust was pushing, but he recognized that the man wasn't going to let it go. "What do you want me to say, old man? That I killed my brother? That he reached out to me when he was in trouble, and I failed him? That I was so fucking busy with my latest operation that I didn't move fast enough? That I didn't believe the threat was real?"

"But you tried to help him. You told me that much." Jessie shook her head, trying to understand.

"Yeah. I tried to help him. But only after he called a second time. And it was too fucking late by then."

"Why are you doing this, Faust?" Jessie asked, her face full of anguish. "Can't you see that you're hurting him?"

"He needs to say it. To put it into words. And if you're going to trust him to help, you have to understand what happened. What he's living with. Why he needs vengeance beyond anything else—and I mean anything, Jessie."

Suddenly David understood. Jessie had been right. The man was here to protect her. To make sure she knew the truth about what had happened. About why he had to make things right. Faust wanted her bargain with the devil to be all signed and sealed with total disclosure.

David blew out a breath. "I told you that my brother was an archaeologist." He spoke to Jessie, ignoring the pain in his gut.

"He was like your mother. He loved everything old."

"Yes. But I didn't get it. I thought they were both wasting their time. That there was more to life than living for the dead."

"Like saving the world?" There was no accusation. Just point of fact. Faust's expression masked.

"Something like that. For what it's worth I really did believe I was making a difference. Improving the world, one operation at a time. So when Jason told me he was on to something big, I pretended to care but really didn't listen. I mean, I was out there protecting liberty and he was obsessed with an old box."

"The Protector of Armageddon is far more than just a box."

"I suppose on an intellectual level I understand that now. But I didn't then. And I still don't believe it has special powers."

"There are a lot of things in this world we don't understand, David." Faust's words sounded like a reprimand, but David was far more interested in Jessie's reaction.

"So you didn't take your brother's quest seriously. That's hardly a reason to blame yourself for his death." She shook her head in denial, as if in so doing she could make it so.

David sighed. Better to just get it out. He wasn't convinced it was necessary, but the door had been opened, and if he wanted Jessie to trust him—he had to tell her the whole truth. She wouldn't settle for anything else now.

"I wish it were that simple," he said, bowing his head to order his thoughts. "Jason was always into academic things. Which meant that most of the time we never really saw eye to eye growing up. But he was my brother, and when he had trouble—like older kids picking on him—I was there to put an end to it."

"You protected him."

"Yeah. My mom used to tell me it was my job. That without my father in our life, I needed to be the man. To make sure my little brother was all right." He picked up his glass and drained the contents. Fool's comfort. "But once we were out on our own, I went my own way. I talked to Jason now and then. And of course I was aware that he was a rising star in his field. But that's pretty much it. And the deeper I got into espionage, the further I pulled away from my family."

"That's understandable," Jessie said. "But when he needed you, you were there." She said it with so much confidence he felt doubly ashamed.

"That's just it. I wasn't. Jason's dream had always been to locate the stuff of legends. To find the reality in the myth. And to that end, he concentrated on stories about the Protector. He used to go on and on about the thing. Its purported powers, its relevance in Christian doctrine. The kind of academic bullshit that drove me to distraction." He walked over to the drinks table for a refill.

"The truth is I didn't care. Not even when he told me he was heading out to the Sudan."

"He thought the Protector was there." It wasn't a question, but David answered it anyway.

"Yeah. Some backer had found evidence of what he thought was a long-forgotten tomb. There was conjecture that it might be the hiding place of the Protector. Jason called me. He was so goddamned excited. And I blew him off. I was in the middle of busting up a cartel and so I didn't have time."

"Did he know who the backer was?" This from Faust.

"It's a question I ask myself every damn day. If he did, and I'd bothered to ask, then maybe I would have realized it was dangerous. But I didn't ask. And so he left and for all practical purposes fell off the radar for a couple of months. It wasn't all that unusual. And I was pretty damned occupied with my supercilious attempt to save the world." He knew he sounded bitter, but there wasn't a goddamned thing he could do about it. The floodgates had been opened and the poison was spewing.

"Anyway, one day, out of the blue, I get a call from him." David paused. He could still hear his brother's voice, remember the excitement that had crackled across the satellite connection.

"He said he'd found it. That it was beyond anything he could possibly have imagined. And he asked me to come and get him."

"Was that a normal thing for him to do?" Jessie asked.

"No. It wasn't. In all honesty, he didn't approve of a lot of the things I did. Never mind that for the most part they were for the greater good, the methodology needed to accomplish some of said good was a bit more than he could stomach. So I should have recognized that his asking meant something. I mean, I was trained to read people after all. It was supposed to be my specialty. But all I felt was annoyed. I had better things to do than babysit my brother.

"Anyway, I forgot about it. Or at least pushed it out of my mind. But then I got a second call. This time he wasn't nearly as excited, just asked if I'd made arrangements to come get him. I asked him why he needed my help. But he wouldn't say. Just kept insisting that he needed me to come."

He took a long swallow of scotch, the burning in his throat helping him to keep focus, to fight off the demons.

"He told me where he was. The exact coordinates. And I promised I'd be there. Only it was two days before I managed to wrap things up and get out of the country." David stared down into his glass, seeing Jason's face reflected in the dregs of his scotch.

"And you were too late." Faust, it seemed, was good at cutting to the chase.

"Yeah. By the time I got around to chartering a plane, my brother was already dead. Only of course I didn't know it. I should have realized something was wrong. That Jason was trying to tell me something. But I missed it." He closed his eyes, memories swamping him—the heat, the sand, the smell.

A hand closed around his, and he opened his eyes to find Jessie on the floor by the chair. He turned his hand, palm up, taking solace in the contact, even though he didn't deserve it.

"It was hotter than hell, and the guide I'd hired didn't want to be there. Bad juju or some fucking nonsense like that. But I pressed on, without him, and found the place, just as David had described it. As tombs went it was understated. Not much more than a hole in the base of a sand dune.

"There was no activity. No sign of a camp at all. In fact it was so goddamned quiet I started to think maybe the guide had been right. I even had the thought that Jason had been yanking my chain. That this was all his idea of a practical joke. But that wasn't the case. He was there. Just inside the tomb.

"I don't know your experience with the desert, Faust. But it's not like any other climate I know. Any life that survives there preys on the things that don't. Which means there wasn't a hell of a lot left of my brother. In fact, if I hadn't recognized the ring"—his thumb moved automatically to the gold signet ring on his fourth finger—"I might have believed it was someone else."

"But it wasn't." Jessie's voice was gentle, the sound soothing. Except that there was nothing that could ever erase the memory of his brother lying there, his corpse rotting while he waited for his big brother to ride to the rescue.

"No. It was Jason. I think I'd have known it even without the ring. But it was a gift from my mother and I don't think Jason ever took it off."

"There was nothing to give you an idea of who'd done it?" Faust asked, frowning.

"Nothing. And I'm pretty good at ferreting out overlooked details. He'd been shot, but they were through and throughs. No casings. No bullets. Nothing that could identify the shooter. In fact, with the exception of Jason's body and the improvised opening into the tomb, there was no sign that anyone had been there at all.

"My guess is they figured he'd just disappear and no one would ever be the wiser. The whole expedition was cloaked in secrecy. If he hadn't called me, the tomb and his remains would have been buried beneath the sand, quite possibly forever."

"So in a way you did save him—at least from the speculation that would have surrounded his disappearance," Jessie said.

"I don't give a shit about speculation. The point here is that I killed my brother. My arrogance killed him as surely as the bullets that shattered his skull. If I'd listened—really listened—I'd have known he was in trouble. I'd have gotten there in time."

"Which means you'd probably be dead, too." Faust was only stating the obvious, but David wanted to shut him up. To make them both understand the horror of what he'd done.

"All my life I've had one simple responsibility: watch out for my brother. And the only time it ever really mattered, I wasn't there. So all that's left for me is to find the man who did this to him, and make him pay. A life for a life."

"Yours." Faust stood up, trading his teacup for whiskey.

"Maybe. If that's what it takes."

"And that's why you're here."

"Yes. If Jessie finds the box, then there's a chance it'll lead me to Jason's killer. Quid pro quo. I help Jessie, she helps me."

"And you're okay with this, Jessie?" Faust asked.

Jessie pushed to her feet, her expression inscrutable. "Even if I didn't need the box for a client I'd want to help. I tried to before."

"But I stopped you," David said, the room suddenly seeming to hold only the two of them. "Threw you out on your ear actually. I can't believe you're willing to risk that again."

"I'm not risking anything. We said it before. It's all about mutual goals. I get the box, you get Jason's killer. It's win-win. Everyone gets what they want."

"Things rarely turn out that neatly, Jessie." There were undercurrents that had nothing to do with Jessie's client or David's torment, but he couldn't seem to stop the words.

"It's like I told Faust. I'm a big girl. I can take care of myself. And the simple fact is that I need your help. Faust's, too, if you're okay with it. He really is good at logistics."

David turned to study the older man. On the surface he seemed harmless enough, but that was often the first sign of trouble. Still, Jessie trusted him. And in all honesty it was probably a good thing to have someone else in the mix. Even someone as enigmatic as Faust. "It's your ball game. If you think Faust can help us, I can deal with it."

Faust nodded, his expression making him seem suddenly older. "All right then, we're in agreement. Cards on the table. Jessie wants the box, you want vengeance, and I want to be sure Jessie comes out of this little mission in one piece." There was a warning there, but David chose to ignore it.

"Look, if you two can't get along, then I'll figure out how to do this by myself. I've got enough on my plate without having to play umpire for the two of you." Jessie stood up, any hint of softness disappearing as she eyed them both. "Seems to me we're overly clear on everyone's motives, but the skill set is what interests me. You obviously think you have something to bring to the table, Faust—besides playing watchdog. So it's your turn for confessions. What exactly have you got?"

Faust leaned forward, both hands on his knees. "It's simple actually. You see, I know where the Protector is."

Chapter Four

David was halfway out of his seat, anger making his face flush. Jessie reached out to restrain him, her gaze on her brother's friend. "What do you mean you know where it is? The actual location? Why didn't you just tell us?"

"I needed to make sure David wasn't a liability."

David sat back on the chair, a vein in his temple pulsing. But at least he hadn't tried to throttle Faust. Not yet anyway. Jessie blew out a breath. Truth be told, she was still reeling from David's confession about his brother. She'd known that he blamed himself for Jason's death, but she had no idea that the guilt ran so deep. It explained a lot, but it also left her feeling strangely bereft.

She shook her head, clearing her thoughts. What mattered now was finding the Protector. It was what they both needed. Whatever else lay between them, it was far too late to mend it now. She turned to Faust, summoning the strength she'd spent centuries perfecting. "I'm not sure that questioning David's loyalties was your call to make. But since we all seem to be working toward the same goal now, I'll leave it at that. So where's the box?"

"In Milan. At least that's what my sources tell me."

"And just who exactly are your sources?" David said, his anger still simmering under the surface.

"I'm sure you can appreciate the fact that in my business contacts prefer to remain anonymous."

"But you trust them?" His eyes narrowed as he studied Faust.

"Of course I do, or I wouldn't be here, would I?" The two of them rose, gazes locked, clearly posturing for one another. Jessie resisted the urge to throw them both out on their asses. Men could be such idiots sometimes.

"It doesn't matter where the information originated; as long as Faust believes it's accurate then I believe him," Jessie said, working to keep her exasperation in check. "And you'd be wise to do the same."

"Well, it's a little easier for you. You know the man." David fisted his left hand, then released it and fisted again, the gesture mirroring the frustration in his eyes.

"And you know *me*. Whatever problems we've had in the past were personal. When it comes to business you trust me, right?"

"Yes." The pronouncement was grudging but immediate.

Jessie nodded. "All right then, I'm telling you I trust Faust. With my life, if it comes to that. Which means that you can trust him, too."

"Or at least for the moment, give me the benefit of the doubt." Faust shrugged, the tension in the room easing a little with the gesture.

"Fine." David sat down. "Do you know where in Milan?"

"In a vault below the Club Azure," Faust said, moving over to refill his whiskey.

"That's one of Max Braun's clubs, isn't it?" Jessie asked, following Faust to the table to refill her own glass.

"Max Braun," David said. "I've heard that name. He's a big player in the international entertainment scene, right?"

"Yes. He owns a dozen or so casinos and at least that many clubs. They're scattered around the world. Ibiza, New York, L.A., Paris, Nice, Monte Carlo. Azure is the jewel in his crown."

"I don't remember his name coming up with regard to the Protector." David folded his arms. "Does he have an interest in religious relics?"

"If you're asking if he's the one selling the Protector, I don't know," Faust said. "He owns the vault, which at least points to his involvement on some level. But even if he is the one who's selling it, there's no guarantee that he was behind your brother's murder."

"Yeah, but there's also nothing to say he's not." David looked as if he wanted to sprint for the nearest door. Jessie held her breath, wondering if Faust was testing him again.

"Agreed," Faust said. "But if you jump to conclusions and launch a vendetta against him, it's only going to drive the box deeper underground. What you need is leverage. And to get that, we need the Protector."

Jessie nodded, hoping that David could see the wisdom of Faust's words.

"All right, so we need to break into the vault. Any suggestions on how we do it?" David asked, accepting the drink Jessie offered. They were all going to need fortification if they were going to figure out how to get into Braun's vault. The man wasn't the kind to skimp on security.

"We'll need blueprints of the club to start with. And information about the kinds of security Braun has in place." Jessie sat on the arm of the sofa, her mind considering options. "I ought to be able to locate both with a little digging."

"Already ahead of you as far as the blueprint," Faust said. "I brought it with me."

"How did you manage to get it?" Jessie asked, not really all that surprised. Faust had been around even longer than she had. His immortality a quirk of fate rather than parentage. He and Marcus had met on some battlefield or another. Killed each other, actually—more than once, to hear them tell it.

"You're not the only one who can ferret out needed information," Faust protested, but not with any real conviction. "Unfortunately I wasn't as successful with plans for the security system."

"Don't worry. I can get that. And once we've got that figured out, David can get us into the vault. Right?"

He nodded. "Yeah. I can get us in, if we know what we're up against. The key, though, is going to be getting information about the vault. Once I've got that, with the right tools, getting to the box should be a piece of cake."

"We'll make the perfect team," she said. "I'll handle the security systems, you'll take care of liberating the Protector."

"And I'll have your backs," Faust said. "Keep watch to make sure nothing unexpected gets in your way."

"So, we on?" Jessie was surprised at the excitement she felt over the prospect of working with David. Despite everything that lay between them.

"Yeah." He nodded. "We're on. I'll help you secure the Protector, and in the process I'll finally be able to nail the bastard who killed my brother. Like you said, we'll kill two birds with one stone."

"All right, then," she said, surprised to see Faust frowning.

"Looks like Faust has a problem," David said, clearly aware of the other man's displeasure.

"I just don't want you to let your quest for vengeance do anything that could jeopardize the operation. Or put Jessie at risk."

"I'm not going to hurt Jessie. How many different ways do you want me to say it?" They were back to posturing, but this time Jessie failed to see the humor.

"I can take care of myself. I don't need either of you. So get off the testosterone merry-go-round and give it a rest. If we go into this, it has to be with the understanding that David's overriding goal is to find out who killed Jason. For him that's all that matters."

The minute the last words were out of her mouth, she wished them back. She hadn't meant them as a dig, but they'd still come out that way. She ducked her head, avoiding his gaze, wishing to hell she could just quit thinking about it. They'd had a brief affair. People did it every day. And then they went their separate ways. Finito. It's over. No looking back.

Besides, it wasn't as if she wanted a relationship. Given her longevity, any commitment was destined to be a one-sided affair. Everything was as it should be. Better to keep her focus on what mattered—fulfilling her quest and finding the box for her father. Then maybe she could put all of this behind her once and for all.

"Why don't we have a look at the blueprints." She crossed over to a library table in the corner, moving books out of the way to make space for Faust's schematics. "How old are these?" she asked as he spread them out on the table.

"Fairly new actually. The club just went through a remodel. Nothing major, but a few walls were shifted here and there. So it required an updated blueprint."

"Do you have photographs as well?" David asked, leaning over to take a look at the plans.

"Yes," Faust said. "Aerial and outer façade. Braun is peculiar about cameras inside his clubs, so I couldn't get any photographs of the interior."

"That's all right. We can run recon when we get to Milan."

"Fine, and in the meantime, I can download the pictures, if you'll let me use a computer," Faust said.

Jessie looked up from the blueprint. "There's a laptop in the corner. Help yourself. The password is Hades."

Faust's eyebrows rose, but he refrained from comment, heading over to the computer instead.

"Looks like there are four stories including the ground floor," David said, studying the crosscut of the building. "I assume the vault is in the cellar?"

"Yes," Faust replied, the computer clicking and whirring as he waited for it to boot up. "The whole building is set into the side of a hill. The vault is set back into the bedrock, and from what I've been told has all the latest safeguards. This isn't going to be easy."

"But easy takes all the fun out of it," Jessie said, more comfortable now that she'd dodged the emotional bullet.

"Access from the ground floor?" David asked, frowning down at the blueprint. "There's no sign of a door to the cellar."

"That's because there isn't one," Faust said, returning to the table with the laptop in tow. "At least not on the ground level. The club occupies the first and second floors, with storerooms and coatrooms on the ground level. The third floor, at the top, houses Braun's private offices. And an apartment that I'm told he uses when he's in Milan."

"He doesn't live there?" Jessie asked.

"No. He spends most of his time in Seville." Faust turned the computer so that they both could see the screen. "This is a picture of the building."

The granite structure was almost austere in its presentation, its angles cold and unforgiving. Not exactly what one expected of a nightclub.

"It looks more like a bank," David noted with a frown.

"Well, considering what we're planning to do, that seems appropriate, don't you think?" Jessie asked, the question meant for no one in particular.

Faust clicked a button and a second photograph filled the screen. "Here it is at night."

"Whoever it was that said it was all about lighting was right. If I didn't know better I'd say you were showing us a totally different building." Jessie shifted so that she could see the screen better, her arm brushing against David's in the process. Heat rushed down her arm to pool deep inside her. For a moment she met his eyes, then pointedly looked away. "This is the same place, right?"

"Absolutely. Just a little neon here and there and the occasional spotlight." He enlarged the photograph until only the front entrance was visible. "This is the only way in. There are no windows or back doors on the ground level."

"Sounds like somebody violated the building code," David said, moving to the other side of the table, the action somehow insulting. It was one thing for her to move away, but quite another when he was the one creating distance.

"Italians are pretty lax about building codes," Faust responded, ignoring the simmering undercurrent. "Especially when it involves someone like Braun."

"So how hard is it to get into the club?" Jessie frowned down at the blueprint. "I can see elevators and some stairs, but they're all located at the back of the building. I assume this hallway"—she pointed to the drawing on the blueprint of the ground floor—"is meant to serve as a funnel, leading to access to the club."

"Exactly." Faust nodded. "There's a small security office to the right of the entrance and the gatekeeper, so to speak, is behind a podium that fronts the hallway. In order to get into the club you have to get past the bouncer at the front door and then be cleared for entrance into the club. If you're not on the list, then you're not getting in."

"So how do we get on the list?" David asked. "Pay someone, I assume."

"Actually I think I can manage that," Jessie said, chewing the side of her lip as she considered the possibilities. "Is the guest list automated?"

"Yes. There are PCs at the reception stand and at the security office." Faust pointed to the corresponding points on the blueprint.

"So all I have to do is hack in, and make sure we're on the list."

"You make it sound easy," David said, his expression skeptical.

"It is. Or it will be after I've gathered a little more information. I can take care of the VIP clearance at the same time."

"Okay," he said, "so once we're on the VIP floor, all we have to do is figure out how to slip the guards and take the elevator up to the offices. And then from there we can take the second elevator down to the vault."

"Right," Faust said. "I'll keep watch for any unwanted attention, while the two of you break into the vault and steal the box."

"So what happens once we get the thing?" David asked. "We can hardly stroll through the club carrying the Protector of Armageddon. Even with you running interference."

"No. I think that would be a bit much," Faust said, "but according to the blueprint, there's a shaft that was cut through the rock to the cellar. I assume that's how they got the vault in. Anyway, you ought to be able to get the box out that way. Although you'll have to cut through a steel panel to do it."

"Shouldn't be a problem," David said. "So what's next?"

"You all get a good night's sleep," Jessie said, "and tomorrow we'll head for Milan."

"And what are you going to do?" David asked, his dark eyes inscrutable.

"I'm going to break into a computer." And try her very best not to think about the man who, at the moment, was driving her to drink.

The sun hung low in a gap between the hills surrounding the lake. The reflection colored the water pink and orange, ripples sparkling as they crested. In the distance, David could see a fisherman pulling his boat to shore, the day's catch stored in a red and white cooler.

The breeze was cool, a counter note to the still warmth of the dying day. The sound of olive trees moving in the wind was soothing, a sort of white noise against the backdrop of the darkening landscape.

Pinpoints of light flickered across the lake. Normal people going about their normal lives. No thoughts of vengeance, or of religious relics. No thoughts at all, really, except that another day was ending.

A picture of Jessie flashed in his mind, laughter cresting in her eyes as she wrestled with him on the bed. Amusement had crescendoed into something more and suddenly it was just the two of them standing together against the rest of the world.

The door behind him slid open, and he turned, thinking it was her, allowing himself, just for the moment, to pretend that this was his normalcy. The dying light, the villa, the lake—Jessie.

"I thought maybe we should have a talk." Instead of Jessie, it was Faust, holding two large glasses of whiskey.

"I think we've already covered my motivations and the reasons behind them."

"That's not why I'm here," the other man said, offering David a glass.

"All right, then, what do you want to talk about?" he asked, taking a long sip of the scotch, the amber liquid glowing in the half-light.

"The Protector." Faust moved to the railing, staring out at the murky waters of the lake. "I assume since you've been trying to find the thing, you know a bit about it."

"I've done my research, but I'll admit I've been more interested in who has the thing than the myths that surround it."

"But you know what it's supposed to signify."

"More or less. The box was created by God in the ancient times. It's purported to be made of gold, covered with jewel-encrusted carvings that depict the Four Horsemen of the Apocalypse. According to legend," he said, stressing the last word, "the box holds the seven trumpets and seven bowls mentioned in Revelation. And once the seal is broken and the box opened, the contents will be freed and bring about the end of the world. Hence the name: Protector of Armageddon." He took another sip of his scotch, eyeing Faust over the rim. "Of course I don't believe any of that—except maybe the jewel-encrusted gold part."

"A nonbeliever." Faust's smile looked ghostly in the dimming light.

"Let's just say I don't go in for all that mystical claptrap."

"Well, what if I told you there's some truth to the legend?"

"I'd wonder how you could possibly know that for certain."

"No one knows anything for certain, David," Faust sighed. "But some things have to be taken on faith."

"And you believe the box is one of them."

"What I believe is that the box has power and that it isn't as simple as you'd have it be. Part of the legend includes the fact that the box was to be guarded by the Seven. Men chosen for their honor and loyalty."

"Like the Knights Templar. I read about them. So, are you telling me my brother was killed by the Seven?"

"No." Faust shook his head to underscore his words. "For centuries the box remained hidden, under the careful watch of the Seven. As long as it remained hidden it was safe from anyone seeking to uncover it."

"But there are references to it surfacing now and then. I've seen my brother's notes. And verified the documentation."

"Yes, once or twice there were slipups, times when for whatever reason the box needed to be moved, and someone happened to see it. The sightings of course only added to the stories. But there was never any serious threat to the box or its protectors."

"If it's always been in their possession, how is it that my brother found it?"

"Well, that's where the story takes an unpleasant turn. The Seven are not immortal, although they possess certain powers. They are simply men of uncommon valor charged with protecting the box. And as they age they are also charged with finding an equally worthy replacement. So the Seven are constantly changing, at least from generation to generation, but somewhere along the line, within the last century or so, a mistake was made."

"What do you mean, a mistake?" David asked, frowning as he swallowed the last of his whiskey.

"The story is that one of the Seven wasn't pure of heart. In fact, his desire for the creature comforts of this world far outweighed any obligation he felt to protect the next. In short, he made a deal with the devil, so to speak, and in return for earthly riches, he arranged things so that the box could be stolen. His defection was discovered, but the box was not. And, at least according to the legend, the Seven, in whatever incarnation, have been searching for it ever since."

"And my brother found it."

"It would seem so."

"But if this is all part of the legend, then why haven't I heard it before? God knows I've talked to pretty much everyone who has information about the damn thing."

"Let's just say I came into possession of some very unique documentation."

"From your nameless sources."

Faust's smile lacked humor. "The point is, David, that this isn't a task to be undertaken lightly. If you're going to make sure that you and Jessie come out of this alive, you need to understand what it is you're dealing with. "

"A hell of an artifact, which, even without supernatural powers, has corrupted many men, one of them enough to kill for it."

"I know you believe that your brother was murdered, but there's something more you need to know. If anyone but the anointed one tries to open the box . . ."

"What?" David asked, a sudden prickling of worry chasing down his spine.

"They die."

Chapter Five

Jessie stared at the flashing letters on the monitor. Password. *Password*. These days everything required one. She closed her eyes, shutting out the muted colors of her bedroom, as she reached out for the correct combination of letters and numbers.

She'd first discovered her somewhat peculiar gift when she was still quite young. Her mother had received a letter, the words robbing her face of color. Jessie had asked, terrified, what the missive contained, but her mother had only forced a smile, reassuring her daughter that everything was fine.

That night, Jessie had tried to find the letter, to no avail, but alone on her cot, she'd suddenly pictured the parchment, the words as clear as if she'd held the correspondence herself. Her mother had been accused of treason. The letter was a summons by the king.

The next morning a coach came to take her mother away, and Jessie was left to fend for herself, in a world that did not cherish children, especially those that were female. She lived on the streets, getting by on scraps and handouts, never certain where she would lay her head or get her next meal.

It was only when she remembered the letter, and the odd way in which it had appeared to her, that Jessie's life had begun to change. Using her gift, she had worked her way up in society, exchanging purloined information for protection and favors, finally achieving a status that allowed her to stand on her own two feet.

It was only when she found herself alive after an unfortunate shooting accident, that she'd realized stealing information wasn't her only asset. The knowledge of her immortality brought the first of her father's visits. His unexpected addition to her life a paradox she'd never quite grown comfortable with.

But all of that was a hell of a long time ago, and thinking about it now did nothing to help find the password. She blew out a breath, clearing her mind, reaching out for the information she needed.

Slowly the password appeared. *REV1318.*

Certainly apropos.

She opened her eyes and typed the password, the computer obediently presenting her with the inner workings of Max Braun's computer system. It took only a few minutes to find the guest list for the club and add their names. And only another two or three to figure out the appropriate designation to allow them access to the VIP floor.

The security system information presented a bit more of an obstacle. Two additional passwords were required and even then she was only able to identify the system and verify the location of the vault. She still needed a schematic. But to do that, she'd need direct access to the computer.

Even magic it seemed had its limitations.

With a few keystrokes, she instructed the computer to print the information she had managed to obtain, and then quickly made her way out the back door she'd opened in cyberspace. With any luck, they'd never even know she'd been there.

The door to her bedroom swung open as David strode through it. "I thought I might find you here."

Jessie frowned and reached for the papers coming off the printer. "Haven't you heard of knocking?" It wasn't as if there was anything she was trying to hide; it was just that she was unsettled enough around him without his just appearing out of nowhere without any kind of warning.

"I did. You just didn't hear me." He was standing in front of her now, glaring down at her. "I've just had an interesting talk with Faust."

"Knowing Faust, that could mean almost anything," she said, forcing a smile she didn't feel. "Want to be more specific?"

"All right. How about the notion that the Protector kills the people who come in contact with it."

"That's only a legend, David. There's no empirical proof that it's true."

"But there's also nothing to say that it's not true," he said, still frowning. "And I don't like the idea of your taking that kind of a risk just so that you can score one for a client."

Sometimes being an immortal was a pain in the ass. "Look, just take my word for it when I say that I have every reason to believe that the box won't pose that kind of threat. At least not to me."

"Care to say why?"

"Well, principally because if there is a danger, it only involves trying to open the box. And I have absolutely no interest in doing that."

"What about Faust?"

"He's a man who keeps his own counsel, but since his main purpose for being here is to help me, I feel fairly confident that he's not interested in opening it either."

"Well, that's another thing that bugs me. Why the hell would Faust want in on this, anyway? I mean, there's no payoff. He said himself that he and your brother like to think of themselves as pirates. So why would a pirate agree to take the kind of risk involved with stealing the Protector without some kind of cash cow at the end of the road?"

"Maybe for the fun of it. I realize that's a concept beyond your understanding. But sometimes people do things just for the rush."

"I don't buy it."

"You're just angry because he backed you into a corner."

"No one backs me into anything, Jessie. I just figured it was better for everyone if I laid out the truth."

"The truth as you see it."

His laugh was harsh. "Maybe that's all that matters."

"You didn't kill your brother, David."

"We were talking about Faust," he said, obviously trying to change the subject.

"Fine," she said, walking over to the window. "It's none of my business anyway."

The lake was calm, the moonlight weaving silver beams into the water, the tiny crests glistening like scattered sequins.

"It's beautiful," he said, coming to stand behind her, his breath stirring the hair at the nape of her neck.

"That's one of the reasons I chose this place," she said, nodding at the velvety blue of the mountains towering above the far shore. "I love the solitude. It's the only place I've truly felt peaceful."

"You mentioned that before. It's funny, I don't think of you that way."

"Nor do I, but that doesn't stop me from wishing for it."

"I've never understood the need for stillness. Give me life at full throttle and I'm good to go."

They were inches apart, and yet Jessie still felt alone. "There's nothing quite like an adrenaline rush. But I think maybe it's possible to have too much of a good thing." Five fucking centuries of it. "Maybe I'm just looking for a counterbalance."

She tightened her hands on the windowsill, thinking of all the times she'd imagined him being right here in this room. Somehow the dream wasn't the same as the reality. But then maybe that's why dreams were dreams—and suddenly she'd become a sentimental sap.

"So have you had any luck with the security system?" He moved away, and while she missed the contact, she was relieved that he'd brought the topic back to safer ground.

"I've gotten us on the guest list and I've nailed the make and type for the security system."

"Sounds like you've made significant progress."

"I have. But we'll still need a recon mission. I can't get the actual schematics without tapping directly into Braun's computers and to do that I've got to get inside."

"And I assume you're counting on me to get you in?"

"It did seem the logical choice."

"Are you're certain you want to do this? I mean, is your client really that important?"

She blew out a breath and attempted a smile, feeling for the first time that maybe they really were in this together. "More than you'll ever know."

"Right, then, I guess it's up to me to get your back. After all, I do have a vested interest in your success."

"Vengeance." And with one word, any sense of camaraderie was gone.

"You know where I stand, Jessie."

"And you know what I think." She turned back to the window, staring out at the lake. "There's no way that Jason would want you to throw away your life because of him."

"Maybe he wouldn't. But then he wouldn't have wanted to die either."

"Believe me, living isn't all it's cracked up to be."

"What in hell do you mean by that?" His voice was sharp, colored with his confusion, but there was really no way to explain.

"Nothing. Just the cynic talking." She felt him move to stand beside her. "I just meant that we all cling so desperately to life, and maybe it isn't really worth all the fuss."

The silence was broken by the song of a cricket somewhere out on the lawn. Jessie sighed. "Sorry," she said, shaking her head, "didn't mean to get maudlin. It's just that with everything going on I'm suddenly second-guessing myself. I thought I knew what it was I wanted. Or at least what would be for the best. But now I . . . well, I just don't know. I don't suppose that makes any sense at all, does it?"

"Yeah, I guess in a sort of fucked-up way it does. I think a person can spend too much time trying to figure out the right path. Sometimes it's better just to play the game and see where the pieces land." He reached out to catch a strand of her hair and tucked it gently behind her ear.

"David, I . . ." Her hand came up to cover his, her heart beating a staccato rhythm.

"I've missed you, Jessie." The words seemed to come out of their own accord, surprising them both.

She opened her mouth to respond, but he didn't give her the chance, instead, pulling her close, his lips finding hers, the touch sending sparks of fire racing through her.

She traced the line of his shoulders, reveling in the feel of his muscles beneath her fingers. His hand found her breast beneath the soft cotton of her shirt and with a tiny moan she pressed against him, all rational thought fading away against the power of his touch.

His thumb rasped against her nipple, sending shards of pleasure dancing through her, and she deepened their kiss, breathing in his essence, holding it deep inside her. His hand moved lower, caressing the skin of her abdomen, soothing and exciting her with one touch.

His lips moved, too, following the hollow of her cheek until he reached her ear, his tongue sending more fire rippling through her as he traced the curve of its shell, his teeth toying with her earlobe, moist and hot against her skin.

His head dropped lower, his mouth trailing along the line of her shoulder, his kisses teasing in their simplicity, his hand continuing to move across her skin. His mouth found the crest of her breast, the hot, sweet suction tantalizing with its promise of things to come.

Urgency built within her. The need for something more. For connection, belonging. The part of her she kept locked away, clamoring for release. She'd promised herself she'd not allow this. Not give in to the sensual need he evoked in her. But the physical pull was so strong now. So essential. Like breathing.

With desire shimmering between them, she pushed closer, grinding her hips against his. Her hands slid to his waist, undoing the buttons on his jeans, her fingers brushing the velvety tip of his penis. With a groan, he pulled off her shirt, at the same time pushing her backward until she felt the cool plaster of the wall against her skin.

His gaze raked across her, sending shivers dancing along her oversensitized nerves. "I want you, Jessie. Right here. Right now. So now is the time to tell me if you're having second thoughts."

She opened her mouth, but she couldn't form the words, instead shaking her head, her heart pounding a rhythm in her head. With a swiftness that threatened to rob her of breath, he removed her pants and panties, following suit with his jeans, and finally they came together, the contact of her breasts against his chest beyond exquisite.

She closed her eyes and opened her mouth to his kiss, drinking him in, wanting nothing more than this moment, this man. Their fervor increased, each touch, each movement raising the stakes, heightening the pleasure.

He pulled her tighter against him, sandwiching her between his body and the wall, his sinewy strength the perfect foil for her soft curves. This was what she remembered. The smell of his body, the heat radiating through her setting flash fires in places she'd forgotten existed.

And for a moment she simply reveled in the contact.

Then her need took over. With a passion she'd almost forgotten, she began to taste him. All of him. The salty skin at the corners of his eyes. His beard-stubbled chin. The softer skin of his neck, and the silky strength of his chest.

She took his nipples into her mouth, caressing first one then the other with her tongue. Delighted when they responded to her touch. Moving lower, she sampled the skin of his work-hardened belly, tracing the line of it with her tongue.

And finally, finally, her lips found the velvety heat of his manhood. She ran her tongue along its length, pleased to feel him tense in pleasure, his hand stroking her hair, urging her onward. With a smile, she took him into her mouth, feeling him grow harder, even as her own desire burgeoned.

And then he was urging her upward again, his hands settling beneath her hips, lifting her until her legs circled him, their gazes locked. There would be no turning back. She was cognizant enough to know that. This wasn't a casual dalliance. And a part of her, the rational, sane side, was screaming a warning, but the rest of her cherished the moment. And the man.

He moved back slightly, still holding her in place, and with one long thrust was inside her, the pure pleasure of the movement threatening to shatter her into pieces. And together, they began to dance. In and out, in and out. Each stroke taking them higher, until she could no longer tell where he ended and she began.

She closed her eyes, letting sensation carry her away. Aware of only the feel of him inside her, filling her, holding her, binding them together with every stroke. And just for the moment, she forgot about her immortality. About the fact that the two of them could never be more than casual lovers.

For just one moment, she allowed herself to pretend that together they could somehow manage to transcend forever.

David lay in the bed and watched the moonlight as it danced across the room, bits of dust glimmering in the reflected silver. Jessie slept with one leg slung over his thigh, possessive in her sleep in a way she would never allow when awake.

Their coming together had been predictably combustible, but

there'd also been an undercurrent he hadn't expected. A connection that somehow had made him feel complete. He'd felt it before when they had been lovers, but it was even stronger now, surprising him with its intensity.

He'd never really been attached to anyone. Not even Jason. Maybe that's why he felt so damn guilty about it all. If only he'd taken his brother more seriously, then maybe Jason would be alive. The thought brought cold comfort.

Hell, he didn't deserve connections with anyone.

But then maybe it wasn't about deserving.

The thought was oddly consoling, as if there might be some higher force out there pulling the strings. Someone or something that could see the chessboard from a bird's-eye view—who knew how each move affected all the other players.

God, he was losing it in a big way. It had just been about sex. Mind-blowing, fucking amazing sex. But still, at the end of the day, it was only physical pleasure. Anything more was just his imagination working overtime.

Jessie moaned in her sleep, then snuggled closer against him. She looked almost innocent in moonlight. And he was surprised by the strength of his need to protect her, but that too was just an illusion.

Jessie was more than capable of taking care of herself. And not even the heat of their coming together was going to change that. She didn't need him, any more than he needed her.

It should have been a comforting thought.

But it wasn't.

Chapter Six

"All right. Let's go over it one more time." Jessie adjusted her earphone so that it was hidden by her hair. "We're all going in. I'll head for the ladies' room, and then Faust is going to cause a distraction. When the security man leaves his office, I'll head for the computer."

"And I'll make sure no one interrupts you," David said. There'd been an undercurrent running between them all day. Morning had brought another round of passion, but no discussion. Neither of them had been ready for that.

Besides, she wasn't sure what she wanted to say. Which was a new development. She'd never been the kind to find herself at a loss for words, but David brought out emotions she hadn't even known she possessed. Made her long for things she hadn't even known she wanted.

All of which was too confusing to try to deal with right now. Better to focus on the task at hand. "Right." She nodded, not allowing herself to look at him. "You'll have my back while I log on to the computer for the schematics." She raised a handheld hard drive. "I'll copy it here, and then once I'm done, we'll duck out, hopefully with no one the wiser."

"Should go like clockwork," Faust said, adjusting the gold chain at his neck. He was decked out in a silk jacket with black linen pants, a jaunty red kerchief peeking out of his breast pocket, the total look falling somewhere between trendy and laughable. But compared to the other people Jessie had seen trying to get into the club, Faust would fit right in.

"All right then, Faust, you're up first." David's scowl fit right in with his black jeans and T-shirt, the etched tail of a dragon peeking out from beneath one muscle-bound sleeve. Whatever he wore, he was still one hundred percent male.

Faust nodded and slid open the van door. "Can you hear me?" he asked, his electronic voice carrying over the widening distance as he headed for the front of the club.

"Roger that," David replied, checking his watch. "Two minutes and I'm following. Assuming we're both in place, Jessie, you'll follow. Then wait for Faust's go."

"Good luck," Jessie said, giving him a thumbs-up, then turned back to the computer console in the van, running a last-minute diagnostic on the portable hard drive. She'd already checked it several times, but she didn't believe in taking chances.

"Jessie," Faust said, his voice seeming overly loud in her ear, "I'm in place and Bishop is just clearing the guy at the door."

"Good. I'm on my way. "

The mike went dead, and Jessie gathered her purse and donned a pair of Manolos. Combined with her minuscule red leather skirt and sparkling halter top, she had no doubt that she would pass for a member of the international jet set. And if there was any doubt, the diamonds at her throat and ears would seal the deal. They'd been a last-minute addition, courtesy of Faust. Sometimes it took big bait to catch a big fish. Besides, she sincerely doubted he'd paid for the rocks.

She hitched the chain of her evening bag over her shoulder, the hard drive hidden inside, and made her way across the busy street. There was already a crowd outside the club, the neon signage casting everyone in garish light.

She pushed by the hangers-on, keeping her eye on the man at the door. "Sandra DeMarco," she announced as she came to a halt in front of the bouncer, careful to keep her Spanish lilt just this side of bored.

The beefy man checked a computer monitor, scrolling through the list, and then nodded toward the entrance, his grunt passing for affirmation. She waited for the doorman as he pulled open the door, and with her best vacuous smile she walked into the club.

After the neon outside, the ground floor seemed somewhat subdued, small groups of glitterati chatting and laughing as they waited for either a bathroom or the elevator. She stood close enough to one group to look a part of it, but removed enough that they couldn't overhear her conversation. "I'm in. Is everyone in place?"

"To your left," came David's reply. She shifted her gaze and saw him standing alone just beyond the reception desk. The lit cigarette in one hand was a useful prop, the exhaled smoke preventing a clear view of him, while at the same time giving him a reason for his isolation. Even in Europe, secondary smoke was becoming an issue.

Jessie lifted her chin in acknowledgment, then headed toward the bathrooms. "Faust?"

"Everything is ready. Detonation should be in forty-five seconds," he answered. "I'm heading back down now."

The device David had rigged for the explosion on the first floor of the club was designed to deliver maximum smoke with minimum damage, but the panic and confusion that followed would hopefully clear the security personnel from their computer long enough for her to get the information they needed.

Keeping her pace leisurely, she stopped just outside the bathroom door, rooting around in her purse as if she needed a lipstick or perfume or something. Silently, she counted down the seconds and was rewarded with the flash of a red warning light on the wall outside security.

The officer on duty emerged from the little office, barking orders into a two-way, moving quickly toward the main elevators. The man at reception had his hands full trying to prevent anyone else from entering the club, the milling crowds suddenly reacting with a mixture of curiosity and concern.

Moving quickly now, she slid through the open door, quietly closing it behind her. A bank of monitors ran along the wall, each of them with a separate view of the club and the offices above it. Taking a few precious seconds to check them out, she was relieved to note that there seemed to be no camera on the cellar.

Most likely Braun didn't want the hired help to know what he had hidden in the basement of the building. At least not the flunkies who worked general security. She turned her back on the monitors, careful to stay out of view of the lobby, and settled in behind a desk with a PC and large monitor.

She quickly entered the series of passwords she'd been able to locate last night, the computer whirring with activity. However, finding the directory she was looking for took longer than she would have liked, and she'd only just found it when her earphone buzzed with David's voice.

"You've got incoming."

"Well, try to do something to stop them. I need more time." She didn't wait for David's reassurance. She knew he'd handle it.

Still, time was of the essence. She closed her eyes, reaching out for the final password, willing it to form in her mind. At first there was nothing, but then slowly a word began to form. *Rapture.* Braun certainly had a preoccupation with the End Days.

Suppressing a smile, she typed the password into the machine.

"Everything okay?" Faust asked.

"I'm in," she responded. "But I still need a little more time. David?"

There was a beat of silence and then his voice there, soothing even in its disembodied form. "We're good. I managed to convince a redhead her only chance to escape the melee was to stick with security. The guy's not going anywhere."

Jessie suppressed a smile, and concentrated on the files listed on the machine. She had to wade through three dummies before she finally found the right one, but everything she needed was there, including access codes and schematics.

She plugged the portable hard drive into the USB port on the back of the computer, holding her breath as the critical files started to download. The device had been modified to cloak her activity, so at least for the moment she was safe from prying electronic eyes, but that didn't mean there wouldn't be intruders.

David's redhead couldn't possibly distract the guard forever.

She glanced around the control room again, using the time to ascertain that there was nothing else they needed to know. The security cameras were recording, but it looked as if they were on a repeating loop, which meant that they were erased unless the computer triggered the mechanism to stop.

She scanned the list of files again and found the software that controlled the cameras, clicking to download it as well. Might come in handy if they wanted to escape the watchful eye of the security team.

"Damn it, Jessie," David barked in her ear. "Get out of there now. There's a second guard coming off the elevator."

She stared at the computer screen, willing it to hurry, feeling the seconds tick by.

"Jessie."

"I'm coming. Just keep him out for another minute."

"Got him," Faust said, the sound of his voice slurring as he tripped over something and began mumbling apologies.

"It's all clear, Jessie," David said. "But get out of there. I don't care if you've got it or not."

She didn't bother to answer. No sense in wasting time on arguments. Two more seconds passed, and the bar marking progress turned green. "Mission accomplished," she said in a whisper as she pulled the hard drive from the computer and dropped it back into her purse.

She crossed to the door, checking the window for clearance. David had positioned himself just opposite, catty-cornered to the door. "You're good to go." He nodded, his dark gaze connecting with hers across the distance.

She shivered, but pushed her thoughts away. There was nothing more dangerous than letting emotions hold sway during an operation. She cracked the door and slid through the narrow opening, making a play of applying lip gloss as she walked toward the entrance.

Less than half an hour later, they were all safely ensconced in the comfortable villa Faust had managed to secure for them—the property of a friend of a friend of a friend.

"So did you get what you needed?" David asked, stopping his pacing long enough to peer at the monitor over her shoulder.

"I haven't had time to open all the files yet. Why don't you sit down and give me a chance to work?" She shot him an irritated look, partly because of his impatience, but mostly because it was hard to concentrate when he was standing so close.

Faust was seated on an elegantly carved slipper chair, sipping a superior Chianti Ruffino from the excellent cellar that presumably belonged to their host. "Come have some wine. It'll help to clear your head," Faust said.

"My head is fine, thank you," David grumbled, accepting the glass the older man offered anyway.

"Jessie?"

"In a minute." She waved a hand in Faust's direction. "I want a look at this first." She hadn't even bothered to change clothes, although she'd abandoned the stilettos. The files were encoded, but it was easy enough to figure them out. The ones she didn't just "know" she managed to work out on her own anyway.

The security system was sophisticated but still fairly simple in its own right. Just as she'd suspected, the security cameras were limited to the lower floors. Access to the third-floor offices required using a keypad. All those authorized for admittance were issued individual passwords. But there was a fail-safe provided by the security company and from what Jessie could see it had never been deactivated.

It was the kind of mistake she'd have expected even from someone like Braun.

From there, access to the elevator leading to the vault was controlled by fingerprint recognition. A bit trickier to handle, but not an insurmountable problem. She could manage to alter her own fingerprint long enough to fool the machine, but she'd need to see a print that actually worked. And the best bet was Max Braun's.

Question was whether he'd be in the system somewhere. She typed in a series of commands and then a couple of passwords, slipping through a back door into Interpol's database. Braun was a slick character, but if she was lucky he'd have been collared once or twice along the way.

Three files later and she hit pay dirt. A charge of counterfeiting from almost twenty years ago. But fingerprints never changed. With a smile, she enlarged the scanned image of his right index finger and printed it. She'd study it later, although she was already fairly certain she'd committed the curves and ridges to memory.

Of course in order to conceal her ability from David, she'd have to make a latex dummy. The technology was available, and David had no idea what resources she had access to. Besides, if she didn't make a big deal about it, there wouldn't be time for skepticism.

"So how's it coming?" Faust asked, his impatience more contained than David's but apparent nevertheless.

"I can get us around the first two security barriers, provided we keep the watchdogs occupied."

"That's not a problem," Faust said. "I've called in a favor and engaged a couple of Milanese women to run interference. They have no idea what's going on. It's just another lark. So you'll have your distraction, Jessie."

"Okay, so we've made the elevator to the cellar. What then?" David asked.

"Well, that's where it gets a bit more tricky. There's an infrared system as well as security cameras protecting the vault. But I think I can disable the former if I have enough time with their computers. If not, we'll have to try to subvert it another way."

"We could try reflection. I'll make the preparations, just in case," David said. "So what about the cameras?"

"That one's a lot easier." She smiled. "I've got access to the system and a copy of the software they use. I should be able to piece together an endless loop of empty hallway. Then all we have to do is insert it into the feed and they'll never know we're there."

"So what did you find out about the vault?" Faust asked, turning to David.

"It's a Burg Wachter," he said, setting his glass down on the table. "Composite construction with a seven-inch door, two-inch chrome locking bolts, and dual relocks. It's also got a drill-resistant hard plate layered on top of an additional steel plate three inches thick."

"Combination or keyed?" Faust asked.

"Combination," David said, checking his notes. "But there's a tempered glass relocker."

"What's a relocker?" Jessie asked with a frown. Locks and vaults weren't her forte—she preferred breaking into things more cerebral.

"It means that if I did manage to drill through all that steel, there's still a chance I could break a glass plate that would automatically trigger a permanent relock. I'll have to do it by touch."

"Sounds to me like you've had a bit of experience," Faust said, looking impressed despite himself.

"Let's just say I've had the need to liberate a few things from time to time. Anyway, with the equipment you rounded up, I should be good to go."

"So that leaves us with the steel panel blocking the exit," Faust said. "I tried to get a portable oxy-fuel gas axe or some other high-powered kind of blowtorch but unfortunately my contacts couldn't come up with anything like that within our time frame."

"That's okay, it'd take too much time anyway," David said. "Not to mention the trick of getting it into the club. I think we're better off using explosives."

"Are you kidding?" Jessie asked. "According to the schematics the panel is five inches thick and secured into the surrounding bedrock. No lock. It's meant to be permanent. That's going to take some serious TNT. We might as well just send out engraved invitations."

"No, I can rig it so that it won't be noticeable at all. Faust, can you get your hands on some plastique and a drill that'll support a tungsten bit?"

"It's within the realm of possibility," Faust acknowledged. "What are you thinking? A controlled explosion?"

"Yeah. I'll drill a couple of strategic holes, fill them with plastique—and instant doorway."

"It just might work," Faust said, his tone admiring.

"Oh, it'll work," David said, "but I'll also need fuse wire and a detonator. And some sort of casing to transport the lot through the club without drawing undo attention."

"Shouldn't be a problem," Faust said. "Anything else?"

"Some industrial-grade latex would be nice," Jessie said, her gaze meeting Faust's. "I need to make a prosthetic finger."

David raised his eyebrows in question.

"Fingerprint recognition," Jessie said. "I need to reproduce Braun's print to get us onto the elevator that goes to the cellar."

"I'm impressed."

"Well, maybe you should hold the accolades until we see if it works."

"It'll work," Faust said, "but not if I don't come up with the goods. So, if you'll excuse me." He flipped open his cell phone, already dialing as he walked from the room.

"I guess maybe we should call it a night?" There was an implied question in David's voice. One Jessie wasn't sure she wanted to answer, but it didn't matter because there was something more important to discuss.

"I found something else in Braun's files. Something I think you need to know." She'd debated about waiting to tell him until after the heist, but she knew she owed him more than that. "There are records here that identify Braun as the force behind Jason's expedition." She pulled a DVD from the machine. "I copied them onto disc for you."

"Is there anything about my brother?" He fisted both hands, clearly fighting to contain emotion.

She blew out a long breath and nodded, wishing there were some way to ease the blow. "There's a whole dossier. It was buried deep within the directories, but it was there. I put it on the disc as well. It doesn't definitively prove that he killed your brother, but I think you can probably assume he was pulling the strings. The whole thing appears to have been a setup from the get-go."

David stared down at the disc in her hand, a muscle working in his jaw. Then slowly he reached out to take it from her.

"I'll understand if you want to pull out now. You have the answer you've been looking for." She waited for a moment, but he didn't say anything. "For all we know Braun isn't even in Milan."

"Jessie, I . . ." He looked up, meeting her gaze, and she saw the answer in his eyes. Avenging Jason was his first priority. And next to that nothing else mattered at all.

"Right," she said, not allowing him to finish. Better to get out of the room before she let him see how much the decision hurt.

Chapter Seven

David stood in the middle of the room, staring at the empty doorway. He should have stopped her. Should have told her he'd stay. But when she'd told him about Braun, given him the disc, his only thought had been to find the bastard and make him pay. The sooner the better. It had been his overriding goal for so goddamn long.

And she'd known that. Which was why, despite the chance that he'd leave her high and dry *again*, she'd told him. It was a gift, and he'd taken it without any thought to the ramifications.

"You look like you lost your best friend," Faust said, appearing in the doorway. The man was definitely quiet on his feet. "Or maybe you're just thinking of your brother." His gaze dropped to the disc David still held in his hand.

"Jessie told you what she found?"

"Just now. She also told me she'd released you from your promise to help her get the Protector." Maybe he was transferring his own guilt but it seemed that Faust's words held a note of censure.

"She did." He couldn't seem to come up with more than a few words at a time, his heart twisting as his mind replayed the look on her face as she'd walked out of the room. "I think I may have hurt her."

"She's pretty tough," Faust said, walking over to the decanter to pour himself a drink.

"On the outside maybe. But underneath . . ." He trailed off, not sure what else he could say.

"Underneath she's as vulnerable as the rest of us?" Faust finished for him. "Maybe more so, actually. Especially when she allows herself to care about someone. I've seen the way she looks at you, David. Whatever's going on between you, it's important to Jessie."

"I'm not exactly good at this kind of thing. I haven't had a lot of practice."

"Neither has Jessie. Sometimes the right people come together despite themselves." Faust's smile was almost gentle.

"Maybe. But even if what you're saying is true, I've still got a lot of baggage."

"Sometimes," Faust said with a sigh, "it's easier to hate than to love."

"You think I'm afraid?" David asked with a frown.

"I'd be surprised if you weren't. Love is the most complex of all human emotions. I don't pretend to understand it, but I do know that when it's real, you can't just throw it way. It's more tenacious than that."

"I don't know if it's love. Truth is, I don't know what the hell I feel. I only know that I don't want to hurt her."

"Which is why you ran away the first time."

"I was trying to find Jason's killer."

"Well, now you've found him. Or more to the point, Jessie

found him for you. And told you about it even though she believed
it meant you'd leave. That's love, David. It doesn't matter if she
recognizes it or not. The emotion is still the same."

"So what am I going to do?"

"I'm afraid I can't answer that one, but if it were me, I'd go upstairs and find her."

It shouldn't matter that he hadn't answered. That he hadn't even
tried to stop her when she'd left. At least this time she'd been the
one to walk away. After all, she'd come into it with her eyes open.
It was too late to change the game now.

Besides, he'd probably already gone. Which was a good thing.
She didn't want a relationship anyway. This whole thing was a
huge mistake. Except that she needed him. There was no way she
could break into that vault on her own. Not even with Faust helping. She might be able to shift a fingerprint or visualize an access
code, but there was no way she could drill a vault.

So she'd just have to find someone else. Faust was bound to
have contacts. It was worth the effort. She needed to fulfill her father's quest now more than ever. Because as soon as she handed
him the Protector, he'd free her from the hell she was living in. Her
father was offering the opportunity to live the rest of her life in a
world where her immortality was an accepted part of existence.
She'd never want for anything.

And she wouldn't have to watch David grow old and die.

She wrapped her arms around herself, trying to contain a shiver,
and walked to the window, looking out at the graveled driveway
that led to the main road. Faust's ancient Mini was parked out
front.

David's car had been parked around back. So there was no way to know for certain if he'd left, but he'd been pretty damn clear about his priorities. As if taunting her, two yellow lights cut through the darkness—the car moving down the road, past the driveway, heading north.

She sighed, leaning against the windowsill, letting the smell of gardenias and jasmine surround her, the soft cry of a dove mixing with the plaintive wail of the wind as it blew through the eaves above her. Sometimes she just felt so damn alone.

"Jessie?" His voice was tentative, as if he were afraid to interrupt her thoughts.

She spun around, her heart caught in her throat. "You're still here. I thought . . . I thought you'd gone. I saw a car and lights, and . . ."

"I don't know what you saw, but it obviously wasn't me." His smile was crooked and her heart gave another lurch. "I owe you an apology."

"No, I shouldn't have—"

With one stride he closed the distance between them, his finger covering her lips. "Just this once, why don't you let me do the talking."

She nodded and moved back, needing a little distance.

His eyes narrowed, but he held his ground, his gaze still locked on hers. "When we were downstairs—before—you gave me a gift. And I should have acknowledged it. Hell, I should have done a lot more than that."

"I told you about your brother because you had every right to know. It wasn't a gift."

"No. But trusting that I could handle the news. Allowing me to make my own choices about what I did with the knowledge—that was a gift. And had I been a better man, I wouldn't have let you walk away without acknowledging it. And I also shouldn't have let you believe even for a minute that I'd leave you on your own to steal the Protector. I made you a promise, and I intend to honor it."

"I don't want you to stay because you have to, David. Because you made a promise. I want you to stay because it's what you choose to do. "

"I'm here because I want to be here."

"Even if it's only for tonight?" She wasn't sure what she wanted from him. And she definitely couldn't even begin to consider the future, but she damn well didn't want him to walk out the door either.

His smile was slow and a little bittersweet. "I'm here for as long as you want me, Jessie."

They stood for a minute, the distance between them seemingly unbreachable, and then with a sigh, she launched herself into his arms, ashamed for yielding to her weakness, but unable to stop the driving need to feel the rhythm of his breathing as he held her close to his heart.

They stood for a moment locked in embrace and then his mouth found hers, his kiss passionate—possessive. The feel of his skin moving against hers was intoxicating—sensual beyond belief. Heat seared through her as they moved together, his tongue thrusting deep into her mouth, the sensation sending tremors of need racking through her.

He stroked the curve of her breast, her flesh responding beneath the shimmering gauze of her shirt. His thumb circled one nipple, his other hand stroking the exposed skin on her back. The rhythm hypnotic—carnal.

She pushed against him, desire spiraling out of control, and his mouth left hers to trail kisses along the line of her jaw, the shell of her ear, his tongue whipping her passion to a fever pitch. They moved, locked together, their steps choreographed by a connection both physical and spiritual. Each movement bringing them closer. Hearts beating together, clothing becoming an unwelcome barrier.

They moved backward, until she could feel the edge of the bed at the back of her legs, but before she could pull him down, he stopped, naked desire etched on his face. "You're sure this is what you want?" he asked, the vulnerability in his eyes making her heart skip a beat.

"I want you, David. Only you." It was a promise. Perhaps one destined to be broken. But for now, in this moment, he was all that she wanted—repercussions be damned. She reached up to untie her halter top, the gossamer fabric floating down to the floor.

With a crooked smile, she released the zipper on her skirt, letting it slide slowly down her legs, and then, with a boldness she hadn't realized she possessed, she pulled off her panties, standing before him naked—ready.

The cold air surrounded her and for one moment she felt doubt, but then he was there, his heat consuming her, his mouth and hands worshipping. His lips closed on hers, his hands cupping both breasts, massaging, stroking, fanning the flames inside her.

Fumbling with buttons and zippers, she worked to free him from his clothes, desire exploding with a power she'd never experienced before. It was as if she stood on a precipice, some intrinsic force urging her onward with the promise that she could fly.

Somewhere in the rational part of her mind, she knew that this couldn't possibly last, that if nothing else the secrets she kept would destroy it, but she didn't care. Maybe tomorrow, but not tonight— not now. Finally, skin to skin, they lay down on the bed, the cool cotton of the sheets a sensual backdrop for all that was to come. He ran his hands down the length of her body, caressing her, learning her. She closed her eyes and let sensation carry her away.

His mouth was warm, and his touch delicious. He started with her shoulders and worked his way slowly down the length of her arms, stopping to kiss the tender skin on the inside of her elbows. From there he moved to her neck, his mouth tracing along the valley between her breasts, his tongue circling each nipple, the action sending her writhing against the sheets. Then he pulled one into his mouth, sucking deeply, the resulting sensation cresting deep between her legs.

Then his head moved lower. The soft silk of his hair teasing her breasts as he slowly licked and kissed the tender skin of her belly. Anticipation built inch by inch, until she wanted to cry out. But she stayed silent, forcing herself to wait, knowing that it would be worth it.

Finally, finally, his hands moved between her legs, his mouth following the curve of her inner thigh, his hot breath teasing her with its nearness. She arched her back, wanting more, and just when she thought she couldn't stand it, his tongue found her.

She cried out, the pleasure almost more than she could bear. Clasping the headboard behind her, she arched her back, urged him on, her need building with each stroke of his tongue, the fire inside her building higher and higher, until finally she reached for his hands, screaming his name, the world splintering into glittering shards of light.

David felt her body shudder and knew she had found release. Sliding up beside her, he pulled her close, cradling her body against him, He'd meant to give her pleasure. To atone somehow for wounding her with his doubt. But he was surprised at the contentment that rocked through him. It was as if he'd come home, found a place of safety he hadn't even known he'd been seeking.

His body ached for her, but still he held her. Wanting to prolong the bliss, the peace. He couldn't remember the last time he'd felt this way, and he knew it was a moment to be savored.

Her breathing was still erratic, her heart pounding against his, but she moved, pushing the hair back from her face, her gaze meeting his, eyes full of lust, the desire there making it impossible to ignore his throbbing penis.

With a groan, he pulled her into his arms, his kiss demanding, absorbing her with each taste, each touch. She met him halfway, her tongue dueling with his, taking as much as she gave. He shivered as her fingers caressed the hard planes of his chest, whispering butterflylike across his skin, tracing circles of fire.

She tasted his neck, then slid down to take a nipple into her mouth. Sucking and nipping, she savored him, the warmth connecting directly to his groin, tightening almost to the level of pain. If it was possible, it seemed his penis grew even harder, impatiently pressing against the soft skin of her thigh.

"I need you." The words came from someplace deep inside him and were almost guttural in pitch and fervor. He'd never felt like this. As if possessing her were the only way he could possibly feel whole.

She smiled up at him and slid farther down, taking him into her mouth, the moist suction almost his undoing. Circling him with her tongue, she moved her hand as well, the rhythms combining to create pleasure so intense he thought he might explode on the spot.

Up and down, squeezing, stroking, he fought his body for control. When he came, he wanted to be buried deep inside her.

Connected.

Fighting for breath, he moved slightly, the shift enough to separate them. Then, still fighting to hang on to his control, he flipped them over, the friction of their bodies sliding into position almost sending him over the edge. Unable to wait any longer, he braced himself above her, and then with a single thrust, slid home, her wet heat embracing him.

They stayed that way for a moment, eye to eye, linked together as man and woman, the age-old dance suddenly taking on new meaning because it was Jessie.

Then she pushed against him, driving him deeper, her hands pulling him closer, urging him onward. Together they began to move, finding their own private rhythm—until there was nothing but the two of them, and the incredible sensation of the dance.

Their bodies locked together, moving faster and faster, until the pleasure exploded into an inferno of heat and light, David's body and mind oblivious of everything except the power of his orgasm and the feel of her breath against his skin.

The first rays of sunshine slipped through the open window and danced across the tangled sheets on the bed. Jessie lay propped on one elbow, watching David sleep. He seemed more innocent somehow. The harsh realities of his life temporarily subdued. She wished there were some way to preserve the magic of the night. But she knew from experience that it was a hopeless endeavor.

She'd been selfish last night. Taken what she'd wanted without thought to the repercussions. And now it was time to pay the cost.

After the heist, she'd do the one thing she'd promised herself she'd never do. Lie to him. Tell him that there was no future. That what they'd shared was only sex—amazingly toe-curling sex—but nothing more.

The alternative was unthinkable. Explaining that while he was going to age and eventually die, she was never going to change. *Ever.* Ironic that most humans would kill for the chance at immortality and here she was wishing it away, simply so that she could spend what would then be left of her life with David.

Almost as if he'd read her thoughts, he reached for her, pulling her close against him even as he slept. She burrowed into his warmth, memorizing the feel of his skin. If everything went as planned, it would all be over tonight.

The Protector would be safely in her father's hands. David would be free to pursue Braun and exact vengeance for Jason. Faust could go back to Marcus and their escapades in the name of beauty. And she'd be free from this world—and the memories it held.

If she was lucky, maybe she would be able to forget him. To erase the memory. But even as she had the thought, she knew it was impossible. Nothing, not even her father's magic, could make her forget. She had, after all, made a fatal mistake—she'd fallen in love with David Bishop.

And now, quite literally, there would be hell to pay.

Chapter Eight

The music in the VIP lounge at Azure swelled, combining with a cacophony of voices to form a deafening roar. And when one added in the olfactory onslaught of overly perfumed, badly bathed bodies it was almost impossible to tolerate. Usually immune to that sort of thing, David felt as if all of his synapses were firing at once. And he was more than aware of the reason.

Jessie.

Last night had been beyond anything he'd ever thought possible. A connection so intense that it scared him. But he was also wise enough to know that what they'd shared last night was something rare and precious. Only he hadn't been able to convince Jessie of the fact.

Actually, he hadn't had the opportunity to tell her much of anything. He'd woken alone in her bed. And when he'd made his way downstairs it was only to find her with Faust, immersed in the details of the heist.

He'd tried to show her at least how much their lovemaking had meant to him, but she'd rebuffed even the simplest of contact, passing it off as a need to concentrate on the task at hand. He'd have been questioning his memory of the night if it hadn't been for the look in her eyes—a flicker of desire tamped down with a sadness that threatened to take his breath away. It was as if there were something tangible standing between them. Something he couldn't see, let alone understand.

Finally, unwillingly, he'd accepted her moratorium on emotion and settled in to prepare for the caper. Faust had amazingly managed to get everything David had requested, and it had taken most of the afternoon to put together their final plans.

And now he was here, in the club, waiting for confirmation that everyone was in place. "I'm in, and on my way up," Faust said, his voice barely discernible over the frenetic discord of the club.

"Jessie, you there?" David prompted—holding his breath as he waited.

"Yes. I'm in position." Just the sound of her voice made his heart rate slow considerably. "To the left of the elevator."

He shifted his gaze to run the length of the dance floor, settling at last on Jessie standing in the shadows. She held a drink in one hand, and she was smiling at a man with a green blazer and equally garish tie. Jealousy reared its ugly head for a moment, and then David quashed the emotion. Jessie was working and if he didn't do the same, it would all be for nothing.

The far elevator doors opened and Faust emerged with a crowd of laughing women, two of them, seeming to hang on his every word. They stood talking for a moment and then separated. The girls heading for the bar, Faust passing Jessie to station himself just to the left of the passageway leading to the private elevator to the third floor.

There'd been no movement at all toward the elevator. No one coming or going. Only a single stationary guard blocking the entrance. Hopefully, if Faust's beauties did their magic, that obstacle would soon be removed. "Guard's in place. He hasn't moved since I got here," David whispered into the microphone, nodding at a man who was pushing past him in search of the restrooms.

"Anita and Analise should be providing their little side show in the next few minutes, so everyone get ready to move. David, I'll give you the go."

"Right." He fingered the bag he carried over his shoulder. It was a sleek leather style favored by Italian men. Inside, in carefully padded compartments, were his drills and the components he needed to break into the vault as well as the explosives Faust had secured. Thank God the club hadn't employed the use of screening devices. Although at most it probably only would have meant separating the various components. "Jessie, you set?"

"I'm ready," Jessie answered, her voice holding a note of excitement. In that way they were two of a kind. The rush of adrenaline as addictive as the challenge. She'd moved closer to Faust, making a play of finishing her drink and handing the glass off to a passing waitress.

David pulled his attention away from her, turning back to the bar and the two women Faust had brought. They were laughing at something, one of them practically falling out of her dress. But then, that was the point. Distraction.

Suddenly the brunette pushed the blonde, as if urging her on to something. The blonde threw back her hair, and then before anyone had time to realize what she intended, she leaped up onto the bar and started to gyrate in time to the music.

Patrons turned, at first surprised and then egging her on as she started to move more sensually. Her friend, apparently not to be left out of the party, joined her barside in a similar undulation, both of them already beginning to shed their clothing.

Leave it to Faust to come up with a lascivious red herring.

The crowd surged forward, cheering and leering, everyone trying to get a view of the now topless women.

The security man responded to a command in his ear and began to push his way forward toward the bar, the two goons stationed at the other elevators also making their way toward the impromptu go-go dancers.

"He's on the move," David said, already slipping past the fracas into the hallway leading to the private elevator.

"I'm right behind you," Jessie said, appearing around the corner, followed by Faust. Faust stopped at the entrance, keeping an eye on the security guards. He'd stay there, playing the part of a drunk, and then once they made it safely to the cellar, he'd make his way to the rendezvous.

Jessie stopped just short of the elevator. "I'm afraid we've got a little problem. I prepared a video loop for the security cameras in the cellar, but nothing for this camera. It wasn't on the schematic." She turned to David, her bottom lip caught in her teeth.

"No problem," David said, shooting her a smile. "I've got it covered." He reached in his pocket for the retractable mirror he'd stashed there. The idea had been to use it if Jessie failed to disarm the infrared system. But it would work here as well.

"All I have to do is extend the mirror and then slip it into place.

Should be relatively easy." At least in theory. He pulled out the extension arm and then, waiting until the camera had panned away from the elevator, he lifted the mirror up and slid it into place just as the lens moved back, the reflection bouncing the eye of the camera into an empty corner.

It wouldn't work for long, but they only needed a few seconds. "You're on," he said, waving Jessie toward the door. "Go." The camera whirred as it started to pan away from the mirror.

"Got it," she whispered, the elevator doors sliding open on cue. Faust held to his post, gesturing for David to move quickly. He maneuvered past the camera and then disengaged the mirror, waiting for the machine to continue its pan before sprinting aboard.

The doors slid shut, and the two of them rode up in silence. Stage one was accomplished but they still had a hell of a long way to go. The ride was quick and fortunately not recorded. Apparently, Braun believed his elevator safe from infiltration. But then he hadn't counted on Jessie. The doors opened on an empty corridor, the door across the way closed, its window black.

"All right, we've only got a few minutes," David said. "Faust, is everything still clear?"

"So far so good," came the answer.

"All right, I'm off to the security station," David said, opening his case and quickly assembling the parts of his hidden gun. "You head for the computer."

"Already one step ahead of you." Jessie smiled, opening her purse to hand him the video loop.

He nodded and moved down the hall, his mind laying out the schematic he'd studied. The security room was open, the guards safely downstairs. It only took a minute to switch the tape. Out in the hall again, he worked his way back the way he had come, checking for unwanted visitors before stepping into the main office, looking for Jessie.

The room was empty, and his heart plummeted. "Damn it, Jessie, where are you?" he hissed into the microphone.

"Inner office," she said over the static. "Through the double doors."

"Right," he mumbled, more to himself than to her, "I'm on my way." He checked the hallway again, just to make certain everything was still a go, and then walked to the back of the room and pushed through the double doors.

Jessie, engrossed in the computer, did not even bother to look up as he stepped inside.

"You need to pay more attention. What if it hadn't been me?"

"But it was you," she said, with maddening simplicity.

He watched her work for a moment or two, then moved so that he could see into the outer office. "Faust, everything still okay?"

No response.

Jessie looked up with a frown, opening her mouth to speak. David shook his head. "Faust?" he whispered again.

"Sorry," came the reply. "I was too close to security to take the chance of talking. They're interviewing patrons now. Apparently someone's purse was stolen."

"Faust . . . ," Jessie scolded.

"We needed the further distraction. So I improvised."

"So we're still good."

"Yes, but I wouldn't dawdle."

David shot a look at Jessie, who nodded reassuringly. "Almost there. Just need to make sure I've got the command right." She sat back, closing her eyes, almost as if she were in a trance of some kind. David shivered. There was something otherworldly about her expression.

"Jess, are you all right?" He was across the room in an instant, his hands on her shoulders. Her eyes flickered open, at first confused and then hardening to something he couldn't quite define. Regret, anger . . . maybe both.

"I'm fine. Just making sure I got everything we needed." She pulled away, turning off the computer. "Let's get out of here." She brushed past him, and he followed her, his brain scrambling to understand what had just happened.

They stopped in the hallway, checking the main elevators for signs of life. Nothing moved. Jessie reached into her pocket, producing the latex digit she'd jerry-rigged with Braun's fingerprint. He wasn't convinced it would work, but she seemed certain that it would. So who was he to be a doubting Thomas?

"David, you there?" Faust's voice crackled over the wireless. "Afraid you've got hostiles on the way."

David pushed Jessie toward the cellar elevator, following behind, keeping his gun trained on the main elevator's doors. At first he thought maybe it was a false alarm, but then he heard the shoosh of the doors opening.

"Jessie, move," he whispered into the microphone. "We've got company."

Jessie disappeared around the corner, and he followed suit, holding his position as two of Braun's men emerged from the elevator, followed by the man himself.

David froze, a lash of anger whipping through him. His quarry was standing not fifteen feet away. In his mind's eye, he'd pictured the devil. But instead Braun had the anemic bearing of inbred aristocracy. David leveled the gun, narrowing his eyes to take the shot. All he needed was for Braun's goons to step out of the way.

One shot and . . .

"Not here, David," Jessie said, her hand on his arm.

"You need to get out of here," he hissed, still watching his quarry. They'd moved closer now, and he could see that at least three of the entourage held guns.

"No. I'm not leaving you," she whispered. "It won't help Jason if you get yourself killed trying to take Braun out. You'll get your chance. You just need to wait until the odds are in your favor."

Her voice seemed to come to him through a haze, his rage threatening to engulf him, but some part of his mind recognized the truth of her words. There were at least three armed men, not the best of odds. He might not care about himself, but he cared about Jessie.

Gut churning, he lowered his gun and turned to follow her into the now open cellar elevator. "It's going to be all right," she whispered as the doors slid shut. "I promise, David, we'll make it right."

With one touch, she'd managed to banish the fog, send his hatred scuttling back under its proverbial rock. But he knew it was only a temporary reprieve. It would be back. And when it came again, not even Jessie would be able to stop it.

Jessie fought to control her tumbling thoughts. She'd known, the minute they'd found out that Braun was connected to Jason, that David would want to kill him. But she hadn't expected the depth of his hatred. His rage had almost had a physical presence, sucking the energy from the room. It frightened her. Not for herself, but for David.

It made him reckless, to the point that not even life mattered. Had she not managed to stop him, Braun would be dead, but so would David. And she'd led him here. Dragged him deeper into his own hell. Without Faust's information and her quest, David would still be searching. Maybe in the end it would have turned out the same. But the idea that she had somehow been responsible for sending him over the edge was untenable.

"Do you think they heard us?" she asked, trying to focus on the task at hand.

"No." David shook his head, the anger he'd exhibited earlier gone—almost as if it had never existed. But she knew it was still there, like a snake waiting to strike. "We're in the clear for now," he continued, thankfully oblivious to the turn of her thoughts, "but we need to hurry."

The doors opened and they stepped out of the elevator, stopping short of the pressure-sensitive floor. David reached into his bag and produced an aerosol can. He sprayed the area over the floor, waiting to see if color developed. The air remained translucent.

"Looks like your code did the trick," David said, taking a tentative step forward.

Jessie followed, relieved when there were no flashing lights, no alarms. "Don't count your chickens yet," she said. "I buried my work behind dummy code, but that doesn't mean it can't be found. And Braun is upstairs right now. That wasn't part of the plan."

David waved a hand at the security camera, nodding when it failed to illicit a response. "But it's something we can deal with if we have to. You keep watch. Shoot at anything that moves. I'll start on the vault."

He pulled out a stethoscope and pressed against the vault door, listening as he turned the dial of the combination lock. Occasionally, he stopped to write a number on the vault, eliminating choices by striking through the losing digits.

She turned away, keeping her gun trained on the elevator doors. "Shouldn't I be drilling the holes for the explosives?"

"No. I think it's better that you keep watch. See if you can rouse Faust. Maybe he can do something to call off the goons."

"Faust," she whispered into the headset. "Faust, are you there?" She waited for a couple more seconds. Then called his name again.

No answer.

"I don't think we're receiving down here. Which means we're operating blind."

"We'll be fine," he assured her, still concentrating on the vault.

Jessie blew out a breath, wondering why in hell she'd agreed to steal the damn box in the first place. *Because you love your father,* came the answer, unbidden but definitely true.

Love was a strange animal, defying logic and convention to survive in places it shouldn't. Her gaze fell on David, watching as he listened to the inner workings of the vault's lock. The back of his neck and the line of his shoulders were as familiar as if they were parts of her own body. Which made their impending separation that much harder to accept.

Sometimes doing the right thing hurt like hell. But she knew it had to be done.

"I've got it." David's words broke through her reverie.

"So quickly?" she asked. "That's amazing."

"Let's hold off the congratulations until after we've got the Protector and make our escape. This is your show. You should go first." He stepped back, waving her ahead of him, as she passed.

Thanks to the thickness of the walls the interior of the vault was much smaller than it appeared from the outside. Directly in front of her were some shelves with stacks of papers and several piles of bound currency. She pushed them aside, but there was nothing behind them. "There's nothing here," she said, fighting her frustration. "After all this, there's nothing here."

"Easy, Jessie, looks can be deceiving," David said, walking over to the shelves, running his hands along the tops and sides.

"You're right. I'm not thinking clearly. This is probably just a decoy." She knelt to feel along the base of the shelves, and was rewarded with an audible click. They both scrambled to move out of the way as the entire shelving unit swung open to reveal a space about half a meter square. Inside, sitting on a square of blue velvet, sat the Protector of Armageddon.

Chapter Nine

After all the effort they'd expended to get here, she was surprised at how ordinary the Protector looked. It was certainly beautiful. There could be no denying the fact. The carving was every bit as intricate as David had described, the jeweled corners winking at her in the diffused lighting of the vault.

But it was still just a box. No herald of accompanying angels or dark paladin appearing to protect it. It was merely an ancient artifact that paid empty tribute to man's never-ending need to impress the gods.

Looking at it sitting on its blue velvet shelf, she almost felt disappointed. As if she'd wanted some greater sign. Something that proved that some part of the legend was true. It was a ridiculous notion. She should be grateful it had gone down so easily.

She started to reach for the box, but David stopped her, his hand on her wrist. "Maybe I should do it."

"Why?" she asked. "You don't believe that it has any power."

"All the better that it be me over you," he said, his expression inscrutable.

"Oh, come on. Does this look like it has the power to end the world?" She hadn't meant to sound mocking, but after all the talk she'd expected something more awe-inspiring.

Before he had that chance to argue with her, she reached past him and picked up the box, the metal surprisingly warm to the touch. The carvings up close were more impressive than they'd appeared from inside the vault, but still it was somewhat underwhelming. "It's just a box." She held it out to him. "See?"

"Well, I still don't like the idea of you having any kind of connection with that *thing*." David frowned at the Protector again. "Maybe it isn't metaphysical, but it certainly invites trouble. Look at what happened to Jason."

"Stop worrying. Once we're out of here, I'll give it to my client and that'll be the end of that." Even as she said it, she knew it wasn't the truth. Once she gave the box to her father, everything would change. A few days ago that had seemed like a good idea. But now, suddenly, she wasn't as certain.

"Look, we can debate the merit, or lack thereof, of the box later," David said. "Right now we need to get out of here." He moved around the side of the vault, kneeling beside the steel panel that blocked the exit. With the precision of an expert, he assembled the drill and in short order sparks were dancing off the rocks that abutted the sheet of steel. "Shouldn't take more than a minute. I want you to get behind the vault door."

"I thought it was going to be a contained explosion."

"It is," David confirmed. "But you never know."

"What about you?" Jessie asked, trying not to let her imagination take her places she didn't want to go. "Where will you be?"

"Don't worry. I'll be right beside you. Now go."

She pulled her gun out just to be on the safe side, moving toward the vault, her attention split equally between David and the elevator. In only seconds, he'd finished with the drill and was inserting the plastique. Then he attached the fuse, rolling it out as he moved backward toward her and the comparative safety of the vault.

She opened her mouth to urge him to hurry but the mechanical whir of the elevator stopped her cold. "Someone's coming."

"Shoot the panel. Maybe it'll short out the elevator, or at least slow them down."

She aimed and fired. Electricity sparked from the control panel, followed by a puff of smoke. For a moment the noise of the dropping elevator continued unimpeded, then with a grinding lurch it came to a stop.

"Come on, Jessie," David called, hitting the detonator.

She whirled around and ran toward him, the reverberations of the explosion vibrating beneath her feet. They rounded the corner of the vault just as a gaping hole opened to the left of the steel panel. Dust filled the air, small pebbles raining from the ceiling.

"This way." He motioned to the improvised entrance. "Quickly. Before they manage to circumvent your handiwork."

As if spurred on by his words, the elevator groaned once and then began to descend again.

"They're coming." She dashed through the hole into the passageway beyond, stopping long enough to make sure that David made it through as well.

"Go ahead," David yelled. "I'm going to try to close the hole."

Jessie pulled out a flashlight and started forward, the light bouncing off the hewn rock of the tunnel. Then she stopped, turning around to retrace her steps. No way was she leaving David on his own. If nothing else she could keep him covered, and handle anyone who managed to get through before he could reseal the tunnel.

Reaching into his pocket, David produced a metal tube with protruding wires. He touched the wires together and threw the makeshift bomb into the opening. This time there was no controlled blast, the sound almost deafening as the explosion bounced off the stone walls, the reverb throwing David to the ground.

Mindless of the falling rock and debris, Jessie ran forward, her hands in front of her, feeling for David, reaching out to him with her mind. For a moment there was nothing. Then she felt a wall of anger, and the hard muscle and bone of an arm. Closing her hand on his wrist she jerked him back, using adrenaline-induced strength to yank him clear of the cave-in.

They rolled to the ground, David covering her body with his. It was over in seconds, the resulting silence almost louder than the blast had been. "Damn it, Jessie," David said, grasping her shoulders. "I told you to run."

"Well, if I had you'd have been buried alive back there."

"Better me than you," he mumbled under his breath, his hands searching her face and arms for injury.

"I'm fine, David." She pushed him away and struggled to her feet, immediately tripping over a fallen rock. "Shit."

"Jessie?" David's hand found hers, his voice more gentle this time. "I didn't mean to . . ."

"I know." They stood for a moment, the dark surrounding them, communicating only by touch. As the dust cleared, Jessie could see the pale beam of her flashlight. By some miracle it had survived the fall.

"Looks like the explosion worked," she said, pulling away to pick up the flashlight. "But I dropped my gun."

She moved the flashlight in slow arcs, the beam illuminating rocks and debris. No gun. "It must have been buried in the explosion," she said, cursing her stupidity.

"Doesn't matter," David said, blotting at the scrape on his arm. "I've got mine. Where's the box?"

"I put it down over there." She moved the flashlight to the far wall, the beam bouncing off the golden box. "Before the explosion."

"Great," David said. "So what do you say we get out of here?"

She nodded, then bent to retrieve the box. David turned on a second flashlight, and together they began to make their way through the tunnel. It twisted and turned for twenty meters or so then suddenly bent in a sharp right angle.

"Hang on a minute," Jessie said, shifting the box from her right hip to her left. The damn box seemed to be getting heavier with every step.

"You want me to take that?" David's expression mirrored only concern, but Jessie had been part of a man's world for too long not to take his offer as a challenge.

"No, I've got it," she replied, shaking her head, hoisting the box higher.

"Maybe you should just give it to me." A string of lightbulbs sprang to life, the rock walls of the tunnel sparkling silver in the resulting illumination. "It was mine, after all, to begin with." Max Braun stood at the curve of the tunnel, a very lethal-looking Walther in his hand. Flanking him on either side were two of his security goons, both armed to the teeth.

"Well, if you want to be technical," David said, "the box isn't yours either. You stole it from my brother."

"Your brother was a hired hand." Braun's disdain was almost a tangible thing. "An expendable one, at that."

David sprang forward, anger marring his features as he aimed the Sig. "You son of a bitch."

For one moment everything seemed to be moving in slow motion, Jessie saw David fire, Braun shifting just at the right moment to avoid the bullet. Then his henchmen both fired and she screamed David's name, diving in front of him, the force of the bullets slamming her back against the wall of the tunnel. The Protector flew through the air, coming to rest against the opposite wall.

Seeing an opportunity, David hit the ground on a roll, returning fire, his first shot picking off one of the security guards, his second meant for Braun, but the shot embedded in the ceiling instead as Braun dove for the golden box.

The second security man shot again, but the bullet went wide, ricocheting off the tunnel walls. David fired again, nailing the bastard between the eyes.

Jessie fought to hang on to consciousness, needing to be certain that David was safe before she allowed herself to sink into the oblivion of regeneration. For the moment she was soaked in blood and although she felt no pain, she knew that, for David, it would appear that she was dying.

To that end, she struggled to her feet, kicking Braun as he moved past her for the box.

David stood less than a meter away, the anguish on his face breaking her heart.

She shook her head, trying to reassure him, but couldn't find the words, the blackness creeping around the edges of her vision now. He yelled something, his voice seeming to come from far away, and then Jessie saw Braun—the Protector in one hand, one of the guard's weapons in the other.

"No," she screamed, watching as the man leveled the gun, aiming for David's head.

Gunshots seemed to come from everywhere, the accompanying sound seeming overly loud—a rumble that echoed through the tunnel. Braun dropped the box, staring down at the now rapidly spreading stain on his shirt. For a moment he looked almost comically confused, then he fell.

Jessie managed to move her head, her rapidly fading eyesight searching for David, and then he was there, his hands on hers, his mouth moving in a silent plea for her to live. She tried to smile, but her muscles were frozen. The regeneration had begun. One minute they were standing in the tunnel and then everything was gone— lost in a cloudy haze of black.

Chapter Ten

The air was thick with dust, the particles filling David's nose and mouth. The lights flickered once and then again, as if they, too, were fighting for life. The tunnel ceiling had collapsed under the barrage of bullets, the resulting cave-in burying everything in its wake.

"Jessie, can you hear me?" He knew she had to be nearby, but he couldn't see her. "Jessie?"

From his vantage point by the wall, he could see Braun's body crumpled a few feet away. And beneath the fall of rock, the feet of one of the bodyguards. There was no sign of the other man. But David knew that he was dead.

"Jessie?" he called again, pushing to his feet, searching the rubble as he moved. And then he saw her, thrown against the wall, blood spattered across her shirt, her hands splayed out as if she'd been trying to stop the bullets.

He dropped down beside her, cradling her head on his lap,

moving his fingers to her neck—trying to find the carotid artery and some sign of life.

There was nothing.

His heart pounded with each intake of breath, his mind leaping to conclusions he wasn't ready to face. She couldn't be dead. It just wasn't an option he would allow himself to consider.

Again, he felt for a pulse, this time trying both wrists as well as the arteries in her neck. The result was the same.

Jessie was dead.

Pain shot through him, hot and heavy, crescendoing with his rage. He couldn't lose her. Not now. Dear God, not now. He hadn't even told her that he loved her. Hell, he hadn't even admitted the fact to himself.

And now it was too late.

He pulled off his jacket, carefully placing it under her head. Even in death she was beautiful. He leaned back against the hard rock wall, his mind filled with self-loathing. He'd failed Jessie as surely as he'd failed Jason.

He'd gotten his vengeance, but at what cost?

Across the way, as if mocking him, the Protector gleamed in the dust-filled light. Fighting against a surge of emotion that threatened to devour him, he pushed to his feet and stumbled across the tunnel. If not for the damned box, Jessie and Jason would both be alive.

He picked it up, surprised at how heavy it was. The jeweled corners winked as he turned it so that he could see the seal. The Seventh Seal. If the stories were accurate, all he had to do was open the box and chaos would rule. The End Days coming in a swath of evil and darkness.

It was heady to hold so much power.

Maybe he'd just open the box. It wasn't as if he had anything to lose.

"David, put it down."

He spun around, his heart threatening to break through his skin.

"Jessie . . ." He trailed off, unable to find words. She was standing in front of him, very much alive, her eyes dark with worry.

"Please put it down. You don't want to do that."

He frowned, his mind spinning as he watched her. "How did you know I was going to open it?"

"Because I know you. And because I could feel your rage."

"I thought you were dead," he whispered, dropping the box, crossing the room in one stride to pull her into his arms. He stroked her hair, kissing her eyes and mouth, savoring the feel of her skin against his. For a moment she returned his kiss, her urgency matching his, and then she pulled away, her eyes troubled.

He stepped back, his gaze falling to the dark blood still staining her shirt. "You didn't have a pulse."

"I know." Something in her tone made him certain he wasn't going to like what she had to say next.

She sighed and lifted her shirt to reveal the smooth unmarred skin of her belly.

At first he was confused, trying to grasp what it was she wanted him to see. Then, in a flash, understanding hit like lightning. There were no entry wounds. Her shirt was stained with blood, but her body was unblemished.

"I wasn't dead, David. I was regenerating."

"What the hell are you saying?" He held out his hands, as if in doing so somehow he could avoid the answer.

"I'm immortal. I can't die."

"But I saw you. I held you. There was no breath."

"When something catastrophic happens to my body, it heals it-self. The worse the injury the longer it takes to heal. And some-times, I can appear to be—"

"Dead," he said, using the word like a shield.

"Yes."

"Why didn't you tell me?" His mind tumbled in on itself as he tried to make sense of what she was saying.

"It's not something I usually bring up in casual conversation."

"Well, I'm not a casual contact. I'm . . ." He trailed off again, anger robbing him of words.

"—your lover?" she finished for him, disappointment flickering in her eyes. "And if I'd told you?"

"I'd have dealt with it."

"Like hell," she spat. "You'd have run for the hills. You couldn't handle our relationship when you thought I was normal. I can't even begin to think how you'd have dealt with it if you'd known who I really am."

"Well, we'll never know what I'd have done, will we? You didn't give me the chance."

They stood for a moment glaring at each other, and then with a sigh, he ran his hand through his hair. "So what happens now? Best I can tell we're trapped. I blew up the Azure side, and now our little shoot-out has blown the other." He waved a hand in the direction of the cave-in. "So does that mean you're here forever?"

She looked away, clearly debating the answer.

"Jessie, this isn't the time to gloss over the facts." He watched as she considered his words.

"Fine." She blew out a breath and leaned back against the wall. She might be immortal but just at the moment she looked vulnerable as hell. It was all he could do to keep from rushing to hold her. But he needed the distance. "If we're truly trapped here, someone will find me."

"Faust." He said the man's name, truth dawning. "I take it he's an immortal, too?"

"Yes." She shrugged, the gesture seeming inappropriate in light of the circumstances. "And if Faust doesn't find me, then my father will."

"Your father is immortal as well?"

"In a different kind of way."

"And your mother?"

"Very mortal. She died when I was a kid."

"And that was . . ." he looked at her askance, then changed his mind. "Never mind. Don't tell me."

"Suffice it to say it was a long time ago." She pushed off from the wall. "Look, I realize this is a lot to handle. And I also realize that in light of my . . . condition, you probably don't want anything more to do with me, but for the moment I'm all you've got. So maybe we should see what we can do to get you out of here."

"In case the rescue party comes too late?" He couldn't stop the bitterness that colored his voice. He'd fallen in love with a woman who wasn't even human.

"I'm real, David. Just as real as you are. I just have a longer life span than most."

"So—what?" he growled. "You can read minds, too?"

"Sometimes," she admitted. "When I really want to."

He stood for a minute fighting his rioting emotions, not certain what he was supposed to be feeling. But in truth, despite her amazing pronouncement, all he wanted to do was hold her. To reassure himself that she was in fact alive. "That's why you're so good with passwords and information?"

"Yeah. I can find things sometimes. If I concentrate long enough. But it isn't always a sure thing. Sort of like finding the needle in the haystack. Only I'm using my mind to find it."

"And you got this talent from your father? You said he was immortal, too."

She grimaced, staring down at her hands, then looked up, her expression deceptively calm. "My father is the devil."

If she'd flummoxed him before, she'd managed to gobsmack him now. "The devil," he repeated, as if by framing the words he could comprehend the enormity of what she was saying.

"Beelzebub, Azazel, Satan . . . he goes by a lot of names."

"Your father." He seemed to have been reduced to two-word sentences.

"Yes." She waited, chewing on her bottom lip. He recognized the gesture, a sign of insecurity, and wondered how many people had rejected her when they'd discovered who she really was. How often she'd been persecuted. Left all alone.

He could see it in her eyes. The reflection of a pain she worked so hard to hide beneath barriers she'd spent centuries building. For reasons he couldn't possibly fathom, she'd let him in. Opened herself to him, knowing what would eventually happen. Beyond the bravado, he saw the real Jessie—the woman he loved.

And suddenly, he didn't care who the hell her father was. Or what her life expectancy might be. Those were problems they could deal with together. He reached out to take her hands, both of them cold as ice. "It's a lot to swallow, Jessie. But right now all that matters is that we're alive and we're together. The rest we'll figure out as we go along."

They stood for a moment, linked by so much more than their hands.

"All right." She nodded, her eyes still full of doubt.

"If it helps at all, my father was a real son of a bitch."

Her smile was a lopsided effort, but at least the doubt faded. He leaned forward to give her a kiss, a covenant of sorts. "Now, what do you say we get the hell out of here?"

"We're not going to get out this way," Jessie said, tossing the rock she held into the growing pile behind them. "For every one we're pulling out, three more replace it." As if to emphasize the truth of her words, another tumble of rock filled the void she'd just created. "This isn't working."

"Well," David said, tossing another rock aside, "I, for one, don't like the idea of spending my last few hours watching you get locked in this hellhole—no pun intended—for eternity. There's got to be another way out."

"We studied the blueprints, and I don't remember there being anything."

"If nothing else, there's got to be a ventilation shaft of some kind. The air still smells fresh. And there's a definite air current. Look at the dust." He waved his hand at the cloud that had risen when he dropped the rock. Sure enough, it was swirling as if caught in an invisible breeze.

"It could just be us moving around." She hated to be a spoil-sport, but it was a credible explanation.

"Trust me," David said, "it's here somewhere. This hill is littered with caves. That's probably what gave them the idea for the tunnel in the first place. So if we're lucky the ventilation shaft will be some kind of natural chimney. One that we can navigate."

She picked up the remaining flashlight and turned it toward the ceiling, the soft white glow enhancing the rapidly dimming light-bulbs. She ran the beam as far as she could, the illuminated ceiling looked frustratingly solid.

"Come on. It's got to be here, we've just got to keep looking." David took the flashlight and started down the tunnel. "Bring the box."

"Maybe we should leave it." She didn't like the idea of disappointing her father, but right now all she really cared about was getting David out of here. If he was afraid of leaving her here for eternity, she was absolutely terrified of watching him perish here— like this.

"It can't hurt to bring it. And after all it is the reason we came."

"You the mean the reason *I* came. You came to kill Braun." She tipped her head toward the man's body as she bent to retrieve the Protector.

"I did. But I wound up killing him because he'd hurt you. In that moment, Jessie, you were all that mattered."

"I don't know what to say." She slowed her pace, her emotions threatening revolt.

"You don't say anything. Any more than I'm going to talk about your sacrificing yourself for me."

"But it wasn't a real sacrifice. I mean, I wasn't in any real danger."

"Well, I didn't know that at the time. And I think you'd have done it anyway—even if you weren't immortal."

She glanced over at him, trying to read his face, but it was impossible to see clearly in the dim light. He hadn't shunned her when she'd shared the truth. In fact, he'd made it fairly clear that he wasn't going to let it stand in their way. But then, he hadn't had time to consider all the implications.

She shook her head and shifted the box to her other hip. Better to concentrate on getting out of here. She scanned the ceiling as they made their way back down the tunnel. "I don't see anything."

"It's here somewhere. Search the walls, too. It could come in on a slant." As if on cue, the beam of the flashlight hit something dark, a sliver of space no more than a meter wide.

"That's it," David said, moving forward to examine the opening.

"How did we miss it the first time?"

"Angle's wrong. And we weren't really looking."

"So what do we do now?" Jessie asked. The flashlight beam carried on ten meters or so, then petered out into the darkness. "I don't see an end, but there's no way to know for sure."

"No guts, no glory."

"An overstatement, surely, but you've got a point." She smiled, the gesture wasted. He was already in the opening, moving forward, arms and flashlight first.

"It gets wider after the first bit," he called back, his voice sounding hollow against the tunnel walls.

"I'm right behind you." She'd never been particularly fond of small spaces, but she wasn't about to let David go in without her. Sucking in a breath, she stepped into the darkness, David's light muted by his body. The box felt hot against her skin as she tucked it to her chest, using it as a buffer against protruding edges of rock.

The going was tight at first, but David was right, the crevice

widened a little as it sloped upward. It was impossible to see anything but his silhouette and the pale beam of the flashlight ahead of
him. She could feel cool air on her face, and there were occasional
signs of tool marks when the passageway narrowed again. All of
which made her hopeful that they'd found a way out.

"Hang on," David said, raising a hand. "It's really steep here. I
think it'll be best if I go first and then come back for you."

"No fucking way." The words were out before she could stop
them. "Sorry. I didn't mean to be crass. It's just that we seem to do
better when we have each other's backs."

"All right," David said, accepting her protest without comment,
"you take the flashlight and I'll take the box."

She nodded, handing him the Protector, and grabbed the flashlight, moving past him into the lead. The floor was slick with mois-
ture, and she had to brace herself against the wall to keep from
slipping. But despite the obstacles, she reached the top of the in-
cline with only a minimum of effort, David following right behind.

"You were right," she said, sweeping the light across the open
room. "We're in a cave." Faint light showed around a rock forma-
tion just to their immediate left. "That's got to be the way out."

She took a step forward, then stopped as a powerful beam of
light struck her full in the face. She whirled around, reaching for
David, comforted when his hand closed on her wrist, pulling her
back against him, the box sandwiched between them.

"Do you have the gun?" she whispered.

"No," he said with a shake of his head. "I lost it when the roof
caved in."

"So what do we do?"

"Bluff."

She fought the fear gnawing at her gut, telling herself that as long as they were together they had a chance. "Who's there?" she asked, raising her hand to shade her eyes from the glare.

A man emerged from the light, the illumination shifting so that it was no longer blinding. Six others stood behind him, three of them holding halogen lights, the others holding what looked to be assault rifles. "We are the Seven."

"We don't want any trouble," David said, edging in front of her, still holding the box.

"I think you passed that point some time ago," the man said, his gaze settling on the Protector. "Give me the box."

Jessie shook her head, grabbing the Protector from David before he had a chance to react. "I'm afraid that giving it to you isn't an option. At least not until I have your word that you'll let us go."

The Templar sighed. "That's simply not possible." His colleagues lifted their rifles.

"Then we have a problem." She stepped in front of David, ignoring his protest. "Those guns aren't going to stop me. But I think you already know that. Which means that as long as I have the box, there's room for a bargain."

"What do you want?" the man asked, the others still holding their rifles.

"I want you to let us go."

David growled something behind her, but she kept her attention on the group's leader. She could feel his confidence even from here.

"I can't allow that." The man's eyes glittered silver in the light. "Your friend wanted to open the box. Its power has touched him. There must be payment."

"But he didn't open it."

Again David tried to move around her, but she shook her head, and he stopped, his frustration a palpable thing.

"He wanted to," the man said, "and that alone is enough to condemn him to death. The power of the Protector is not to be taken lightly."

"Then we're at an impasse, because I can't give you the box." She held his gaze, shifting slightly in front of David to be certain that her body blocked the shooters' line of sight.

The older man smiled. "Despite your claim, we both know that your regeneration will give me the necessary time to take the box and kill him. In front of you. Is that what you want? To watch him die?"

The thought terrified her, but she had a final card to play. "If you make so much as a move toward him, I'll summon my father. And believe me, when I call, he comes. Especially now that I've got the Protector in my possession."

"And your father would be . . . ?" For the first time she felt a flicker of worry emanating from the man in front of her.

"Obviously you haven't done your homework," David said, stepping around her, his eyes blazing with anger. "Jessie's father is the Devil. Capital D."

The man frowned, turning to converse with one of his comrades. "I must confess I underestimated you both." He was watching her now, as if he could find some sign that David was telling the truth.

"No cloven hooves or forked tail, if that's what you're looking for. But I assure you my father is very real and very interested in obtaining the Protector."

Even with the diffused light, she could see the man blanch, her pronouncement hitting him hard. "You could summon your father," he said, his eyes meeting hers, "but in the time it would take him to arrive, we can surely manage to kill your friend."

"Possibly, but the Protector will go to my father. Is that what you want?" It was an empty threat. She wasn't going to call her father. Not if it put David at risk. But she couldn't hand over the Protector either. She struggled for a solution, trying to find a way to keep David alive.

"Perhaps there is another way," the Templar said, taking a step forward, his wrinkled face offset by the intensity of his eyes. "It is true that we cannot kill you by traditional means. But if you allow it we can take your life."

"But I'm immortal. No one can kill me. Not even me. And I know because once, a long time ago, I tried."

"Jessie . . . ," David started, but she waved him quiet.

"So what is it exactly you think you're going to do?" She frowned at the Templar, trying to read his expression, to make sense of what he was saying.

"Accept your sacrifice. It's that simple. Your life for his. The power is yours, Jessie, not mine."

"And you'll let him live."

"Surrender yourself and give me the box. And in return, I'll allow him to go free."

"You can't do that." David's voice echoed off the walls of the cave, his anger vibrating between them.

"In point of fact, I can." The man shrugged, turning back to Jessie. "So it's up to you how you want this to end. His life or yours." The Templar waited, his gaze reaching out for her across the space that separated them.

"Earlier you said he *had* to die. Why the change?"

"It turns out that you are the greater prize."

"You mean that because of my parentage, my death is worth more to you?" She kept her gaze steady, her tone defiant.

The Templar studied her for a moment, then held out his hands, waiting.

"You can't seriously be thinking about doing this." David's hand closed on her arm.

"I want you to live," she said, fighting tears. "And this is the only way."

"I'll have your answer." The leader was flanked now by the other members of his sect, their eyes reflecting the wisdom of the ancients.

"I accept," she said, squaring her shoulders. She'd never been surer of anything in her life. "My life for his."

David's hand tightened on her arm. She could feel his anger, the emotion colored with his fear. "This is just a ruse, right?" he whispered. "They can't really kill you. I've seen it myself. You can't die."

For a moment she was tempted to tell him the truth, but knew that if she did, he'd never let her go. "I'll be fine. Just stay here and let me do this."

"But we can't trust them."

She turned to face the Seven. "Swear to me that you'll honor our bargain—on all you hold holy."

Again there was silence as the man considered her request. Then he nodded. "You have it. In the name of our Lord."

"They're just words, Jessie. They don't mean anything." David's eyes were pleading now, his love a tangible thing.

"In my world, they mean everything." She leaned forward to kiss him, memorizing the taste of him, the feel of his lips. Then she pushed away and walked toward the Templars, their leader meeting her halfway. He reached for the box, and she placed it in his hands, his face curiously devoid of expression.

"I'm ready," she said.

"Jessie." David's voice was sharp, her name echoing in the cavernous dark.

"It is done." The light flashed white, blinding in intensity. One minute the men were there and the next they were gone. Pain seared through her, robbing her of breath and speech.

David rushed to her side, his arms enfolding her, his gaze locking with hers. "You're just regenerating, right?"

She struggled to breathe, the pain crashing through her body in waves. "Dying . . . ," she whispered on an exhale. "I'm dying. . . ."

"What have you done?" The blood drained from David's face, his eyes dark with fear.

"I . . ." She struggled for air, enough to support the words. "I did it for you." Oddly enough, despite the pain, she felt almost peaceful. Finally, after centuries of searching, she'd found meaning in her life. How ironic that the knowledge came on the heels of her death.

"Jessie," David cried, rocking back and forth, cradling her like a baby, "you can't leave me. I need you. You've got to fight it."

"Nothing I . . . can . . . do." She sucked in a breath, summoning the last of her dying strength. "David . . ." She felt his hand close around hers, and turned her fingers so that their palms were touching. "I love you."

Tears streamed down his face as he held her. "I love you, too, Jessie."

"Histrionics aren't going to help anyone, young man." With a flourish the voice was followed by her father's dapper figure. His cravat white against the black of his goatee. "What have you done now, daughter?"

"Leave her alone. She's been through enough." David rose, hands clenched, and moved to stand between her and her father.

"You can stop with the macho posturing," her father said, dismissing David with a wave of his hand. "I'm here to help."

David stood firm for a moment, studying the older man, and then with a muttered oath stepped aside.

Her father knelt beside her, his hands steady as they slid behind her shoulders to lift her up. "You could have called me. I would have come for the box."

"But David would have died." It wasn't really an explanation, but her father seemed to understand anyway.

He stroked her hair. "I want you to breathe deeply now, and listen to me."

She nodded, aware of David, kneeling now, just within sight.

"I can take you with me now, Jessie. And the pain will all go away. All of this will just be a distant memory." Her father searched her face, and then sighed. "Or I can restore your mortal life."

"What are you saying?"

"I'm saying that if you choose to stay here, I can grant you a limited life."

"With David."

"Yes." Her father nodded, his face reflecting her pain. "But you have to understand that if you choose the path of mortality, I won't be able to protect you anymore. And everything you had—your immortality, your special talents—all of it will be gone. There'll be no turning back. You'll be on your own."

"She'll have me." David's hand closed on hers, his voice filled with emotion.

The pain intensified, her ribs seeming to compress over her heart.

"It's time, Jessie," her father said, rising to stand over her, his cane lifted toward the ceiling. "Make your choice."

She fought for the words, her gaze locked on her father's. "I'm sorry, Daddy, but this is what I want. I choose David."

"So be it." With a last look, her father waved his cane and disappeared in a flash of red smoke and light.

David wrapped her in his arms, his heart pounding next to hers. "Is it over? Are you really okay?"

Jessie tested a breath, and then another, the air flowing freely into her lungs. The pain had diminished, leaving only a dull throbbing in her head. "I have a headache."

"You sound like that's a good thing," David said, pulling back to frown down at her.

"I've never had a headache before, David," she said, grinning like an idiot. "Don't you see? I'm human. Really, truly human. If you cut me, I'll probably bleed."

"I'll take your word for it," he said with a laugh.

She leaned back against David, staring at the spot where her father had disappeared. She'd never see him again, and yet she knew that in setting her free, he'd proved his love. And that she'd carry with her always.

David pulled her close, his arms warm, his heart beating a rhythm against her ear. His eyes settled on the spot where her father had disappeared. "Are you sure you won't miss it?"

She tipped back her head, looking at the man she loved. "All I want is you. Nothing else matters at all."

He bent his head, his lips hard against hers, the kiss a covenant— a promise of things to come. For the first time in her very long life she had everything to live for.

"Looks like the cavalry's arrived a bit too late," Faust said, stepping into the cavern, his lantern banishing the shadows once and for all. "I always miss out on the fun. I take it everything is all right now?"

Jessie snuggled closer to David, smiling up at her friend. "Everything is perfect, Faust. Absolutely perfect."

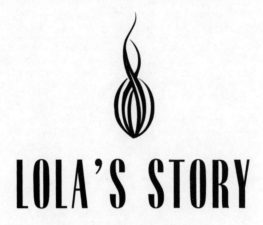

LOLA'S STORY

Kathleen O'Reilly

Chapter One

The dance club was crowded, people squeezed together like sardines, which was the curse of the It clubs. Lola de Medici didn't like the crowds, but she hated being alone even more.

Fernando, her agent, sat across from her, chatting into his cell phone, blowing her kisses every now and again, just to make sure she didn't think he was ignoring her. She really didn't need an agent, but she liked the sound of it. *My agent.*

Across from Fernando was Sylvia, her publicist. Next to Sylvia was Viktor, her stylist. And next to Viktor was Angela, her personal trainer. Lola didn't need a personal trainer, either, but Angela was Sylvia's sister-in-law, and Lola really liked Sylvia, so if Angela needed a job, well, personal trainer was better than most. They were her entourage. Her single link to the real world. As reality went, it was tenuous at best.

The music kicked up to a heavy bass, and the latest Hollywood movie star smiled in Lola's direction. It would be so easy to smile back, wave him over, and take him to bed, but La-La Land really wasn't her scene. Vanity might be *her* biggest flaw, but it didn't mean she had to like it in other people.

Instead of gracing Mr. Superstar with her favor, Lola wiggled her fingers in Fernando's direction.

"Dahling?" he asked, pausing in his conversation.

"I need a drink," she said, blowing him an air kiss.

"Of course," he replied and click—the cell phone gone, the rest of the world forgotten. Except for Lola. Just the way she liked it.

She gave him her trademark smile, first successfully used in the Bourbon court under Henry IV. After four hundred years, she had perfected it.

"Champagne?"

"Veuve Clicquot," she said. "A bottle for the table. We should celebrate, don't you think?"

"I can't believe this," Angela said. "My first time in the VIP room, and now you're ordering VC. God, this is awesome! What're we celebrating?"

Sylvia glared at her sister-in-law, bringing her down to a suitable level of ennui. Lola shot her a look of gratitude. Such maladroitness should never be encouraged.

The waiter brought their champagne, glasses were clinked, and all was well until Sylvia's eye's grew large, even larger than Angela's.

"Who is he?" she gasped.

The man walking through the room was devilishly handsome, turning female heads as he passed. Dark, brooding, with a goatee that Lola had always despised and eyes that promised every woman a good time.

Hell.

There was only one person in the world who could upstage her. The devil himself.

Daddy.

Life really wasn't fair.

Lucifer smiled in Lola's direction and in response she shot him the finger. It would make the papers tomorrow, but as Sylvia always said: there's no such thing as bad PR.

As the devil walked toward her, more than one woman brushed up against him. He was the world's ultimate bad boy. God, women could be so gullible. Lola turned around to face the wall.

"Lola, Lola, Lola."

"Is someone talking to me? I don't think I hear anyone talking to me. Viktor, is someone talking to me?"

Viktor cocked his head. "He's very cute, Lola. I think you should talk to him."

Lola turned to glare at Viktor, the man formerly known as her stylist. Traitor. For that she wouldn't even give him a good reference—or at least that's what she'd tell him.

"You're acting very juvenile, my darling," said her father.

And wasn't that a fine thing to say, when she hadn't seen him in over fifty years? Sometime after World War II he had sent her a postcard: *Wish you were here.* Lola hadn't thought it was very funny. And now, after all this time, he was just popping into her life, like his absence didn't matter.

"I'll have security kick you out," she said, full of bravado. It was easy when you were the devil's spawn.

"I own the place," he answered with a yawn. He looked at the table, at her entourage, her friends. "Leave," he commanded. And in one heartbeat the table was empty. Just Lola and her father. Estranged father, thank you very much.

He seated himself across from her and took up a champagne glass, toasting her.

Lola scowled.

"I have a proposal."

"No."

"You don't care what I'm about to tempt you with?"

"Oh, puh-lease. That might work with some of your other little minions, but I'm beyond temptation. Very beyond temptation."

She studied her nails, deciding that she needed to get a new color. Something bolder, more innovative. Red was getting a little . . . stale.

"I need a soul."

"Have you tried Wal-Mart?"

He laughed then, not the way she remembered. Deeper, older, like an aged wine. "You were always my favorite."

It was such a lie that she didn't even call him on it. Instead they could both pretend.

"You need *me* to get a soul for you?"

"It's a particular soul," he continued. "One very special soul."

"You've never come to me with a request before." It was true. Lola had a unique gift, although "gift" was her father's term. When Lola slept with a man, he gave up his soul. Literally. In exchange for that small price, Lola stayed beautiful, immortal, and—sadly—heartless, as well.

"There's a reward if you bring it to me," he added, as if bribes would work with a Medici.

"Oh, goody."

"There's no need to be churlish. And what's that I see? A wrinkle on the brow? Are you starting to lose your glow?"

Just like the devil, knowing exactly which button to push.

She fought the itch to pull out her mirror, instead digging her fingers into her palms. "I could have any man in the room," she bragged. Although was it bragging when it was the truth? She gave her father her most confident smile.

"Then why haven't you?" he said, his eyes curious, probing, staring deep inside her, looking for answers that Lola didn't have herself.

"Who is he?" she asked, needing to change the subject.

"No one special. Not special at all."

"Then why do you want his soul?" she asked, not trusting her father one inch.

"Does it really matter to you? Is one man any different from the others?"

She thought of the elaborate fantasy world she had made surrounding her father. The dreams of vacations by the sea and long dinner conversations that never existed. The times she'd looked in the mirror and saw her heritage reflected back. Was he any different from all the others? Lola met his dark gaze evenly. "No, you're all the same to me."

Another lie that they both would ignore.

"You'll do it. For me?"

"What do I get out of it?"

Her father laughed again. "I've taught you well."

"You've taught me nothing."

"Feeling a little pissy, are we? Consider this my way of making amends."

"Too little too late," she snapped, because she really didn't want to hear this.

"You won't do this one little favor for me?"

"Why should I?"

"I'll give you the keys to hell."

"Right." What a laugh. The father who had never given her the time of day was suddenly entrusting to her his entire enterprise?

"Mock me if you want to, I'm retiring. I want to play golf, go fishing, chase women."

"Retiring? When hell freezes over. Without you, where would the world go for all its pain and suffering?"

He leaned in and stared at her soulfully, a look that at one time would have made her day. "So you're not going to help?"

"Your charming homeland means nothing to me. *Daddy*."

For a second she saw a flash of pain. About time.

"What does, Lola?" He steepled his fingers together. "What would mean something to you?"

Her thick lashes fluttered downward, because she couldn't let him see the torture in her eyes. "You have nothing that means anything to me."

"Not even eternal beauty, a body that all men would kill for?"

She tossed back the long fall of her hair and smiled through full, voluptuous lips. "I already have that."

"But there's a cost. I'll give it to you gratis. Along with my kingdom."

When the devil smiled like that, there was always a price. Her mother had known it, and Lola knew it as well. Unfortunately, Lola wasn't nearly as strong as her mother. The temptation was potent, pulling her into the whirling pit of purgatory that was her father.

But still . . .

Liberté. Such a simple word, so underestimated.

"No strings?"

"None," he said, his smile never faltering, always so sure of what little Lola would do.

"Maybe I will. Maybe I won't."

He rose from the table, an explosion of camera flashes following in his wake. "Think about it," he said, leaning down to kiss her cheek.

She sat in cold silence until he was gone from the room and the crowd came back to life. Her father could do that. Suck the life from a room.

Lola snapped her fingers, and her entourage assumed their positions at the table. Lola smiled at her friends, smiled flirtatiously at the Hollywood type across the room. She had everything she wanted here. *Everything.* But her fingers betrayed her, creeping up to touch her cheek where he had kissed her.

Yes, his offer was tempting, but her father didn't deserve her help with anything. How many times had she called for him, only to be ignored?

She moved her fingers away and lifted her glass in Mr. Hollywood's direction. Before she could take a sip, he was by her side, his hand possessively on one bare shoulder. Lola fought the urge to move the hand away, gazing at her reflection in the mirrored walls. Maybe her father was right. Maybe she was losing her glow.

She pulled the man closer and gave him a practiced kiss. He sighed, his hands slipping into her hair.

Losing her glow? *Not for long.*

Christopher "Crash" St. Clair sat on a bar stool, drumming his fingers on the bar, more than ready to take care of business and leave. It would have been nice to play in St. Kitts, kick back with a froufrou rum drink and a beautiful woman by his side.

He laughed to himself. Now *that* sounded like paradise. Instead he was stuck waiting on some old gypsy crone who probably wore a turban.

Spiffy.

He took a deep breath and scoped out the place. The run-down cantina wasn't much on the eyes, and the afternoon crowd was tiny. The "bar" was nothing but two planks balanced on barrels, although the bar stools were nice. Two tables sat along the back wall, filled by a couple of locals passing the time. The floor was dirt, the roof was thatch, and his gut told him the beer wouldn't be cold, but then again, Crash wasn't here for the beer.

While he waited, he pulled the tiny green plant from his pocket. His lucky charm. Deep in his own thoughts, he twisted the leaves between large fingers, before placing it carefully on the bar. Wouldn't need that anymore.

An older blonde occupied the next seat over, well on her way to an afternoon drunk. She gave him the eye, looking him over once, then twice. It was a look he'd received lots, but Crash had learned many hard and painful lessons. His last relationship had ended with a shitload of yelling and crying, and he wasn't about to repeat the mistake, mainly because his relationship before that had ended badly, too. And the relationship before that. And so on. And so on.

He smiled politely and then looked down, tracing a pattern in the dirt on the bar.

"You from around here?" the blonde asked, her words slurring together.

"Nah. Just passing through."

"Too bad. But smart," she said, tapping a finger against her brain. "Hurricane season."

Crash looked out the window at the pristine blue sky, the wind so still not even the palm trees were moving. "Hurricane season?"

"Yeah, that's why I'm here. Chasing the story. Any story. Government corruption, natural disaster, sex scandal, civil war."

"Hurricane season?" he repeated stupidly.

"You didn't know?" she said, and then started to laugh.

"Yeah, I know, I'm a riot." *Hurricane season.* Shit. Crash stayed inland for a reason.

"Sweetie, after five beers, everybody's a riot. Or else you're going to slit your wrists." She laid her head on the bar, grime and all, and he could hear the pain-filled sniffling.

Crash really wanted to ignore her. God knows, it was the smart thing to do and he really needed to work on that smart thing. He even went back to tracing patterns with his fingers, examining the fine craftsmanship involved in distressing the rotted planks. People paid big money for crappy-looking stuff. He didn't understand it, but hey, he didn't want to judge. . . .

Oh, fuck.

"What's wrong?" he asked.

She looked up, tears cruising down her cheeks. "It's my job."

"It's not that bad of a job. I know your people get a bad rap, but it could be worse."

"I'm old."

"Nah. You've got plenty of years left in you. I've seen a lot of sick people. You look really healthy."

"I'm forty-seven."

"See. That's not old."

"You don't understand."

"That's a very chauvinistic attitude. Just 'cause I'm lacking in sensitivity, emotional depth, estrogen, I can't understand? Who made those rules?"

"They gave the evening slot to Trixie. Trixie! How am I supposed to compete with an anchor who's called Trixie?"

"I thought they liked male anchors. Rock, Stone, names like that," he offered helpfully.

"Not in Idaho."

That explained much. "Oh."

She fell silent and Crash went back to studying the planks in the bar.

"Marjorie Newman," she said.

He sighed, because no matter how many times he tried, it was impossible to walk away.

"Crash St. Clair."

"Crash? Where'd you get that name?" she asked. Then she pulled out a tissue. "You could be a news anchor."

"You seen the bartender in this joint?" he asked quickly before she could start up the waterworks again.

"In the back. He's feeding the goats."

"Quaint."

She cupped her hand to her breasts. "Do you think there's anything wrong with these?"

Crash tried not to look. "No."

"The station manager does. I've exercised, lifted weights, Botoxed and acupunctured."

And what am I supposed to say to that? "I think it shows," he said cautiously.

"They want me to get a boob job. I bet they don't ask Christiane Amanpour to get a boob job. Just one story. One great story.

That's all I need." She buried her head in her arms and began to cry again. Huge, noisy sobs.

Just then, salvation arrived in the form of the bartender. Glory be. He was a native type with long dreadlocks and a Hawaiian print shirt. "She with you?" he asked, one thumb pointing in Marjorie's direction.

Crash shook his head. The reporter would survive. He'd seen worse. "I'm looking for someone," he stated.

"Ain't dat the truth?" said the bartender. "But first, you must drink, mon. What can I pour for you?"

"Surprise me," said Crash, because he wasn't thirsty.

The bartender pulled down a mug from the shelf, but the mug slipped through his fingers and crashed to the floor, the sound like a bomb in the quiet room.

Another accident. Crash slid his gaze away.

The bartender bent to pick it up, and promptly cut his finger.

"Sorry for the trouble," the bartender said, after wrapping the bloody hand in a rag. "Who you looking for?"

"A gypsy. Mama Leone," he said, keeping his voice even. He didn't want to get his hopes up, but deep down, Crash was an optimist. A moronic optimist, but an optimist.

"Whatcha need with the gypsies?"

"I'm looking to get my fortune told. What do you think? Just get Mama Leone. I need her help."

"She won't be helping you today, mon."

Crash put a hundred-dollar bill on the bar, because he knew how the world worked. "I'll pay whatever I need to."

The bartender gave him a sad smile. "You won't be needin' dat. Mama Leone died," he said, and then he crossed himself. "She's restin' in peace now."

Cold settled over Crash like a shroud. A damp, nasty, hurricane season shroud. "There's a mistake. She can't be dead. I talked to her son last week."

"It just happened a few days ago. Heart attack."

Crash stared at the crumpled green leaves that he'd abandoned, and tucked the remains in his pocket, because life never changes after all.

All his life Crash had dealt with bad thing after bad thing, like his father before him, like his grandfather before that. He wasn't sure why the St. Clair males were bequeathed a hellish existence. A disaster gene, a curse, but he'd always thought that he could find the solution.

Somehow.

"You got a problem, too?" asked the reporter, lifting up her head. And now she pays attention.

"Nah," said Crash, shaking his head. No problem. Not a problem at all. He took a long drink on his beer, draining his glass. "Fill it up," he told the bartender. "Until the money runs out." He pointed a thumb at the blonde. "And her, too. In fact, drinks on the house." Alcohol wouldn't change things, but for a while he might be too bleary-eyed to know it.

A grin split the bartender's face, white teeth flashing against tanned skin. "You make many friends on the island, mon."

As Crash lifted his second glass, a man in the corner of the room caught his eye. He was sitting alone, his head low, shoulders sunk.

The hairs rose on the back of his neck. It was the hinky awareness that had dogged him his entire life. When his Boy Scout troop had gone camping, he had known before the compass broke, and then they'd spent three days wandering in the woods. And when his mother had driven off to get a haircut one morning, Crash had given his dad an extra hug. He would need it when his wife didn't come back.

Not the time, St. Clair. Really, not the time.

Quickly he scanned the room. Three bystanders in the back, plus Marjorie and the bartender. His fingers found the cold steel of the blade he carried. He didn't think he was going to need it, but old habits died hard.

Marjorie looked back to where Crash was looking, noted the tension in the room, and then her eyes began to gleam. "Are you a cop?"

"You should get out of here."

"That's a joke, right? Does he have a gun? Will there be hostages, you think? I've got a camera in my bag."

The man raised his head and reached into the pocket of his hoodie, a desperate plea in bloodshot eyes. Crash didn't know if it was drugs, or just the crazies, but in the end, who gave a shit why? It was what people did—or didn't do—that defined them.

Crash gave the reporter his most intimidating stare. Since he was a big guy, it wasn't so hard.

"Look. I'm not a cop. But you need to leave."

"This is *my* story. Island paradise marred by crime, drugs, maybe death. A cop springs into action and saves six lives with his quick thinking. It's fab!"

"I'm an accountant. A goddamned, law-abiding, flag-waving accountant," Crash answered, sighing heavily as he watched the man rise and walk to the bar, his movements unsteady.

"You'll be wanting another round?" asked the bartender.

Hoodie Man jerked his head to one side, his hand reaching into his pocket. Crash pounced on the hand before it could go further.

"Hey, got a buck?" Crash asked, holding tight to the arm. Hoodie Man tried to shake off the hand, but Crash held strong. "Don't," Crash said.

The man looked at him, stared through him.

"What d' you need? Food, shelter, money, a babe? You know, I could give you some pointers," said Crash, still trying to make conversation. Get 'em talking. That was important.

"You can't help me," he whispered. "You can't help me. Nobody can help me."

"That's a very defeatist attitude; we'll work on that next," said Crash. "But first things first. We need to get rid of the gun."

The man looked up, his head listing to one side. "It's all I got left."

"You need money? Let me buy your gun. A thousand dollars."

"You're crazy, man."

"Yeah, I know. Humor me."

"A grand for a gun?"

Crash reached into his pocket and peeled off a wad of bills. "Here, take it."

The man pulled the gun out of his pocket, laid it on the bar, and then pushed it over to Crash.

A cap gun.

Marjorie looked at the toy, looked at Crash. "You've been suckered."

He shrugged nonchalantly. Sometimes things ended good, sometimes not so good. He'd rather be suckered anytime.

Chapter Two

So this was paradise.

Silky white sand covered the quiet Caribbean beach, framed by a line of trees and tropical gardens. The air was salty, tinted with the sweetness of jasmine and the tang of rum. There were no crowds, no paparazzi, no comforting hum of the masses. Instead all you could hear was the quiet sound of the surf lapping against the shore.

Frankly, Lola was bored. The thatched umbrellas that studded the beach kept her out of the sun, and there were special sun shades to pull when the heat became too much. Waiters wandered back and forth, ready to quench your every thirst, but everyone was just . . . sitting, including Christopher St. Clair.

Dark sunglasses hid her eyes as she studied him, trying to discover his secret.

What the hell did her father want with him?

He sat on a wooden chaise lounge, watching the sunlight glint on the aquamarine waters, although he really needed a bigger chair. His long frame—she thought he was over six feet—wasn't made for a regulation lounger. And his body, well, it wasn't that skinny, ripped look that was all the rage currently. No, this man was big and brawny, like a fortress, with a smattering of hair on his chest, and Hummer-sized shoulders. Everything about him was hard—his legs, his arms, even his jaw. Everything except his hair. Surprisingly enough, the top of his head was covered with a tousle of brown silk, quite unkempt, and yet . . . touchable.

Lola had always thought the Cro-Magnon look was overdone, but something about this one made her rethink her position.

He sipped on his cold beer as if he didn't have a care in the world, as if he didn't know the devil was out to get him.

Lola stretched her legs in front of her, and the waiter, mistaking the move for a beverage request, ran to her side.

"The beautiful lady needs a drink?" he asked.

Lola didn't bother to look up. "The beautiful lady needs privacy. *Por favor*," she added as an afterthought, because there was no point in rudeness. The man looked disappointed enough—they always were—but he departed, leaving Lola alone.

Alone. Lola glanced around for Sylvia. Or Fernando. Even Angela. She considered calling the waiter back, but not only would she look neurotic, but seduction was a solitary job, although there was that one time during the seventeenth century when she'd taken on three bawdy members of the French Musketeers. Her glow from that one night had lasted for weeks. Sadly, she wasn't that young anymore.

She pushed her sunglasses up on her head, so Mr. St. Clair could appreciate the full power of her tip-tilted green eyes, which she had always thought were her best feature. Deliberately she stared in his direction, until at last his head turned and she met his eyes.

Mon Dieu.

There was trouble there. Looking into the deep depths was like staring into a well, yet she couldn't look away. There was something insistent in the way he studied her, watching, instinctively finding her weakness. She fought the desire to cover herself up, as if he could see into the blackness of her heart.

Then, like Houdini with his tricks, the darkness in his eyes changed. He smiled politely and then leaned back in his chair, taking a long sip from his beer.

As if she were nobody.

Ha. She was Lola de Medici, daughter of Catherine, daughter of Satan.

There wasn't a man alive she couldn't take.

She forced herself to breathe, slowly, relaxing, letting the tension ease from her body.

Mr. St. Clair turned.

The dark eyes flickered over her, lingered on her breasts, her long legs, the tanned expanse of skin strategically exposed by the black micro bikini.

A purr rose in her throat as she moved in for the kill, stretching her legs out even further. She arched her back, her breasts silhouetting nicely.

His eyes flared with desire, and she waited for the carnal smile.

And waited.

And waited.

Instead he looked away.

Bastard.

Her sultry aura deflated some as she contemplated her next move. Since she'd never had to make more than one move, this process wasn't quick.

Unbidden, the waiter brought her a strawberry daiquiri with a fat strawberry and this time she didn't even snap at him. On the contrary, disheartened by her first rejection *ever*, she flirted with him shamelessly, leading the poor man on until he was literally drooling. The devil on her shoulder whispered for her to slip a hotel key into his hand, mainly to assure herself that she still had the touch. But this really, really, *really* wasn't the time to feed her own neurosis.

No, she had a job to do.

Once again she shooed the waiter away and pondered the mysterious—and possibly poor-sighted—Mr. St. Clair. It was the only explanation, and there was only one way to find out.

Lola rose and walked to the water, her hips rolling back and forth in a patent-pending rhythm that females had tried to emulate for centuries. When she reached the sea, Lola bent at the waist, pretending to study a seashell, but in actuality, she was displaying an artistically sculpted derriere that had once started a revolution.

It didn't take long before her performance was rewarded, a wolf whistle splitting the air. She straightened, her face displaying the perfect amount of surprise and indignation, and looked up.

A lifeguard was standing on the edge of the beach, legs splayed, chest muscles displayed to maximum advantage.

Poser.

The lifeguard whistled again, and her chest heaved, partially in frustration, partially in a Pavlovian response. She looked in Mr. St. Clair's direction, happy to see the dark gaze fixed her way. Wary and uninterested.

She blew out a breath and stalked back to her umbrella, abandoning her patent-pending walk.

This should not be that difficult. God knows, she'd been seducing men for four hundred years. Hell, once she had seduced a man in her sleep.

She was a Medici, born to the most powerful family in Italy. Her mother became a French queen, her half brother a king. Yet Lola had always been damned to want the one thing she couldn't have. She wanted the ability to fully make love to man. To wake in the morning, look deep into his eyes, and know that he was just the same as before. A soul was a small thing, nothing more than a wisp of air, yet if you took a man's soul, you might as well have taken his heart.

This time, the father who had damned her had given her a way out, and she was going to do this, whatever it took.

A desperate idea popped into her head, and for one devil-may-care moment she considered sunbathing topless. Unfortunately, very few men could survive the sight without protective lenses and besides, she had always considered such displays of flesh vulgar and somehow needy.

Lola popped the strawberry into her mouth, racking her brain for something new and different, something original, something fresh and sexy.

Something she'd never lacked before . . .

Then, from the hotel side of the beach, a young couple approached, the chunky woman walking far in front of the man, her posture as stiff as the anger in his jaw.

Trouble in paradise.

Lola watched as the woman threw down a beach towel in close

proximity to Mr. St. Clair, flashing him a shy smile and thighs bigger than the French Riviera.

Merde. Some women truly let themselves go.

The man took cover under a nearby umbrella, close enough to keep an eye on the woman, but with enough distance to signal that peace talks weren't forthcoming.

Then, as if that weren't enough, Lola watched as the little hussy tried to engage *her* target in conversation.

Women didn't compete with Lola, especially women who were less than physically perfect. They knew they would lose. This woman obviously didn't realize whose pool she was swimming in.

As Lola watched, Mr. St. Clair began to joke, laugh, his hand waving in the air. The woman's lips curved in a size 2X smile, the aura of gloom left her, and even the woman's previous companion was looking at her strangely.

He had taken a stranger under his wing. And not just any stranger, a woman who was less than pretty. What sort of magician was he that he could transform clouds into smiles? And more importantly, how was she going to get this, this *cow* away from him?

No, this was war. And you went to war with all the weapons that you had.

Her lips curved in a steely smile.

Lola called over to Carlos and ordered a cold bottle of beer, pretending to be overcome by the heat. Next, she sat upright in the beach lounger, placing the bottle deep in her cleavage, arching sensually, letting the icy cold droplets bathe her breasts in Technicolor splendor. Then she waited until she was sure that all eyes were focused in her direction and all conversation had ceased.

She didn't have to wait long. Slowly, lazily, as if she had all the time in the world—which she did—she unknotted one tie, then the other, slowly removing the bikini top with a subtle shimmy, exposing the two perfect globes that had never needed a plastic surgeon's knife. She froze for effect, even the ocean seeming to pause and watch.

Lola slipped her sunglasses down over her eyes and took out her bottle of suntan oil—not that she needed it.

Lazily, she poured the oil over one breast, rubbing the plump flesh, "accidentally" tweaking one dusky nipple in the process.

Round and round her hand went, a massage here, a caress there.

Her heart thudded as she went through the motions, dying to see if he was watching, but she knew that attitude was everything and so she continued.

She poured oil over her other bare breast, her fingers twirling in slow, seductive circles, her tanned flesh glistening nicely.

When she was done, she stood, Venus rising from the sea, well, actually the chaise, taking her beach bag with her. Acting as if unaware that every eye within a fifty-mile radius was watching her, she walked half the distance to where Mr. St. Clair sat, letting the sun rays heat her golden skin.

Not that it needed heating. Lola wasn't a huge believer in self-gratification—Hello! Not necessary when men were willing to kill to have you. However, this time she'd turned herself on, and there was a heavy pulse beating between her thighs.

Fortunately, there were other, more sociable ways to ease the ache. She spread out her towel, lay down, and then closed her eyes. Time to hope that Mr. St. Clair was ready to make his move.

There was a rustle of movement around her, and she nearly smiled with triumph. Instead she peeked open one eye and saw that eleven strange men had set up camp next to her.

Fools.

"Space, please," she said in her royal voice, not bothering to sit upright.

Of course the men picked up their towels in a big tantrum of motion and obediently moved away from her personal space. Even the flirtatious cow moved back to her original companion, leaving Mr. St. Clair alone.

The seconds ticked by, the sun beating down on her, no longer so pleasurable. The tension became overpowering, the seagulls laughing at her antics. For the first time in her life, Lola felt exposed. Flagrantly exposed. No, not her body, because she'd gotten over modesty long ago, but this uncertainty within her was new. This suspense, the waiting . . . as if she were a virgin again.

Then her skin tingled and a smile bloomed inside her. He was watching her. She felt the dark gaze poring over her flesh, and her nipples tightened with excitement.

Stay still, don't move.

"Sunburn would really hurt like hell," he said from across the sand. His voice quiet, but rough and uncultured. "Maybe if you used a towel . . ."

The man really knew how to kill a moment.

She jerked upright, lit up with some Molotov cocktail of desire, frustration, uncertainty, and anger.

She had pride, dignity, and best of all, looks. He flirted with Chunky Monkey, but when faced with a bowl full of exquisite French vanilla, he was telling her to cover up?

"I'm trying to enjoy the sun," she said with a tight smile.

"No, what you're enjoying is taking every man's balls and squeezing. Hard. Who was he? Did he leave you for somebody else?"

Her eyes narrowed, the flames of hell licking at her soul.

Insulting.

Her.

"I do not have a problem," she snapped, sounding just like a woman with a problem.

His mouth curved in a grin. "We all got problems, lady. Some bigger than others. But from where I sit, when a woman slinks over, flashing her highbeams in my direction . . ." He took off his sunglasses and gave her a long, thorough, toe-curling once-over, from thighs to breasts and then back again. "He really must've done a number on you."

The intimate gaze went far beyond anything she'd felt before. It was as if he were the one stealing souls, reaching deep inside her, farther than any man had ever touched.

At that moment she knew exactly how his touch would be, felt his hands caressing her breasts, yet he hadn't moved from his chair.

Lola let out one deep shuddering breath, thinking that perhaps Mr. St. Clair's seduction might be harder than she thought.

Damn her father. This was all one of his little games.

"I didn't mean to cause such a fuss," she said, the accompanying smile not nearly as faked as it usually was.

"Right," he answered with a laugh. "You want to keep your secrets, go ahead."

"Do you mind if I share the umbrella? It's getting so hot," Lola said, lifting the heavy fall of her hair off her neck.

His eyes flickered downward and again she felt the whisper of a touch. "Don't let me stop you, not that I'm sure I could."

She smiled innocently, scooting her towel in closer. He was miles away, sitting in his beach chair, but she could fix that momentarily. "I love the beach. It's like heaven should be, I think." She picked up a handful of the silky sand, letting it glide through her fingers.

"Yeah," he answered noncommittally, his eyes narrowing as he focused on the horizon where a dark cloud was forming.

"Are you here on vacation?"

"No."

"Business?"

"No."

"Talkative, aren't you?"

"Sometimes."

"Where are you from?"

"New York. You?"

She shot him a coy look from under her lashes. "Small world."

"And getting smaller by the minute. Look, I don't know what agenda you're working on, but I'd feel better if you didn't look at me like I'm a side of beef."

Lola's mouth fell open. Slightly. In an appealing way, until she realized what she was doing and closed it. "You really believe that's why I'm here?"

He looked her over. "Duh."

She stared down her nose, very snooty, very Continental. She did it well.

"Okay, so why're you here?" he asked, as if she wanted something from him.

Lola stared down at the ground, because to be frank, she was feeling something new—and uncomfortable. She'd heard the word was "guilt."

"I was lonely," she answered, picking up another handful of sand and pouring it over her thigh. "You looked lonely, too," she said, meeting his eyes.

She didn't think she'd made an effect, but then his breathing slowed, the rise and fall of his chest almost nonexistent. His easy

248

grin faded, his mouth a hard line, and in his dark eyes she could read each and every thing he wanted to do to her.

With her.

For her.

Lola gulped, floundering, four hundred years of composure shot to hell from just one little look.

His hands flexed, rough, large, capable.

Lola wanted to feel those hands on her. Badly.

"Are you lonely?" she asked.

His hands stilled and the promise in his eyes faded. "You don't know what you're doing."

"Yes, I do."

Sitting this close to him, she noticed something else. A force that radiated from him. Not exactly power, but strength. Safety. His shoulders were even bigger than she'd thought, his chest like a brick wall, a sprinkling of chest hair begging to be touched.

She blinked the thought away because there was no point in getting too sentimental or too attached to any man. Still, the feeling persisted.

Mr. St. Clair shook his head. "I'm going to walk away now. All you need to know is that it's hurricane season, the gypsy is dead, and my plane had an emergency landing. You look like a really nice lady. It's the smart thing to walk away."

"Why?"

"My ex-girlfriend was bipolar. She was suicidal."

"Did she succeed?"

"No. I stopped her. The girlfriend before that? Her parents were killed in a plane crash two weeks after we met. Are we getting the picture here? The list goes on."

He moved to stand, but Lola put a hand on his thigh. When she touched him, his jaw locked like a vise, the tendons in his neck stretched to breaking. But Lola held firm.

"But you took care of them, didn't you?"

He shrugged.

As if it were nothing. Lola looked at him with new eyes. People needed him and he didn't even realize. Fascinating. "Let's stay here," she whispered.

Their eyes met, and the air turned. Hot, heavy with musk. This was the world she knew.

Mr. St. Clair raised a brow. "There's a lot of people watching. Are you into that? I think it's very edgy myself, but I'm not sure—"

"No. Lower the shades," she answered with a slow smile. "They'll never guess."

"They might imagine," he said, unrolling the material.

"Let them," she said, watching him with impatient eyes as he efficiently sheltered them from the rest of the world.

He truly was a marvelous-looking specimen of man, his legs long and lean and bronzed by the sun. The cutoff shorts he wore hugged buttocks that could have been sculpted by the masters. And his shoulders . . .

Lola sighed.

They were shoulders that a woman could dig her hands into. Shoulders that held the weight of the world. Shoulders that could keep a woman safe.

Safe? Safety was irrelevant to an immortal. She didn't need safe. Still her eyes were drawn to the strength of him, the muscles in his back cording as he moved. There were some scars here and there. Like a soldier.

"Are you in the military?"

He sat cross-legged next to her on the sand, a hint of his cologne tickling her nose. "Not even close. Should I ask your name, or is this one of those times when I'm better off not knowing? In fact, don't tell me. I don't think I should know."

She took his large hand, discovered the worn calluses there, and smiled with delight. "Touch me," she said, her fingers discovering the width of his palm.

"Will you bring me luck?" he asked, something gleaming and desperate in his eyes. She had seen men desperate for her before, but not like this.

"Of course," she answered.

"I can't do this."

"You can."

"I'll hurt you."

What a strange idea, but Lola was touched by his concern. "No man can hurt me," she answered, fascinated by the lines on his hands. He had marvelous hands, large and warm. Rough. Yet his fingers were long and thin. A worker's hands, an artist's fingers.

Perfection.

"You don't even know who I am," he answered. "I could be a serial killer, a monster, a man responsible for more disasters than FEMA."

"No, I know you," she told him, and, staring into his eyes, she did know him. "You're steadfast. It's in your jaw, your mouth, your chin. You don't move from a task."

"Some people call that pigheaded."

"You're strong," she whispered, her hands exploring his biceps, tracing over the defined lines of his chest. His shudder thrilled her.

"Clumsy," he muttered.

"You're loyal," she said, placing a hand over his heart.

"A sucker," he answered, stilling her hand. "What about you? Tell me about you."

"I'm pretty," she said, because "beautiful" sounded too arrogant, and even if she was, she didn't want to flaunt it.

He nodded. "Yeah, you're easy on the eyes. And what else?"

"I'm determined. Focused. I always get what I want."

He grinned. "Always? Mighty sure of yourself, aren't you?"

She ignored that and tried to come up with more nice things to say about herself. After a momentary lapse, she thought up another one. "I take care of those around me," she said, rather proud of herself.

"Are you strong?" he asked, running his hands down her arms. "Or weak?"

"Always strong," she lied.

"Good or bad?" he asked, taking her chin in his hands, studying her face intently.

Her smile turned sly, because this one was easy. "Always bad."

He pulled her closer, so close that his chest just brushed against her own. Lola bit her lip.

"Lucky or unlucky?" he asked.

"Always lucky."

Then his mouth covered hers, gently, softly, a butterfly kiss from such a strong man. Lola was charmed by the idea of strength restrained. He was so careful, like she was something fragile, to be cherished, and a warmth blossomed inside her.

His hands tangled in her hair, pulling her closer still, until she was sheltered in his lap. She could feel his erection jutting between her legs and she realized with a shock that everything about this man was huge.

Her intentions turned urgent.

She deepened the kiss and heard his groan. He pressed her against the sand, his body covering hers, and his tongue began to tangle with her own. Back and forth he went, slow, seductive, a luxurious rhythm that her body knew well.

Mon Dieu, the man could kiss. For all of her life, she'd been waiting for this. To be swept away. To forget.

After four hundred very long years, Lola de Medici, master connoisseur of seduction, found herself being seduced.

Crash St. Clair knew he was going to burn in hell for what he was about to do, but sweet mercy, he really didn't care. She was perfect, all fire in his arms, all softness.

And so strong. Oh, merciful God, the woman didn't have a problem in the world.

He kissed her as if his life depended on it, because right now, if he didn't taste her, he was going to die. Keeling over from a hard-on the size of Alaska.

Her lips nipped against his neck and he heard himself growl, teetering on the edge of control, but he needed to be careful, so careful.

She rolled over, rising up over him like a conquering Valkyrie, and he took one breast in his mouth, tasting her coconut oil, the salt from the ocean, the spice that was her.

She threw back her head, her eyes glazed with pleasure. This strong and confident woman was this close to coming apart, and that was a sight he was primed to see.

Lola collapsed onto him, her body hot with sweat, feverish from Mr. St. Clair. Her heart was pounding as if she'd run a million miles, but he didn't let her rest. His mouth covered hers, so quietly, full of hope. She felt it, felt his lightness in her, even as her darkness inside him grew.

For four hundred years, she'd dealt with the hard realities of sex. Men took, woman gave, but this time, this was new. This wasn't just sex.

Lola almost stood, almost pushed him away. Maybe he deserved his soul, but then his mouth took her nipple in his mouth and began to suck and Lola's whole body jerked, like a string being plucked. His mouth was hard, the excruciating touch blurring her vision, fire burning between her thighs. She rocked against him, thighs locked around him, and ground her clit against his cock, a poor imitation of sex, but right now it was all she had.

In the back of her mind, she wanted to hold on to the madness, wanted to stave off the final joining. This man was different. Lola wanted to take each second and press it into her mind, keeping it forever.

Why?

His thumbs locked into the strings of her bikini bottom, and she protested, but he pressed a kiss against her lips and eased the material down her thighs.

She nearly cried out, because it was too soon. She wanted to wait, but her body needed to come. He rose up over her and stared, his eyes dark with lust.

"You are so beautiful," he said, tracing a finger down her breast, over her navel. "But you know that. Thousands of men have thrown themselves at your feet. Why do you hurt?"

For a second, the words cut through the madness, and she froze. "I don't hurt," she said, an edge in her voice. Frustration, desire. Pain. The vulnerability scared her, strengthened her resolve. Mr. St. Clair was not different from any man. Not different at all.

She pulled his head down for a kiss, then her hands drifted lower, finding the head of his cock emerging from his trunks. Not long now, she thought, as his moan cut through the quiet sound of their breathing.

But he pulled away, laughing. "Oh, honey. We've got all the time in the world," he said, and then he lowered his mouth to her breast, his tongue tracing a path in the oil, down low, lower, following the trail of his fingers. Following the trail of every nerve ending in her entire body. His hands parted the dark curls that covered the apex of her thighs, leaving her exposed to his gaze. And then, slowly, hellishly slowly, he inserted one long finger inside her.

Lola's heart stopped beating, she was absolutely sure.

His finger slid up, across her swollen lips, up, and then back. A gentle touch against her clit.

Lola's body lifted off the sand.

Mr. St. Clair laughed softly, but his finger stayed inside her. Wickedly inside her.

He moved back, slow, deliberate, inflicting all sorts of pain on her. All kinds of pleasure.

Her clit hardened, and he circled gently. Then not so gently, then gently again.

Lola's head thrashed to one side, and she closed her eyes, welcoming the rainbow of colors that lit the darkness.

His finger circled and traced, and then two fingers were inside her, and suddenly she couldn't think, could only whimper like a puppy, panting for each new stroke. Her hips rose, like a woman possessed, and each stroke was harder, more forceful than the last.

Then suddenly his fingers were gone, slipping out of her like thieves. Her eyes flew open, ready to protest, but then his hands cupped her bottom and his head bent between her thighs.

Oh, God.

She was going to die.

His tongue touched her, circled gently, seducing her into something she didn't want to feel. Her hands clung to his shoulders, nails digging into hard flesh. She, the seducer, was being seduced. The gentle licks turned canny, pulling her deeper and deeper into his world. Lola tossed her head from side to side, the climax building inside her.

She never lost control. She never screamed.

And now . . . she didn't care. For the first time in her long, long life, the façade slipped, and Lola was free. She fisted her hands and beat against him, and then the orgasm took over, starting at the base of her thighs, exploding in her mind.

Oh, God. Oh, God. Oh, God.

She was sweaty, she was oily and sandy, and who knows what sort of dirt was hiding in her hair, but oh, God . . .

"Quick on the trigger," he murmured, his face wearing a tremendous expression of pride.

Lola ran a hand over her face, trying to keep the world from falling off the edge of the ocean. "Not usually."

"That's all right. I like it. Makes you spunky."

She peeked up at him, intrigued by the softness in his voice. His eyes were so warm, velvety dark that danced with golden flecks of lights. Again the feeling of safety washed over her and she found herself smiling. Dirty hair, sandy back, slick with sweat. And she was really, truly smiling.

He lowered himself next to her, their bodies not quite touching. "What's your name? I have all these ideas in my head, but none of them exactly matches."

"Susie?"

He shook his head.

"Jamie? Ashley?"

He frowned. "No."

"Lola," she said, and he laughed.

"That's it, isn't it?" he asked and she nodded. "It's perfect." He bent and kissed her. "What is it about you? A shot of whiskey doesn't have a kick like this."

He pulled out a green clover from his pocket and crushed it into a tiny ball. "Don't need this anymore, do I?"

She studied his face, her finger exploring the line of his jaw. His eyes darkened, grew serious, and then he bent his head, kissed her softly, and again she felt like he was taking some part of her.

Their lips met, clung, and then she turned away.

"Stay with me tonight." He was asking, his eyes intent, probing. "We need a bed. And you'll need a shower," he said, one finger tracing over the oil and sand that coated her. "Maybe two."

Lola shivered with pleasure. She wanted him in her bed, and yet . . .

In the morning, his soul would be gone. That magic part of him that knew exactly how to clear away the clouds. She suspected he could clear away her clouds, too. Even now, the little time she'd been in his arms, she'd glimpsed a warmth she'd never known before.

She looked deeply into his eyes, dazzled by the strength there. In her life, she'd known many great men, seen how they ruled and how they commanded power. Yet here, inside Mr. St. Clair, there was power. True power. Not an iron fist, or a clever tongue that promised the world. His power came from within. He shone with it. The ability to handle whatever came his way.

She wanted to bask in that glow.

Part of her knew that it would be better to seduce him here, on the beach, wham-bam-thank-you-sir, get it over with and exorcise him from her mind. There were plenty of fish in the sea, but she wanted to hang on to this semblance of normalcy. Two lovers away from the prying eyes of the world, and the underworld as well.

Temptation warred within her, but the devil inside her began to laugh at her dreams. Her smile faltered and then blossomed again, stronger, harder, better than before.

She drew a hand down the strong lines of his body, cupping his hardness. "We don't have to wait." She moved in closer, breasts rubbing against him. "You don't feel like you want to wait."

His eyes closed and he pulled her against him. "God, you like to torture a man, don't you?"

"There's no need for torture," she whispered, her hands starting to lower his trunks. *Just get it over with, Lola. Just do it.*

Strong muscles flexed in his butt, and she took a moment to appreciate and explore. Everywhere she touched was hard, firm muscle. Butt, thighs that charmed her fingers.

She lowered the trunks an inch farther.

Cock.

Then a scream pierced the air.

Not hers.

Not his.

"Lo-laaa!"

Her fingers stopped their travels and she drew up his suit with not a bit of regret. Fate had taken away her choice, at least for a little while, and given her a few more hours to feel the soul of Mr. St. Clair. For a few more hours, Lola was going to enjoy it.

There were times when Crash wondered why he tried. The woman was in bad shape, crying on the beach like it was the end of the world.

He hoped he was exaggerating, because there was a nasty cloud gathering just over the water.

Lola handed the woman a tissue from her bag, doing her best to get the woman back to normalcy. "Dry your eyes, Angela. Blot gently, not a lot of pressure. Your mascara is running and the last thing you need is raccoon eyes on top of whatever is giving you fits."

She was something. Crash couldn't decide if Lola was a blessing or a curse. He'd never seen a body like that before, much less been *this close* to possessing it. Because he couldn't help it, his eyes drifted over curves now regrettably concealed by a cover-up. Damn fabric, should've been illegal.

His balls were paining him something awful, which seemed suitable punishment for almost losing his head. Literally.

The wailing woman's—Angela?—sobs got louder and Crash realized he was drifting.

"What's your problem?" he asked, trying to be nice, because she'd probably prevented another bad mistake.

Angela sniffed, pushing her hair from her eyes. She stopped for a minute and stared at him. "It's Tony," she said finally and then launched herself into his arms.

Awkwardly Crash patted her back, and noticed that another storm cloud was cooking up—this one in Lola's eyes. Trouble in paradise.

"What's up with Tony?" he asked Angela, ignoring Lola—mainly because he couldn't think when he looked at her.

"He went to Atlantic City with a friend of his from Rutgers. I had told him that he couldn't go—he's only twenty-one—but he knew that I was coming out here, with Lola, and he doesn't listen very well. Anyway, so they were doing really well—he said he was up by eight grand, but then . . ."

Her voice turned squeaky, she sniffed, and then she broke out in sobs. Again.

"Just tell the damned story, Angela," said Lola.

Angela lifted her head. "He gambled away the deed to the house."

"Can they do that in Jersey?" asked Lola. "I thought the law prohibited putting up a homestead as collateral."

Crash looked at her in surprise. *Where had that come from?* "By law, yes, but there are some financial dodges you can use to get around it. He went through a loan shark, didn't he?"

Angela sniffed and nodded.

"Why do you know so much about loan sharks and gambling?" asked Lola, eyes narrowed with suspicion.

Crash looked at her over Angela's head. "I've seen a lot of this. People get in too deep and then can't seem to find a way out."

Lola looked at him, something new, soft, and appraising in her eyes. "You helped them?"

Crash met her eyes, got lost for a moment, and then shook it off. "Not all the time. Some things are unfixable."

"You think this is fixable?" asked Angela hopefully.

"You can actually do something?" said Lola.

"We'll try," said Crash, because there were ways, but unfortunately, not every one was a happy ending. No, life really sucked when you got right down to it.

The woman looked up at him with googly eyes, and Crash sighed. You listen to a woman, tell her you can fix her problems, and bam, instantly they want to bear your children. There was something really wrong with the female brain.

Which was the wonderful thing about Lola. As far as he knew, she didn't have a problem, didn't have an issue, didn't have a pain or a terminal disease. No, Lola was perfect.

Suddenly the hairs stood up on the back of his neck. Crash looked around, but the skies looked calm, everything seemed fine.

From over at the edge of the beach, some kid began to cry, wandering in Crash's direction.

He handed Angela off to Lola. "Take her back to the hotel. I'll see you later."

The wicked green eyes didn't look happy, but she looked at the kid and nodded.

Right then, the late afternoon rain began to fall like clockwork.

"I'll see you tonight?" she asked, looking up at him.

She looked like a goddess, the sun glinting off her face, her eyes promising him the world, and he knew that most goddesses would kill to have her body. No, Lola was without a doubt the most beautiful woman he'd ever met, ever touched, ever kissed. She made him forget, and that was saying something, but right now, when he wasn't touching her, he knew better.

"Maybe," he answered. Not really an answer, but the afternoon was early. Who knew what disasters lurked just ahead?

"I'll meet you in the bar at eight," she said, as if she never doubted he would show. She led Angela away, but took one last, long look in his direction.

Crash couldn't help but stare, watching the long legs as she walked back to the hotel, heaven walking away. There was a woman, who was strong, could take care of herself. But God forbid, if Crash got ahold of her. They didn't call him Crash for nothing.

To prove his point, two cars collided in the hotel parking lot. Crash spied the remains of his good luck clover and picked it up, stuffing it back in his pocket.

Then he ran over to where the kid was sitting. The little rugrat looked up at him with big eyes, tears waiting to spill out, a hunk of glass embedded in the bottom of his foot.

"I want my mommy," said the kid, trying to be brave.

"Wait a minute. Did you see that out there?" Crash asked, pointing at the ocean.

"What?" asked the kid, his eyes searching the water.

"I think it's a penguin or something," he said, and when the boy's attention was diverted, Crash pulled the glass out of his foot. "Better?"

The kid managed a weak smile and nodded. Crash took off his T-shirt and wrapped it around his foot. "Now off to find your mom."

He hoisted the kid up on his shoulders and trudged up the beach. "Tell me about your mommy. Is she an elephant?"

The kid giggled. Kids were so easy. "No."

"Giraffe?"

"No. You're a silly man."

Behind him, the afternoon rain began to fall in earnest. Ahead of him, the most gorgeous creature to ever walk the earth would be waiting for him to make love to her. And he wasn't going to do it. Yeah, not a doubt in the world. He was a very silly man.

Chapter Three

Lola waited for forty-five minutes in the hotel bar before she realized that she'd been stood up.

If it hadn't been for the eighteen free drinks (she'd stuck with soda water) and twenty-two propositions, she might have wondered if she was losing her touch.

Instead, she wondered what Mr. St. Clair found lacking in her. She'd never known a man who could resist her. Well, there had been Cardinal de Noailles, but Christopher was no cardinal, and he was definitely no monk, either.

Tightly she crossed her legs, remembering the feel of him between her thighs. Not a monk. No way.

Yet instead of taking what she had offered, and what he obviously had wanted, he was standing down.

Why?

When he had helped Angela, she had realized what set Christopher St. Clair apart from every other man in the world, and God knows, she had known a *lot* of other men in the past four hundred years.

He cared. Not in that "what can I get out of it?" way that most men did. He simply saw something that needed to be fixed, and he acted.

Lola stirred the ice in her drink, trying to act like she was engrossed in the task, rather than sitting at a hotel bar alone.

Waiting.

"Can I buy you a drink?"

The businessman was classy, handsome, with tawny gold hair, even a dimple in his jaw. Not one flaw to be found.

"No."

He walked back to the table in the bar, and Lola was, once again, alone. When you were alone, it gave you time to think about your life, and Lola didn't like to think about her life. Better to live it than to analyze it. She liked to blame her father for her flaws, but at times like this, when the bar was buzzing with conversation that didn't involve her, when the music was quiet and calming, when no one was around to pay her compliments, or write sonnets to her beauty, she knew the truth. She chose her life. She seduced men, took their souls, because she wanted to stay beautiful and immortal. What was so wrong with that?

Okay, that was a rhetorical question. The mirror behind the bar showcased her in a far more brutal light. It'd been two weeks since she'd slept with a man, and already a wrinkle marred the perfect line of forehead. She picked up her drink, wanting to throw the glass at the mirror and shatter her perfect image into a million pieces. She couldn't. She'd never been strong.

Instinctively she looked around the darkened bar, searching for another victim, then she froze.

On the far side of the room, he stood. Standing, his hands stuffed in his pockets, watching her.

For a long while she stared, drinking him in with her eyes, not wanting to commit to a right or wrong. The conversation around her slowed, until it was nothing more than a soft hum. So soft she could hear the beating in her heart.

His strength brought low by her weakness.

He started toward her, and she nearly stood, nearly told him to run, but she couldn't move. Feelings shimmered inside her, rushing up, locking her in place.

Before this, the souls she had taken had never borne a name or a face. Now they did. Mr. St. Clair wore the face of the thousands of souls; he possessed their hearts. She'd never regretted seducing a man until now, and Lola wanted to weep.

He sat next to her and didn't say a word. He didn't look at her. She knew he couldn't. The minutes passed, time a meaningless concept, until she caught his eye in the mirror. A look was exchanged and Lola's heart shuddered with regret.

There was love in his eyes. Not lust, not obsession, not desire. Love.

Here was the one moment in the last four hundred years that she had waited for, that she had longed for, a dream so long buried that it had nearly died. He was the one good and noble man whom her soul had cried for.

It was odd to be sitting here, in an anonymous bar surrounded by strangers, and to know the truth.

Why him? Is that why her father had sent her after him? A cruel joke? To meet her fate and then destroy him?

"I didn't want to come," he said.

"I know," she answered quietly.

"I don't want to hurt you, and women always get hurt when they're around me." As he spoke, his fingers traced patterns in the wood.

She longed to touch him, quiet the storms inside him. "You're a good man," she murmured, like Diogenes reaching the end of his search.

He turned and looked at her. "I've tried. I've truly tried. But I can't stay away."

Lola took his hand, quieted the restless movements. She longed to tell him that he didn't have to stay away, longed to take him in her arms and lose herself inside him. It would be so easy. Her father had counted on her weakness.

Not this time.

When he looked at her, his eyes burned with pain. "You have the perfect life. Why aren't you the wife of a king or a senator or some business tycoon? Why me?"

"Because you're a good man," she said simply.

"I'm going to stay away from you, I think."

"Yes," she whispered.

"I should go," he told her, rising to leave.

"Yes," she answered stupidly, because she knew it was past time. Today she would beat her father's game.

"I wish I were someone different," he said.

"If you were, I wouldn't love you."

Her words registered, hung in the air like the final note in an aria. Lola didn't blink, didn't waver. Mr. St. Clair didn't look surprised. He knew.

They both knew.

Then he nodded once, and was gone.

Lola was alone.

Crash had a plane ticket for the nine o'clock flight out of St. Kitts. Only nine more hours until he would be gone, away from her.

He had spent most of the time drinking in the run-down cantina, no longer searching for Mama Leone. No longer searching for a cure for his curse. Oddly enough, now he was at peace. The world could fall around him and he had loved.

The afternoon sun was setting on the water, a ball of fire with a reflection so strong it turned you into a blind man. Crash looked into the fire and raised his glass to the heavens.

It didn't matter that they laughed at him. Lola loved him. That was what mattered.

Someone sat down next to him and he glanced over, thinking it was the reporter, or Angela. Mainly wishing it was Lola. Instead, there sat an old-timer who smelled like fish.

"Howdy, stranger," said the man.

Crash looked at him suspiciously. "You're talking to me?"

The man laughed. "Is there another stranger here? What's your problem?"

"I think that's my line."

"You're an odd one, aren't you?"

Crash laughed harshly. "Stupid is the better word."

"Let me buy you a drink. You look like you need it. Here you are in paradise, and instead of living it up, you look like you're in hell."

"You could say that."

"There's always a light at the end of the tunnel."

"Yeah, always darkest before the dawn. This too, shall pass. Tomorrow is another day. And my favorite: Cheer up, it's not the end of the world. Trust me, I've heard them all and repeated most of 'em."

"I think you could use another drink. Bartender, pour my friend something stronger than the piss he's been drinking."

The bartender obliged, and Crash found himself drinking his fourth scotch of the night. "You really don't have any problems?" he asked, wondering if Lola had released him from his curse.

The old man shook his head. "Nope, I'm too old to have problems. What's eating you?"

Crash stayed silent, staring deep into the gold liquid.

"Maybe I could help. You look like you could use help."

It was hinky, having someone else offer him help. Crash looked into the kindly blue eyes twinkling behind silver spectacles. Like the Santa Claus of the Caribbean.

"It's a woman? Whenever a man sits buried in his cups, there's a woman involved."

"Woman" seemed like such a clumsy word to describe Lola. She burned hotter than the sun, and shone brighter than the stars. For the first time in a long, long time, he had forgotten the weight of the world. He could focus on Christopher St. Clair, the man, not Crash St. Clair, the plague.

"I love her," he said simply.

"That's not love. That's lust."

Lust denied hurt a man in his balls. Love denied kicked a man in his heart. Crash rapped a hand against his chest. "No. I think this is love."

"Love doesn't exist."

"Boy, somebody did a number on you."

The old man stared into his glass. "Nah, with age comes wisdom. Love's for fools."

"Can't argue with that."

"So what makes her special?"

An odd question coming from a stranger. Crash felt the hairs prickle on the back of his neck. "What's with all the questions?"

He shrugged. "Don't know. You've made me curious. Wonder what I've been missing all these years."

Now *that* Crash understood. He'd been missing something for a while, too. "You ever have a bad day?"

The old man stroked his beard and nodded wisely.

"I have a lot of bad days, but she made me forget. It's like this huge weight that I don't have to deal with when she smiles at me."

"Good in the sack, eh?"

God, some people were just dickwads. "Never mind."

"But she's not here with you. You're either a bigger fool than me or else she left you for somebody. Two-timing harlots, all of them."

"No. It just didn't work out."

"Pshaw! Spoken like a coward. A man wants something, he should go after it. Where is she?"

"Here."

The man's eyes got big and he stared around the bar. "Here?"

"On the island."

"Well, go find her, then."

"It's not that easy."

"Of course it's that easy. You say you love her. You think she loves you?"

Crash nodded and the old man clapped his hands.

"You have to sweep her off her feet. Take her away, where she can't say no. Women love that."

"Maybe a long time ago. Modern women are a little more complicated."

The old man shook his head. "Trust me, son. Women don't change. Take away her options. Take care of yourself. Live. Love."

Crash laughed, because life wasn't that simple.

"You'd be surprised," the old man said. "Could be that if you were to go away to some solitary island paradise, just you and this woman you love, it might be just what you've been searching for your entire life. Your lucky charm."

"What are you saying?" asked Crash. "Who are you?"

The stranger shrugged. "I know more about you than you think."

"This will work?"

Santa Claus smiled. "Only one way to find out."

Crash nearly hugged the guy, and by nature, he wasn't a hugger Finally, to be rid of all this. He'd known Lola was the key from the first second he laid eyes on her.

He would take her away. He'd get Angela to help. After the phone calls he'd made to some Jersey financial types on her behalf, she owed him one.

Crash slapped some money on the bar and headed off in pursuit of life.

Back at the bar, the devil laughed to himself.

Mankind was such a simple species. He'd expected differently from his daughter, though. She had surprised him. But with a little push in the right direction, she'd play true to form. She was his daughter, after all.

Chapter Four

Lola came to slowly, her mind swimming through layers of cotton, until finally she was able to think. She was lying on something hard. A cot. God, she'd been in stables that were more comfortable than this.

Rain pelted the roof. Tin, from the sound it, machine-gun bullets assaulting her ears.

And the floor. The floor was rocking beneath her. Back and forth. Back and forth.

Water.

A boat.

Merde, she'd been kidnapped.

Now this was a first. She lay back down against the scratchy blanket, hoping it didn't have bugs. The nice thing about being immortal, imminent threat of death doesn't really scare you like it does everyone else.

She shook her head, bits and pieces coming back to her. Angela had given her a drink before bed, something to help her sleep, and that was the last thing she remembered.

Obviously she'd missed some important piece somewhere.

The boat looked like a fishing boat of some sort, the tiny cabin dark, flashes of lightning casting hellish shadows on the walls.

She had never liked storms.

The rocking increased in intensity and her stomach began to protest. Lola tried to rise, but her feet wouldn't move, and she collapsed back against the cot.

No need to worry. No need to worry. Everything was going to be fine. After all, she was immortal.

The wind picked up, howling like a banshee, the boat pitching from side to side, and water began to seep under the door.

No need to worry.

Thunder boomed, and a rush of water flooded under the door.

Okay, time to worry.

Lola crawled beneath the covers, which was the place she worried best, especially when in the middle of thunder and lightning.

Suddenly, she heard a sound. Wood creaking, scraping painfully aground.

The boat lurched and then the movement stopped.

Nervously she peeked from under the covers.

Outside the storm might be raging, but for the moment, the boat had landed.

Somewhere . . .

Crash donned the backpack with some provisions and made his way portside through the pouring rain to secure the anchor. The wind had been driving at fifty knots, and according to his calculations they were about three miles away from his intended destination. A blast of thunder rattled the boat, laughing at his plans.

Yeah, his calculations could be wrong.

Water splashed over his boots as he climbed below deck. He threw open the hatch, and saw a huddle under the blanket.

Lola. *Is she not awake yet?*

Dear God, Angela was just supposed to give her a double dose of NyQuil.

Crash rushed over and pulled the covers back to find Lola awake, but terrified, her teeth chattering.

Quickly he pulled her huddled mass into his arms. "It's all right. I'm sorry. I'm sorry. I'm so sorry."

She took a good look at Crash, her eyes widening, then cocked a fist and punched him in the nose.

Wham!

Crash rocked back on his heels, an archangel singing in his ear. He felt around his face, checking for blood.

Damn it, the woman threw one helluva punch.

"I hate storms," she said, lifting her chin, long dark hair streaming down her sheer nightgown, every shadow, curve, and line drawn with a loving hand. Impure, yet completely awe-inspiring thoughts revved through his head.

Whoa, really not the time. He grabbed the blanket and covered her up before his cock forgot that they were in the middle of what looked to be a hurricane.

"We need to get to shore and get out of the storm."

"Just get me off this ship."

"Boat."

"Ship."

"Shit. Okay," said Crash, lifting her into her arms before she could argue further. Then he climbed back above deck and out into the storm.

Rain pelted down, stinging against the skin like a mother, and he ducked low, covering her as best he could. The night was black, flashes of lightning cutting above the water, lighting it up like fireworks. But just beyond the shore, a line of trees and rocks promised some sort of shelter.

Hopefully.

Crash stepped into the water and then waded onto the shore. The sea bottom gave way to sand, and he plowed forward, moving carefully, dodging the low-hanging branches of the trees until they got to an overhang of rocks.

"Almost there," he yelled, trying to be heard over the wind.

He ducked underneath the edge of the overhang, easing her inside, then placing her carefully on the sand.

"Not the Ritz," he said.

"At least we're out of the storm," she said, her eyes losing some of their blurriness.

"I'm sorry," he said, then blew out a breath.

They were here.

Paradise.

Right.

It was a little while before Lola started to feel normal. Chris had started a fire, and she was warmer now. Outside the cave, the storm still raged, but she was safe and ready to get answers for the eighty million questions in her brain.

"So you kidnapped me?" she asked, shocked, *shocked* at what he had done, never admitting that a secret part of her was grinning inside.

The incredibly romantic fact was that Chris had kidnapped her and whisked her away to some tropical paradise (the fact that they were originally on an island paradise with modern amenities notwithstanding).

"It seemed like a good idea at the time," he managed. "I thought you'd be happy. Obviously there's a disconnect."

"I thought you'd be happy about it, too. Obviously there's a disconnect."

The rain had darkened his hair, his T-shirt soaked through. He looked wet, miserable . . . and completely edible.

She rubbed at her face, because edible or not, she'd made an agreement with herself to stay strong, and she was going to. "What is that smell? I feel like I've been hung over for three hundred years."

Chris threw a piece of wood on the fire. "NyQuil, I think. Here's some clothes," he said, pulling out a backpack.

She raised a brow and zipped the bag open. "This is my stuff."

"Angela helped."

The plot thickens. "My Angela?"

"Yeah."

She would have to give Angela a raise for that. With a suitable dressing-down, of course. "You're very persuasive with the females."

"A gift, a curse, depends on the day of the week," he said with a shrug, and possibly a flush running up his neck.

Lola stared, entranced. "Who are you?"

"I'm an accountant."

She stared harder, ignoring the flippant answer. "Really this time."

"I told you. Christopher St. Clair, accountant by day, bad meteorologist by night."

"I've never seen an accountant who was so . . . muscular."

"Lola, how many accountants have you met?"

"None."

He cast her a triumphant grin. Lola ignored it; there was something buried here and she cared enough to dig.

"Tell the truth. You didn't always want to be an accountant, did you?"

"Nah."

"So what were you supposed to be?"

"Cop."

"Now see, that makes sense. Why aren't you a cop?"

"Didn't work out," he answered, ducking her look.

"I think you'd make a good cop.

"It was a long time ago."

"And now?"

"I think the lesson here is never trust an accountant with a ship."

"Boat."

"See, you did pay attention."

"I don't mind," she said.

"Mind what?"

"Getting kidnapped." She rested her elbows on her knees and relaxed, staring into the fire. "Although the storm was wretched."

"I'm sorry. I had grand visions."

"Why did you do it?" she asked.

"I'm just a guy in love."

So many times she'd heard those words, and stomped all over them. Now they pierced her heart, precious, yet just as sharp as diamonds.

"We can't do this."

"Why?"

Because I won't let you give up your soul. "I'm not dressed properly."

He started to laugh. "You're kidding."

"No, I'm not."

"What's proper attire for making love, Lola?"

"My hair is a mess."

He sat down next to her.

"Your hair is glorious."

She pulled out a strand of seaweed and thrust it on the floor.

"I have other, more appropriate garments."

"And when we get back to the mainland, you can show them to me. In fact, I can't wait to see them. But right now, that blanket is pretty much the sexiest thing I've ever laid eyes on."

And he meant it. He didn't care that she was at her all-time worst physical state, even worse than when she'd slipped from her horse and had been dragged through half a forest. The French court had laughed for days.

His hand reached out to stroke her hair gently, calming her. "I have wrinkles," she whispered.

"Where?"

"Here," she said, pointing to the tiny crow's-foot at the corner of an eye.

He put his mouth against it. "It's a mark of character. I love everything about you. Even the wrinkles."

Lola met his eyes, saw everything she ever wanted, and promptly burst into tears.

"Aw, don't cry, Lola. I'm a schmuck. A lunatic. I'll take you back," Chris offered.

She looked up, aghast. "In this weather?"

"Well, no, once the storm passes. Right now, we're stuck. And

I actually am a good sailor, when it's not hurricane season. I thought if I took you away here, where other people aren't around, then bad things wouldn't happen."

Bad things. And he thought a storm was bad. Lola began crying again, because she couldn't explain anything to him. He loved her now, but would he still love the daughter of Lucifer, a woman who couldn't make love to him without stealing his soul?

She suspected that was a no, and she only cried harder. Loud, soul-racking sobs.

"What's wrong?" he asked, his voice close against her ear.

"You wouldn't understand," she sniffed.

He pulled her into his arms, and once again she felt that marvelous security. That warm feeling that everything would be all right. Right beyond the rocks, the wind lashed against the waves, but here she was safe.

"I won't understand unless you tell me," he said, his lips nuzzling her hair.

Lola snuggled closer, savoring his warmth. "Just hold me," she said, which she thought was a fine compromise.

"Sure," he whispered, his lips tracing kisses on her nose, her jaw, her neck.

She tilted her head to one side, loving the feel of the stubbled skin against her skin.

So big, so strong. She wanted him so badly, her hands curved into his chest, mainly because she could.

His chest felt so right to her, a coating of dark hair that teased her fingers. He was her port in the storm. His arms reached for her, and weakness took over.

His lips nuzzled against the neck of her nightgown, pulling it to one side, and she began to purr.

His mouth covered her breast on a sigh. Heaven. Slowly his tongue teased against her nipple, circling, building a symphony of pleasure inside her.

He lowered her onto the sand, and she couldn't think to protest. Her entire body turned to quivering mass.

His mouth moved to the other nipple, and she watched the dark head against her breast with tender eyes.

There were other men, who were wealthier, whose looks were more refined, but there was no other man who had a bigger heart than Chris.

She raised his face to hers, met his lips. Once, twice, showing him how she felt. Her tongue slid between her lips, drawing in and out, and his arms tightened like steel.

He growled, low and greedy, and she smiled at the sound. Then his body was on top of hers, covering her completely.

Paradise.

They fit so well together, heaven and hell.

Her hips rose to meet his hardness, cradling him there.

"Lola," he whispered, her gown giving way under his hands.

Oh.

It was a dream, an adventure, a fantasy that she'd never lived, and the world became a magical place.

Maybe she couldn't make love to him, but there were other ways.

Lola rose on top of him, her languid gaze drifting over the massive chest, the lean hips, and came to rest lower still.

He watched her, heavy-lidded, waiting to see what she would do next. She smiled with promise, her full lips closing over him, and Crash felt the pleasure explode in his brain.

Slowly, she sucked, drawing him in, and he knew he wasn't going to last long. But that wasn't the plan, and no matter how screwed up things had been, this was for her.

Drawing in oxygen to his lungs, to his brains, he rolled her underneath him.

"You're going to kill me," he whispered, "and I'm not done yet."

"We can't," she said, and he saw genuine fear in her eyes.

"Lola, do you trust me?"

She nodded.

"Everything's going to be all right," he said. "I swear."

He wasn't sure what she'd been through, but he could make the first time between them as perfect as anything. He drew a finger down her breasts, between her thighs. Slowly he parted her lips, finding her moist and swollen. He traced the flesh, back and forth, watching her face, watching her eyes, seeing the trust there.

"Do you like that?" he asked.

She opened her eyes, green fire burning inside them, and nodded.

"I could lie here, watching you forever," he whispered. It was the truth. She made him come alive, gave him joy, happiness. Things that he thought were outside his reach.

His finger went back and forth, and he added another, her hips matching the rhythm he played.

A place where her problems, her past, her future didn't exist.

Right now, it was a woman and a man. Nothing more. He increased the rhythm of his hand, and her head tossed from side to side. He pushed the dark hair back from her breast, and she looked liked some mermaid tossed up from the sea, bare in the sand.

Her moans grew more insistent and he knew she was close. Crash swallowed, nudged her thighs apart, and in one long thrust, was inside her.

Chapter Five

Mon Dieu.

Lola's eyes flew open, as she realized what she'd done. What they'd done, and oh, God, he was still inside her.

She pounded against his back.

"Open your eyes," she yelled.

He obliged, looked at her strangely. "Are you okay?"

"How do you feel?" she demanded.

Please, please, please . . .

"Good?" he said, still looking at her strangely.

"How good? Really good? Halfway good? Do you feel like something's, I don't know, missing?" she asked, staring into the depths of his eyes, searching, desperately searching.

He *looked* like he still had a soul.

"I feel excellent. Is this a test? How do *you* feel?" he asked cautiously.

"I don't understand," she whispered to herself, hearing the falling rain, the crash of thunder, the still beating of his heart.

"Lola? Shhhh . . . I don't understand either." And then he kissed her gently, calming, soothing, so tender she wanted to weep.

It was a miracle of some sort, but for now, she was going to feel.

He thrust inside her slowly, waves of heat warming her each time he moved. Deep and deeper still, until she felt him touch her heart. Never had she known this glow of emotion inside her, light threatening to spill over the darkness of her soul. It was frightening and thrilling and she gave herself up to it, to him.

Chris.

Her arms curled around his neck, feeling the power as he moved inside her, through her.

His eyes focused on her, dark and full of promise, and the rhythm quickened in intensity. Faster he moved, the world whirling around her, falling apart.

When he finished, their bodies joined together, Chris opened his eyes and stared at her full of love.

A miracle.

A single tear fell down her cheek and he kissed it away. This marvelous man who gave her everything.

Tonight, Lola was going to love.

Outside their tiny cave, the storm raged on, but inside Crash had finally found peace. He had found a woman who was strong, lucky, sexy as hell, and most of all, had no problems whatsoever.

Life was good.

He smoothed back the hair from her face. "Are you hungry?"

he asked. He wasn't, but they'd been at it for a while, and he didn't want to seem like a total asshole.

"No," she said, smiling.

"Tell me about you."

"There's nothing to say."

"Aw, come on. There's got to be something. Favorite color."

"Green."

"Flavor ice cream?"

"Chocolate."

"No shit?"

She nodded.

"Thing you're most afraid of?"

She didn't answer.

"Oh, come on. I mean, your favorite flavor is chocolate. How bad can this be?"

"You're right. I'm scared of storms."

He looked up, stared into the night. "Those sort of storms?"

She nodded.

Then he grinned, feeling confident for the first time. They'd survived the hurricane, made love, found shelter, made love. And the night was still relatively young. No, Crash was on top of the world.

"Don't worry. Got it all taken care of." Thunder rumbled in the distance, and then crackled closer still. The ground shook like a demon, and Lola looked at him in alarm.

"You're nervous, aren't you? No need to be nervous; I mean, what could happen?"

Boom!

The rocks on the ledge above him started to tumble and Crash launched on top of Lola, covering her.

He felt a thud on his back and then a shower of little rocks followed.

The ground stopped shaking and the rocks settled. Crash looked down at Lola. She was quiet in his arms, still, and her face was deathly pale.

"Lola?"

She opened one eye, then another, her gaze woozy.

"Oh, honey," he said, cradling her head to his chest. For a second he merely rocked her close, and then his medical training took over. At the back of her head, found the goose egg. "You're going to have a bump, but I think you'll live. How many fingers am I holding up?" he said, holding up two.

"Four," she said.

He looked at her in alarm.

"Gotcha."

"You're a wicked woman."

"A wicked woman who's hungry."

"I've got some food on the boat."

"Not for food, plebe. Come and perform your love slave duties."

Paradise.

The next morning, Lola awoke like a kid on Christmas morn. This was it. The real test. The moment she'd waited four hundred years to see.

Chris was still asleep, dark lashes shuttering his eyes. He held her tightly in his sleep, as if he couldn't bear to let her go. Lola didn't mind. Didn't mind at all.

However, she really wanted him to wake up.

She coughed, and still he slept. She sighed and still he slept. Her hand slid down his body, circling his amazingly unsleepy erection for a man who wasn't awake.

A smile curved on his lips.

The cad.

"You're awake?" she asked and held her breath.

One eye opened and looked at her. Then the other. Two brown eyes. Full of love, full of soul.

Oh.

"Why are you crying, Lola? You gotta know that I really don't like that. I mean, it's really not fair to men, don't you think? We just sit here like lumps, and you're all falling apart and shit, and we want to do something, but—"

Lola pulled his head down and kissed him.

Paradise.

For breakfast there were energy bars and some bottled water.

"You thought of everything," murmured Lola, crunching through oatmeal and raisin.

"You making fun of my culinary talents?"

"Do you have any?" Lola asked.

"Nary a one. You?"

"Nada."

"We'll starve," he said with a happy sigh.

"But you do have other, more redeeming talents," Lola reminded him, just in case he didn't know.

He quirked a brow. "Again?"

Lola shrugged. She wasn't normally so . . . well, horny, to be frank, but she'd never slept with a soulful man more than once before. It was more perfect than a concerto, more soothing than any sonata.

She looked at him, her big, strong Adonis, and right on cue, his cock began to grow. "That's what I like about you most."

He looked down. "This?"

"No, your dependability. It's very reassuring."

It was more than reassuring, it was perfect. And as if the island weren't perfect enough, there was a small lagoon, fed by a waterfall. The water was cool and clean, and tiny white flowers grew around the edge. Christopher St. Clair was quite the water aficionado, she learned.

He dove under the water, playing shark, grabbing her leg and pulling her under. Of course, he didn't realize who he was messing with. Lola got him back by diving under and swimming back and forth between his legs, catching him in her mouth when he was lucky.

They swam and kissed and bathed. And Lola realized that this was love. This is what drove artists mad, why women burned themselves on pyres, why wars were fought, why men and women traded their souls. All in the name of this joyous madness called love.

She swam through the warm water, letting the spray from the waterfall splash on her face, when suddenly she felt a stinging cramp in her leg. Lola floundered in the water, confused by the sting. She never felt pain. Never.

Chris pulled her in his arms and brought her to the edge of the lagoon, laying her on the soft grass.

"Lola? What happened?"

"Bit. Hurts. Like. The. Devil."

He touched her leg, and she saw an angry red welt.

"It's a jellyfish, I think." He grabbed some pills from his backpack.

"Tylenol?"

"Yeah."

Lola popped the pills in her mouth and swallowed them. Eventually the pain subsided and Chris was pacing on the bank, back and forth.

"This is my fault."

"You have mind control powers and caused the jellyfish to bite me?"

"You don't understand."

Lola looked at his face, and for the first time, saw fear in his eyes. "These things happen," she told him, trying to calm him.

"First the storm, then the rocks, now the jellyfish. These aren't accidents," he muttered.

Just then, Lola put it all together. "No, they aren't accidents."

Quickly she pulled on shorts and a T-shirt.

"I know how to fix this. I'll be right back."

Chris knew the trip had been a mistake; anything that seems too good to be true always is. He wasn't sure how Lola thought she'd fix this, but it'd never been his way to let anyone else take responsibility for a problem that was well and truly Chris's own.

He gathered up their stuff and checked out the boat for the return trip.

"Daddy!" Lola tramped through the jungle, past the rocks and trees to the places where the snakes hung out. That's where the devil would be.

"Daddy!"

"No need to bellow, Lola. My hearing is still better than average."

He was sitting on the rock, clad in a Savile Row suit, examining his nails, as if he nothing mattered, which, of course, it didn't.

"Leave us alone," she said, quietly, with dignity. Better to start out that way, and then go downhill as necessary.

Her father looked at her, all innocence. "I'm not doing a thing."

"The storm, the rocks, the jellyfish."

He held up innocent hands. "It's an ocean. The jellyfish have free will about whoever they choose to bite."

"Whomever."

"Whatever."

"Why don't you quit playing games?"

He threw back his head and laughed. Deep and satanic. For four hundred years she had waited for this man to pay attention to her. To love her.

Merde.

What a fool she had been.

"The games begin when you leave the island," he said, crossing one elegant leg over the over.

"What do you mean?"

"Don't you wonder why he still has his soul?"

Lola smiled, because this one she had figured out all on her own. "Because of true love. It's the most powerful magic. Ever."

The devil just laughed. "Dream on. It's this island. This particular island, Lola. Your Mr. St. Clair has a special affinity to this place and some of your more . . . shall we say, insidious . . . powers don't work here. But once you leave here—poof."

"I don't believe you."

"Go ahead, go off the island. Pick another island. Any island. Fuck the poor fool somewhere else. See what happens? It's only a soul."

She didn't want to believe him, but she didn't dare not.

"It doesn't matter. We don't have to leave here."

"Ah, yes. The powerful magic of true love. Just wait until those wrinkles start to show. And what's that I see on your thighs, darling Lola? Cellulite?"

Lola looked down at her thighs, realized what he was doing, and shook her head. Oh, no. Not this time.

"Leave us alone. And I don't want to be having any more"—she held up quote fingers—"accidents."

"Then you'll have to find a new boyfriend, darling."

"If you think I'll believe that Chris is behind all this, like something that one of your minions would think up, uh, no."

"He doesn't mean to do it. Your Christopher St. Clair is quite the special man. Bad things follow him."

"Why?"

"I'll never tell. You take his soul, you cure his curse."

"Go to hell, Daddy. Oops. Can't, can you?"

"You've grown bitter, Lola. How did that happen?"

"Don't pull that father-daughter bullshit with me. You're four hundred years too late."

"Ah, the power of true love."

"You know, Daddy, for so long I would hang on every moment we spent together. You ignored me and it was like the worst sort of hell. No more. We're done. We're through."

"What? You're cutting me out of your life?"

"Finis."

"You don't want to do that, Lola."

"Good-bye, Daddy."

"Lola! You'll regret this."

Lola never looked back.

Crash had just finished packing the boat when Lola returned. "Lola, we need to talk."

"Don't worry. This time I took care of everything. Some of this is my father's doing." When he looked at her face, he saw the anger in her eyes, the tight line of her jaw.

"No, Lola. It's me."

She just laughed, as if he'd just told the world's biggest joke. "No."

"Yeah."

"Everything's going to be fine," she said, swatting at the buzzing mosquito that landed on her arm.

"You'll get hurt. I'm dangerous."

"I can top that," she answered, hands on her hips, looking like she owned the world.

"This isn't a game. It's over. If anything happened to you . . ."

"You can't hurt me, Chris. I'm—" She stopped in midsentence, her face pale.

"What?"

"Nothing. But you can't hurt me. Trust me."

It was just one more stake in his heart. This was exactly why he loved her. She was so stubborn, so sure that she could handle whatever life threw at her. Crash knew better.

He swallowed air, then gathered his courage.

Easier to rip off the Band-Aid with one clean jerk.

"I didn't want to say anything, Lola, and you know, it's been really nice. You're obviously really great on the eyes, but, uh . . . the weekend's over. Time to pack up. You back to your life, me back to mine."

The faith in her eyes dimmed a little. "You're just saying that."

"It's time to join the real world. We gotta get off this island. Paradise doesn't last. Nothing lasts."

"Stop it, Chris. You can't desert me. I'm beautiful. Men love me."

"Well, you know, I didn't want to say anything, but the sun is really doing a number on you." He rubbed against her cheek. "You were right about the wrinkles."

For a second she stared, as if he'd pulled the blood from her veins. Then her face squeezed up and his heart shattered into pieces.

This was for the best.

"No!" she screamed and then threw herself at him. "You don't mean it. He told you to do it, didn't he?"

"Who?"

"My father."

"Whoa, Lola, darling. You're losing it, sweetheart. It's just us two here."

"You don't understand," she said, and then fell to her knees, tears streaming down her face.

Crash looked away. He couldn't watch this. Not with her.

"I'll pack up the boat. Grab your stuff from the cave. Maybe we could get a beer sometime," he said, turning so that she couldn't see his face, and quickly he swiped at his eyes.

He had seen so much pain in the world. But nothing compared to the hot blade tearing at his insides. Her cries blared in his ears, like the horn of a freight train screaming down the tracks, but he ignored it.

He didn't have a choice.

Back on the mainland, Crash found himself back in the welcoming arms of the cantina. Damn this curse. What had he ever done to deserve it? Hell, he didn't even know where it came from. He'd been born, and there it was.

"Are there any other gypsies on the island? Maybe Mama Leone had a relative? A cousin or someone that tinkers . . ."

The bartender picked up a glass and began drying it. "You be needin' some magic, mon?"

The glass dropped from his hand and shattered.

"You could say that," answered Crash.

The bartender stared at his hand. "It's been paining me, not sure what's happening."

"Look, I'm sorry about your hand, but can you help me with the gypsy?"

"We don't have gypsies on St. Kitts other than Mama Leone. The police say it hurts the image, so every now and then, they crack down. Whoosh. No gypsies. Sorry, mon."

Crash smiled. "Not a problem. Give me some whiskey, will you? Double."

"You still having your woman troubles?" The old Santa Claus settled himself on the neighboring bar stool, joints creaking.

"Your little solution didn't work."

"What's the problem now?"

"What do you know about me—what do you know about the curse? Is it a curse? Tell me. Anything. Just give me some idea of why my life is hell. . . ."

Santa Claus gave him a smile. "A long time ago, there was a line of saints. St. Christopher, protector of the lost and the troubled. He was a large man, a giant, and when people had no place else to turn, they were drawn to him, drawn to his strength. The man found a wife, who gave him a son. And his son inherited his unique gift, as did his descendants. The history of the family was long forgotten, but there is always a first-born male of the family who carries on."

"Why are you telling me?" asked Crash. But he knew.

"You're one of his descendents, Chris. You're not happy?"

"Oh, come on, don't I look happy?"

The old man laughed. "It's not a curse you and your father were blessed with. It's a gift. You don't want it?"

Crash thought for only a second. "What do I need to do?"

The devil looked at Crash and smiled. Mortals were so predictable. "It's easier than you think. You need to try again with Lola," he said, then proceeded to tell Crash what to do.

Back in Lola's hotel suite, Viktor looked at Lola and tsked in disapproval. "Look at what the sun has wrought. Did you forget your moisturizer when you went on your little jaunt?"

"Go to hell," Lola snapped.

"Someone's in a mood," he said.

Lola glared.

"I'm only trying to help."

"Go away. I want to be alone. Can you all just let me alone?"

Fernando snapped his fingers. "The queen has spoken," he said. He gave her a long look. "Are you sure?" he asked quietly.

Lola nodded and they left her room. Lola was alone. She walked to the bathroom, looked in her mirror. The days she had gone without taking anyone's soul were starting to show. There were lines there, nothing major, but when you were used to perfection, every little bit hurts.

She could go down to the bar, pick up a man, have her wicked way with him, and everything would be back to normal. She raised her chin, let the hardness settle back in her eyes, and then made her decision.

Just then, she heard a knock at her door.

"Go away," she yelled to the world in general.

"Look, I don't think that's fair. You haven't heard me out and I think I deserve to be heard out. I was a jerk. But I had my reasons, and I think you should hear my reasons. Unless you don't really love me."

Chris.

No.

Lola walked closer, love warring with pain. Because she had never been strong, she opened the door. "What do you want?" she said, using her most unforgiving tone.

"Can I come in?"

Lola looked at the room, the bed that beckoned like a huge elephant in the middle of the room, and knew that was a bad idea. "No."

"Okay, that's fair. But you have to listen."

"I don't."

His mouth hardened and his jaw set. She knew the look, this was Chris at his most stubborn. "Okay, you don't. But you should."

No, she shouldn't, but she would. "Go ahead."

"You can't leave," he said, his hand touching hers.

Run away, Lola. Run away now.

She shook off his hand as if it burned. And it did. "Yes, I can. I don't think I need an asshole to tell me I can't."

"I'm not a real asshole, Lola. Only a pretend one, and that was to keep you from getting hurt."

"Did a great job with that."

He had the good sense to look ashamed. "I want to be with you. Forever."

At the word "forever," Lola stopped, all the pretend-anger washed away. The reality was so much worse. "That's not a good idea."

"Why?"

"We just can't."

"That's a very defeatist attitude, Lola. I think we could work it out."

Lola backed up into her room, because suddenly he was offering her things that she didn't want to think about. Things she knew she couldn't have. The devil might be lying, but maybe not. "The island is a world apart from the real one."

"Then let's go back to the island, Lola."

"You can't stay in paradise forever," she said, but in her heart, she knew that she could. If that was the only way, she'd do it.

"Yes, you can."

She couldn't believe what she was hearing. "What are you doing?"

"I'm fixing my life. I'm doing whatever I need to do to be happy. And that's you, Lola. You make me happy."

Oh, dear heaven. She closed her eyes, imagining things she'd never let herself imagine. When she opened them, he was there. Strong, steadfast, reassuring.

"You didn't mean all those things you said? Because I have to tell you, they really hurt."

"I'm sorry, Lola. I had to say them. I was the worst thing that ever happened to you."

"And you didn't mean them, right?"

"Are you kidding? Do I look like the superficial, judgmental type?"

She looked over the khakis, the scuffed-up loafers, the tousled brown hair that had never met a stylist. "No."

"You know me better, Lola. You know me better than anyone. Hell, no one ever cared about knowing who I was before. They just needed me, but in one instant, you *knew*. Like I knew. You are the only person in the world for me. All my life, I saw the worst part of magic, a curse, whatever the hell it was. But with you? You make it disappear. You make the weight disappear. I've never felt like this before, and I can't lose it. I won't."

How was she supposed to resist him? Yet fate had given her a solution. "The island? It has to be the same place."

"It'll be romantic," he said, pulling her close.

She cast a fearful glance at the bed. "No kissing until we're uh, not here."

Chris pressed a kiss against her hair, but did put her safely away. "Whatever you want, it's yours."

Lola looked up at Chris and smiled.

Paradise.

The trip to the island was quick, so quick that her doubts couldn't fester inside her. Because she had doubts. A man and a woman couldn't stay locked away from the world forever. He would get bored with her. A quick glance in her compact mirror had shown the tiny lines around her eyes growing bigger. No matter what he had said, she didn't believe that once her body started losing its glow, he wouldn't want to look somewhere else. Who could blame him?

"Ready?" he asked, holding out a hand.

She looked at the shore of the island, looked up in his eyes, and knew it was now or never.

"Ready," she answered.

For now, this was all she had.

It was a night for the angels. Crash was prepared. No hurricanes, no jellyfish. He had brought wine, cheese, even a blanket where they could lie and watch the stars. Tonight he just wanted to see the stars in his eyes.

"You know that I would do anything to be with you, Lola," he said, smoothing back her hair from her face. She looked anxious, but she didn't have anything to fear. Not anymore.

"Anything," he said. He closed his eyes, and their bodies were joined.

Magic had never felt so good.

Lola knew instantly something was wrong. She pounded against his back. She could feel the energy inside her, feel her body recharge. "Chris!"

Dear God, her father had lied.

"Chris," she said, and pushed him away. Maybe it wasn't too late. Maybe she could undo this.

"What have you done?" she yelled, jerking his face up until she could see his eyes. Wanting to see his beautiful, love-filled eyes.

He blinked twice, absently. "I wanted us to be together. It was the only way."

Non, non, non . . .

"What did you do?"

Chris looked at her blankly, with soul-free eyes. "We're on a different island."

Chapter Six

Crash took her back to the mainland. The ride back was pretty quiet. She was still hopping mad, but she would get over it.

What did a soul really matter in the end?

After he docked the boat at the marina, Crash tempted the fates and they walked together down the main boulevard. All was quiet. The weather peaceful, not a cloud in the sky.

What was not to love?

Crash gave Lola a quick squeeze, but she was tight with anger. No matter. This was for the best.

They sat by the pool overlooking the beach. Flowers were everywhere, and for once, nothing was falling over, no disasters on the horizon. No one was crying. Everything was quiet. For once, Crash was at peace.

Lola picked up her glass of champagne and studied him.

"He told you who I was?"

"Yeah."

"It doesn't bother you?"

"Did it bother you that trouble dogged me like a bitch in heat?"

"No."

He raised his glass. "There you go."

Over in the corner of the pool, an old man watched the world with sadness in his eyes. Crash waited to see what the old man would do next.

"What does it feel like?" she asked.

He thought for a second. "I don't know. Everything's nice."

"Nice?"

"Yeah. Not great, but nice."

He really didn't remember what great was anymore.

"What about me?" she asked.

"It's all nice," he said automatically.

He could see her frown and he knew that he'd said the wrong thing, but he didn't remember the right thing anymore.

He was mulling this over when he saw the reporter—Marjorie—walking toward him. His heart stopped for a minute.

Her face when she approached was all smiles. "Crash?"

He stood up. "Is everything okay? You're not, like, gonna slit your wrists or anything?"

She laughed. Laughed? "Oh, no. Everything's really great. The manager at the hotel gave me this great lead for a story on this kid who had lost his parents during the hurricane. And then his dog disappeared, too. Real heartbreaker. And then, the lifeguard from the beach braved fifty-mile-an-hour winds just to save the little puppy, who was clinging to a raft on the water. It was amazing and the Idaho networks ate it up. In fact, the New York stations picked it up, too." She winked. "I'm a star."

"Oh," answered Chris. "That's really nice."

"Yeah. Great seeing you. Have a nice day!"

And then she was off, ready to chase whatever bad news was about to break somewhere else, because it sure wasn't about to break near him. Not anymore.

He rubbed his heart.

He sat back down next to Lola and looked up at the sky.

"Do you think that's a storm cloud?"

"No, don't think so."

They shared another couple of drinks, enjoying the quiet, and Angela showed up.

Crash stood up, and pulled a hankie from his pocket. Just in case. He waved it in Angela's direction.

"Everything okay?" he asked.

She laughed. "Peachy—better than peachy. I've been talking to this new accountant in Jersey. You wouldn't believe this guy. Leon Berkhower. Oh, man, he's a whiz with the legal stuff. Tony is doing so much better. Leon even got him in a twelve-step program." She began to blush. "He even offered to take me out when I got back home."

Lola smiled politely. "I'm very happy for you, Angela."

"Oh, thank you, Lola. If not for you, I wouldn't have met Chris, and if not for him, I wouldn't have known to call Leon."

Crash nodded. "Peachy."

After she left, Crash heaved a heavy sigh. Life slowed down when everything was perfect. He picked up Lola's hand and rubbed his thumb against her palm. Not because he wanted to, but because he knew he was supposed to. He knew what it was supposed to feel like, but it didn't.

Eventually he stopped.

Together they watched the perfect sunset on the perfect beach. Hell.

Lola was miserable. After a perfect dinner at the hotel's five-star restaurant, Chris took her up to the lovers' suite. They made love for several hours. Chris was attentive, with perfect technique, and even went down on her for forty-five minutes, bringing her to orgasm five times.

Peachy.

But Lola still couldn't sleep. Oh, yeah, now she'd won. She would be beautiful forever. She could go out and make love with any man in the world and he would keep his soul. Yippee!

Any man in the world, except for the one man that she wanted.

She rose, padded to the bathroom, rooting around until she found some NyQuil. The stuff packed a great punch. Even for immortals.

In the bathroom, the full-length mirror beckoned. She saw herself there, no wrinkles, her nude body Playmate perfect, no airbrushing needed. She smiled, but her eyes were flat, soulless, and no amount of airbrushing could fix that.

She picked up the bottle of NyQuil and threw it at the mirror, letting it shatter into a million pieces, cold syrup running out over the floor.

Chris pounded on the bathroom door, his voice urgent. "Lola? What was that? Did you hurt yourself?"

"I dropped a glass in the sink, Chris. Go back to sleep. I'll call maintenance. They can fix it. They can fix anything."

She found her father lounging on the beach, sipping a piña colada with a set of blonde twins next to him.

"I need to talk to you."

The devil nodded at the girls. "Come back in fifteen minutes." He took a good look at Lola's face, angry and tight. "Better make that five."

After they left, he gestured to the empty beach chair next to him. "Take a seat."

"I prefer to stand."

"Oh, get over yourself, Lola. You won, congratulations. Hell is all yours."

"I don't want it."

"What do you mean, you don't want it? I'm retired; somebody has to take over. You won. It's yours. I didn't think you had it in you. Actually, it's Mr. St. Clair who had it in you, I suppose."

Lola slapped him. Hard. The mark didn't even show.

"Pity," she said.

"Why are you here?"

"I want you to give Chris his soul back."

"Here at hell, we use our own variation of the Pottery Barn rule: you steal it, it's yours."

"Please."

"My little girl is begging? Quick, grab the cameras."

"I want you to give Chris his soul back," she repeated stubbornly, because she was not going to be baited by her father. Again.

He studied his manicure, blowing on his nails. "And what will I get in return?"

"Hell. It's yours. Take it. Throw a party. We'll have confetti. And champagne. Hell's Grand Reopening."

"Very cute."

"Come on, it's a great deal. What King of the Underworld, what Prince of Darkness, what Speaker of the House of Hell wouldn't just jump all over that?"

"Okay, okay, okay," he said.

Her heart began to lift and for the first time Lola felt hope.

"You don't want hell, I'll take it," he continued.

"And Chris gets his soul back?"

"No."

"Fuck you, Daddy."

"Tsk, tsk."

"Please," she said. She needed to remain calm and in control. There was only one person who could fix that, and unfortunately it happened to be Satan.

"Why didn't we ever spend more time together?"

"You were always too busy. You had all those other children that were somehow more important than me. None were better looking," she added.

Her father laughed. "I shouldn't have ignored you."

"No."

"I should do something to make it up to you."

"Yes," she said, refusing to hope this time.

"Why don't you run hell with me, Lola? I really do want some time off. And think of all those men that you can screw to your heart's content."

It was too much. It didn't matter if Chris didn't have his soul back. They could still be together. She could get used to nice.

Maybe.

Never.

Lola turned to go.

"There might be one thing . . . ," the devil whispered, his voice carrying just above the surf.

Lola froze.

"What would you be willing to give up?" the devil asked, dark eyes dancing.

"Whatever you want."

"Your looks? Lola, beautiful, baby Lola, are you willing to trade the face that kings have died for in exchange for the soul of a mere mortal?"

"Mortal" seemed such an ordinary word to describe Chris. Lola smiled. "Not just any mortal. He needs his soul. He needs to help people. People need him."

"You need him."

"He needs it back. He needs his old life. It's part of who he is."

"Idiot," said the devil, but she knew he was softening. If there was one thing Lola knew, it was men.

"You'll do it?"

"You'll give up your looks?" he asked, with a curious half smile.

"Will I be ugly?" For the first time, Lola contemplated life without her beauty. It was like losing an arm, only worse.

"You'll be mortal. No long life. Wrinkles."

"Will I be ugly?" she repeated.

"I'm your father, not a monster. No, my darling. You'll just be . . . average."

Lola nodded. Anything was better than nice.

Her father's dark eyes began to gleam with mischief. "What if he won't love you if you're not beautiful?"

Ancient fears pushed at her, prodding her, but she stayed strong. "Do it."

"But how would that be? Sacrificing yourself and then he's off with some perky-breasted blonde saving the world from a tornado?"

"*Do it.*"

"Okay." The devil held up a hand. "No, I think I need more."

Lola sighed in frustration. "What?"

"You have to give up Chris."

"What do you mean?"

"My, we are slow on the comprehension station. You. Give. Up. Chris."

"I can't see him again?" she said, because this was worse than losing her looks, or losing her arm, or losing her life. This was cutting out her heart.

"Never," said her father.

"Ever?"

"Never, ever, forever and ever, amen."

Quickly, get it over with. "I'll do it."

"You'll do it?" he said, his voice surprised.

"Yes."

"How did I spawn such an idiot?"

"I love him."

"There are those words again. Good God, can we get rid of the love rainbow and all the little ponies and unicorns that go along with it?"

"Do it."

"All right. But you'll be mortal and average," he said. "No man to keep you company late at night, when the wind gets cold and the sheets get even colder."

"I'll manage."

"Ha. Lola, you couldn't manage an ant colony."

"Good-bye, Daddy."

"Call the girls back, will you? I can't believe my retirement is over, and just when I was starting to get the hang of all this."

That afternoon, another hurricane blew in, the window glass in the hotel shattering all over. Crash immediately felt the change. Everything was normal again. People were screaming in fear, cars colliding with each other, there was pain and suffering everywhere.

He rubbed against his heart. Yeah, it was back.

Instantly he was back in the groove. Barking out orders, leading people to safety, leaping buildings with a single bound. Okay, maybe not that, but he felt like he could. Right now, he felt like he could fly.

He had just gotten the fourth floor evacuated, and was running back through the lobby, when he saw Angela carrying a suitcase. "Where's Lola?"

Angela shook her head, her eyes looking at him with pity.

"Where's Lola?"

"Don't ask me."

"Where's Lola?"

"She's got to leave."

And then it dawned on Chris exactly *why* things were back to normal. "She did this?"

Angela looked confused. "The hurricane?"

Oh, God, he needed to find her. Now. "She did this for me. Where is she? I have to talk to her."

"I can't, Chris."

Angela turned and ran out to a waiting car. The rain was pouring in sheets, turning the world a dark shade of gray. Through it all, he saw Lola's face. Then he remembered how it felt, how love felt.

"*No!*"

She raised a palm to the window, and then the car drove away.

Over the roar of the wind, over the howl of sea, the sound of Crash's pain carried.

Lola closed her eyes and wept.

Chapter Seven

A woman could adjust to having an average face, but the bat wings of flesh that she developed under her arms gave her fits. Every morning Lola exercised, but the two pieces of droopy skin never got any better.

And neither did the ache in her heart. Her father had kept his word. She wasn't ugly. She wasn't pretty. The word most often used was "nice." Life could be cruel that way.

She moved to upstate New York and found a job as a waitress in a tiny one-café town. If the world noticed the disappearance of Lola de Medici, no one commented. No, the world had moved on without her.

She actually enjoyed her job because it kept her busy, kept her from thinking, and she was hardly ever alone. Except at night, and NyQuil worked equally well on mortals as well as immortals.

During the day, she bustled around the café, carrying coffee, making small talk, and in general, surviving.

Her boss, Mary Margaret Taggert, was a little white-haired widow who called her customers "Honey" to their faces and "Jackass" behind their back. Lola understood.

In the fall, the tourist season kicked in. The colors started to change along the Hudson, the trickle of customers becoming a flood. The wind began to blow more and more from the north, and sometimes in the afternoon, a thundershower would burst up from nowhere.

It was just such an afternoon when the coffeemaker broke and Mary Margaret was swearing like mad. Lola was doing her best with instant coffee, but the customers weren't happy, and when they ran out of Mary Margaret's homemade scones, well, you would think the world was about to end.

In fact, Lola was just about ready to tell off the mayor of Philipstown, when the wind changed direction and began to howl. Then a pinging sound began.

"Hail!" wailed the mayor.

Lola went back in the kitchen to get a pan of muffins, and she tripped and fell over the mayor's umbrella.

Her eyes were even with a pair of loafers. Brown loafers on extra-large feet.

Scuffed-up loafers.

Heavens.

She didn't want to hope, but Lola had always been weak.

She raised her gaze an inch higher. And higher still. Long, long legs that seemed to go on forever, and the blue jeans that loved them. Her heart began to beat a little faster and she climbed to her feet.

The shirt had definitely seen better days. Faded flannel, wet, and one elbow was worn to mere threads. But the chest. Ah, that chest. When she saw his chest, she knew. When she had the undeniable urge to launch herself there, curl up in the sanctuary of his torso, she knew.

There was only one man that made her feel this way.

She looked up and smiled, caught a glimpse of her face in the window, and turned away.

He caught her chin with his hand. "I like it."

"I'm not pretty."

"That just means that I'll have less men to kill."

"You're here."

"Your friend finked on you."

"After four months."

"I tried, Lola. I tried every single person I knew. If I could have figured out a way to get to hell—other than killing myself—I would have called on your father. However, eventually I got to her."

"Sylvia?"

"Angela," he said proudly. "Leon's a friend of mine, and I tracked her down after they came back from their honeymoon."

Suddenly in the kitchen, a grease fire erupted, and the cook screamed in pain. "Hold on," Chris said.

He was back in a moment, fire extinguisher in hand.

Her heart began to sing and it didn't matter if hail was ruining car hoods everywhere, or that the restaurant might catch fire at any moment. In fact, she was sure she could hear her father laughing. But right now, nothing mattered except this.

"Chris?"

"You should really get used to calling me Crash."

"But I like Chris."

"I love Lola."

Lola stared at him, an unfamiliar smile tugging at the corners of her mouth. Then, she succumbed to temptation, curling her arms around his neck.

"I love Chris," she answered, and then Crash kissed her, and it was paradise all over again.

Epilogue

Lucifer stared at his desk with melancholy eyes. Piles of work covered the surface. Contracts, requests for information, ancient documents describing yet another damnable religious artifact. He'd been so close—*this close* to retirement—the good life. He thought he'd had it with Lucia, then Jezebel, and then Lola.

The devil collapsed in his chair and with one hand scattered the papers everywhere. "Problem, sir?" asked his butler, Eustace, already beginning to pick up the devil's mess.

"Tell me where I went wrong. I thought I gave them everything, and what do I get in return? Bupkus, that's what. All for love. First Lucia and that bloody do-gooder, then Jezebel gives up everything for a few lousy years of humanity with whatshisname, and Lola. Good God, she picked a man who has been on the scene of every disaster since the *Titanic* over her own beloved father." He reached for the three pictures that sat on his desk. *My daughters. Ha. The little devils.*

Epilogue

"I don't believe Mr. St. Clair was alive in nineteen-twelve."

Lucifer waved a hand. Details. His life was turning into one long detail. "Make yourself useful. Pour me a drink," he ordered. "And put something peppier on the stereo. Maybe a salsa beat."

"After I clean up your mess, sir."

Just one more person not to rely on. "I can't face it anymore, Eustace. I tasted it." He retrieved a little pink drink umbrella from his suit pocket. "I was even going to take up golf. I think I'd be really good at it."

"And what would we do without you, sir?" said Eustace, placing a piña colada on the desk, the strains of a mambo filling the room.

For a moment the devil lost himself in the rhythm of the song, snapping his fingers. Then he smiled at his most faithful servant. "Do I mean that much to the crew?"

Eustace's mustache twitched. "Of course, sir."

"Thank you for lying," said Lucifer, taking a sip of the tangy drink and emitting a heartfelt sigh. "I feel like a rat trapped in my own little cage, every day running and running and running, but never getting anywhere. If only there were some way to escape this . . . this *hell*. But there's no one left."

Eustace began sorting through the papers, shuffling them until all the edges were neatly aligned, but then he looked up, his face suffused with guilt. "Eh-hem. Uh, sir, that's not exactly correct. . . ."